The Griffin's Claw

Sarkin, Volume 3

Rachael S Lucas

Published by Rachael Lucas, 2023.

THE GRIFFIN'S CLAW

First edition. June 11, 2023.

Copyright © 2023 Rachael S Lucas.

ISBN: 979-8223876403

Written by Rachael S Lucas.

Also by Rachael S Lucas

Sarkin
Sailing For Shadow City
A Lonely Wind
The Griffin's Claw

Sci-fi and fantasy short stories
Illusions Of Steel And Sunset

Standalone
Dimensions

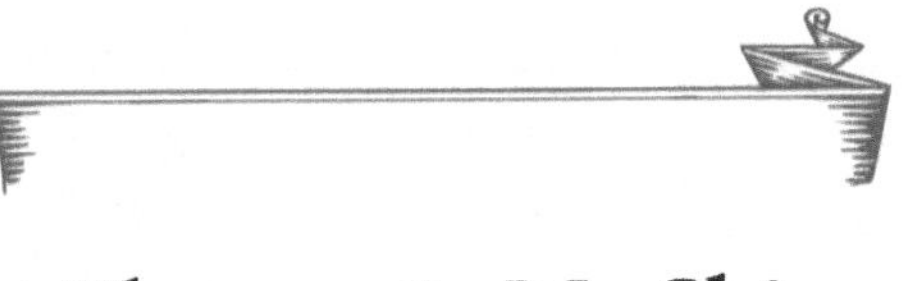

Chapter 1: My Ship

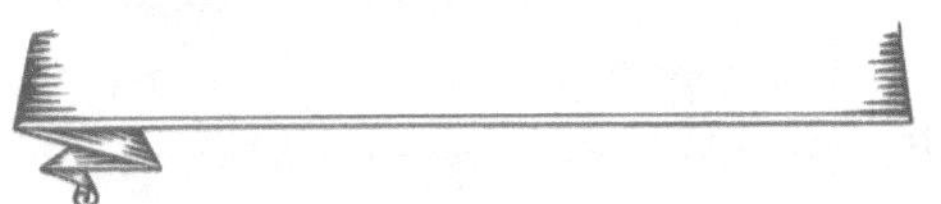

The waves lapped softly against the side of the ship, a sleepy noise in the warm fall afternoon. Sunlight sparkled on the rich blue water, tipping every wave in white. I leaned on the rail for a moment, gazing at the coastal bay around us. The shape of the trees and land was familiar, the shades of green old friends to my eyes. This was Appledock cove, the same place from which we had left four years ago to find a riddle and a shard in a wrecked schooner. Once again we were sitting here, waiting. But this time, we were waiting for passing prey.

With a bigger ship and larger crew, almost any size of single ship was within our means to capture. Our swift frigate made a ketch easy, a barque a good feast and a galleon within possibility. With-twenty five cannon and an average of two hundred men on board, we could either sink a ship or board her, coming off pretty well using the rough fighting methods of pirates. We had captured a lot of treasure this way during the last few years and were not nearly as poor as when we had sailed the *Blue Bucket* with only five crew members.

Though there were downsides to the larger ship as well, I had found. For one, it took much more hard work and hard-earned money to keep her in running trim. Secondly, it was not easy to be the chief mate of a crew which averaged at two hundred men. That was my official position now: first mate. After finishing Skon Yew, I had asked for the sailing ship *Seashooter* as a reward from the officials of Fraistia. This had started a long, heated debate about whether an unknown young man should get a reward for killing the erstwhile King of a country, or if he should be thrown in the dungeon on his head. But as Skon Yew had come in to the position of King by a siege of terror which led to the murdering of his own father, they eventually decided that I could have the ship. Upon receiving it, I promptly made my grandfather Leighton the Captain and part owner. He really deserved the ship after loosing his own, and I was most comfortable with him as the commander. But our previous first mate Bowen had been blinded by Skon Yew and could no longer take the position of a duty officer. He insisted that I take the post of first mate and there was no good reason for me to refuse. Secretly, I thought that I deserved it after all I had been through in Grackland and in the fight with Skon Yew. But once I learned how much hard work it was, I often wondered if I would have been happier as just another one of the crew, or in my old post as second officer. It was exhausting work being the first mate, watching over the whole crew, trying to make sure that every one did their work, did not get into too many fights among themselves and were not planning a mass mutiny.

Things had worked themselves out in the last years and I was finally beginning to feel comfortable with my post. Both Leighton and Bowen had always supported me and, of course, a lot of the real decisions were still the Captain's to make.

Now we lay quietly at anchor, our frigate all in perfect order with the deck washed, the sides recently repainted, and the sails ready to be put up at a moment's notice. I straightened up from my position on the rail, turning at the sound of footsteps heading my way. With a glance I saw that it was Chirn, who had become our cook after we set sail from Fraistia. His pale hair was all spiked up, as if he had been running his hands through it repeatedly, and he had an anxious look on his face. Chirn was always worrying about something, except for the times when he was boasting about his own prowess instead.

"Hey, chief," He came to a stop in front of me, moving a hand nervously to brush it through his hair once again, "I have a problem and I don't know what to do about it. The Captain wanted me to fry the fish for his dinner, but I accidentally put it in the pot and boiled it with the fish for everyone else. What should I do now?"

"Stop giving everyone boiled fish, perhaps?" I suggested ironically, knowing that the crew was just about fed up with it. But when Chirn gave me a pitiful glance, I relented, "Well, there is still some time before dinner. Why don't you just fry a different fish?"

"There is no more left!" He exclaimed, but I did not have any more time to listen to his sob-story right then, because a voice called out to me from the helm, "Sarkin!"

"Then catch a new fish!" I flung over my shoulder, as I hurried off toward the helm. On the way, I passed a few men doing various duties on the deck, such as preparing to tar the masts, refilling the drinking barrel or simply standing their watch. They gave me short salutes or nods as I passed, to which I always nodded back. Limping lightly, as I had ever since receiving the cut on the back of my right leg in the fight with Skon Yew, I made it up to the upper deck and over to the Captain. He was standing with his back to the wheel, looking out to sea through his spyglass. Despite the passing years he was still a strong, active man, with long iron-gray hair and sharp eyes that did not miss much on his ship. The old blue uniform had long since fallen to pieces, so he had found a new maroon one in the chest of a ship's owner aboard a vessel which we had plundered. It was set with bright studs of brass and came with a dark teal sash which he was obviously proud of, as he constantly fingered it while talking to the men. Leighton always liked things a little bit showy, though it had never gotten in the way of his being a good Captain.

"Sark m'lad, look out there and tell me what you see," He passed me the glass, indicating a direction. I took the telescope and fitted it carefully to my eye. At first, all I saw was the branches of a tree on one arm of the bay, sticking up with the pattern of the sea behind them. But when I slid the glass over to the right a few inches I got a better view of the open water. Far out, so that it was just a white billow on the horizon, could be seen a sail.

"It's a sail, cap." I told him, though I guessed that he already knew it and had only wanted me to see, "And it looks like it's coming this way."

"Ah, just what I thought." The Captain took the spyglass back, peering through it for another moment. Then he glanced sideways at me and snorted, "Well, don't just stand there! Get the crew ready for action, up anchor, unfurl sail and set a man in the bows to help navigate us out of here. We are going after that ship."

"Yes, sir. Even though we don't know what it is yet?" I ventured, making a move as if to go and then checking it.

"Ah, but we do know what it is," The Captain told me, tucking the telescope under one arm and pulling a rolled up piece of paper from his shirt, "This new chart which I picked up in Appledock yesterday shows all the shipping lanes in the area and tells which ships are most likely to be in an area at a time."

He rolled the map out onto the rail, tapping the small image of a ship on a dotted line which I could see went right past the cove we were in toward the nearby bay in which the docks of Appledock were located. It seemed to me unlikely that a chart could predict the pattern of sailing ships accurately, what with delays and accidents along the way. But the captain loved to collect different types of maps and usually believed what they said explicitly, even though on certain occasions that I could remember the maps had been wrong. Not wanting to argue just then, I simply agreed with him and asked what sort of ship was predicted.

"A merchant of the Freedor line; the *Feline*." Leighton squinted down at the chart to read the small letters printed above the ship, "A brig, it says, though the pictures are all the same. So, there is your answer," He looked up at me with a smile that was just a touch smug, "Go get the crew ready. We'll be able to take her easily."

With a quick salute, I jumped down to the main deck and hurried to rouse the men from below by banging on the forecastle hatch and shouting for them. This brought a noisy reply of half-heard words, objects being slammed around, and the sound of men's feet hitting the planking. Leaving them to find their own way up, I turned and called to the second mate, who was standing nearby pretending that he was not listening, "Caraway, set a pilot in the prow. And make sure that the extra arms are in their racks ready to use; we're going after a merchant."

"Aye, sir." He turned to begin issuing his own orders, while I went across to the galley, which was beside the Captain's cabin. With a quick glance I spotted Bowen inside, sitting on a stool while peeling potatoes into a large cauldron on the floor in front of him. Though he was blind, so could not be of any use as a normal seaman, he had come along as an advisor and general help on our ship. Really, the Captain and I would not have left our old friend behind even if there had not been a good reason for him to be aboard, but he had often enough proved his worth in the last years. Not only doing odd jobs such as peeling potatoes and mending clothes, but keeping the crew's morale up through his odd native stories we had time to listen, and with his unfaltering courage when the ship went into battle. What man would want to admit that he was afraid to sail into a fight that a blind man did not hesitate to enter?

Rapping on the table with my knuckles so that he knew someone was there, I told him, "Better get everything stowed in here, Bowen. We're going after a prize."

With a nod in my direction, he stood and felt across the counter until he hit the sack of potatoes he had been taking them from to peel. This he shoved into a cupboard, before going to put other items away. Knowing he could get the job done perfectly well alone,

I hurried back out of the galley onto the deck. The Captain was helping to supervise the rigging of the sails, shouting such encouragement as; "You lazy no-good, don't just sit there staring at the line! Heave!" Or perhaps, "You fellows up on the mainmast, stir your stumps m'lads. We don't have all day!"

Meanwhile, the second mate was aiding the men in pulling up the anchor using the capstan. After seeing in a glance that everything was going smoothly on this level, while taking just a minute to admire the square, billowing sails beginning to fill in the east wind, I ducked down the hatch which led onto the gun deck. My shoes thumped down the steeply-angled ladder, then clattered on the smooth-polished deck. This was a low, long space running across the center of the ship, with rafters spanned all along the roof and square port holes running along both sides. Parked in front of every hole was a cannon, barrel a dull, dark gray and wooden frame gleaming softly. The chief gunner had already perceived the stir topside and was having his men haul up powder and balls to prepare for a fight, the round cannon balls being laid in wooden troughs beside the guns so that they would be quick to load when the battle began.

"Dolgan!" I called to the gunner, "Good, you're getting things ready. But no heated shot this time! Just hold some chain shot ready for the command."

With a small shiver, I remembered the time we had set a ship on fire using heated shot. It had been effective, to a point, but we had lost most of the perishable goods on the prize ship when the fire had gotten away from her crew. Personally, I did not like using fire as a weapon, both because of practical considerations and the fact that it was a horrible way to kill the enemy. Though this last reason was not pragmatic enough for me to ever admit to it, so I always claimed to others that it simply ruined the loot and was dangerous for our own crew.

The chief gunner responded to my commands with a salute and I watched for a moment as he went about his duties. Dolgan was our third gunner aboard the *Seashooter*, the first having been killed in an explosion when an enemy shot shattered part of the gun deck. The second had been a quiet, shadowy man, who had disappeared without a word when we were anchored near the town of Littleton. Since his clothes and gear disappeared with him, we figured that he had just become sick of life as a pirate and jumped ship. Dolgan had joined us soon afterwards: he was no seaman, but an artillery commander from Selland who had run away from the army. Desertion was punished strictly, so a life of piracy looked like a good opportunity to him at the time.

Personally, I never really liked our third gunner. He talked too much and often thought that he knew everything better than anyone else when it came to cannons. But he seemed like an efficient officer and I had not yet had a good reason to complain of him to the Captain. Everyone was working well on the gun deck, so I quickly mounted the stairs again and began checking to make sure that Caraway had distributed all of the weapons where they needed to go. The men were armed with short cutlasses, flare-bladed boarding axes, flintlock pistols and an assortment of muskets and rifles. Among them stood my old friend Ramses, who had joined us as a pirate after Skon Yew was defeated. I gave him a nod and he tipped me a wink. Though he could have asked for the position as an officer aboard and I would have been obliged to give it, he had always been content to be just another of the crew. In this role we had made a good pirate of him, even though he had not been a sailor of any sort before he joined us.

The men who would be the boarding crew all stood near the center of the deck, eagerly awaiting the coming conflict. Many of them had come from the dock area of Leveress and showed the distinct caramel-colored hair of most Fraistians. Others we had culled from different ports, so that in appearance and dress they were a motley group of men. But all of them had the same gleam in their eyes now, the same tense expression. Every one of them was ready to fight for a good haul of loot.

Checking briefly with the second mate to make sure that everything was well stowed in the hold below, I went on to rejoin the Captain at the helm. The ship was moving slowly now, feeling its way out of the bay. The pilot in the prow called back instructions as the arms of land which protected the bay glided silently past on either side. Soon we hit the choppy water of the open sea and unfurled all sail. Catching the wind, our fast ship leaped forward like an eager horse and rode across the waves toward the prize ship which was just becoming visible on the horizon. I held the rail tightly as spray blew back across the deck, enjoying the feeling of the wind blowing through my hair. A few steps away the Captain muttered and chuckled to himself, working up to the full tirade which he always carried on while we attacked any ship. It did not matter if he was talking to the *Seashooter* or the crew, it was simply a way to let off steam while in battle.

"What is the plan of action?" I asked him, keeping an eye toward the sail on the horizon.

"The usual!" He called back in a loud voice, "We pull up, give them a chance to surrender and if they don't, then we give them a few sweeping rounds before boarding their ship!"

"Good." I let loose a grin, laying a hand on the silver sword which hung at my side. It was worn, chipped and a little tarnished now, but it was the same weapon which I had taken from Skon Yew after giving him my own full in the chest four years ago. Beside the sword on my belt hung a row of pistols and small blades, including a dagger which matched the sword and which the Dark Prince had once tried to kill me with. That was when I had been working as a mercenary for the Queen of Grackland. I also had a pistol from that time, given to me by the Queen herself. This had been part of the pay which I accepted when I joined her as a mercenary. After the last fight with Skon Yew though, I had left her service to rejoin my captain as a pirate. She had let me keep the gun and even the month advance of pay she had hired me with. Since I had got rid of the Dark Prince, her soldiers and subjects would start returning to her castle, so the Queen had no more need for mercenaries. Though she had still let me off a little reluctantly, giving me the feeling that it was only her kindness that let me go at all.

My guns were already loaded and I checked now to make sure that the firing mechanisms were all in good order. Then I stood gripping the rough wooden rail, watching the ship on the horizon. It's sails gradually grew from being an indistinct blur to the separate shapes of dirty white squares hung along two masts and the triangular staysail in front. It was a brig alright, just as the captain had predicted with his new map. But there was something about the ship that was making me uneasy; it did not seem to be sailing as a merchant should. I know that sounds odd, as you would think any ship of the same basic type would sail in just the same way. But there was an aggression to the way it was coming on, a steadiness that did not fit the way a meek merchantman should be moving. With a sudden misgiving, I decided to check on this ship a little closer, to see what we were really getting in to. Instead of asking to borrow the captain's glass and having to explain myself to him, I simply closed my eyes and slipped through the door in my mind into the inverted world. My mind's eye was no longer in my head, but beyond me in the outside reality.

I had become experienced enough at this skill now to remain standing in one position while through the mental door, though any large shock or bump would still have knocked me right off my feet. Through the door the colors of our ship and the sea were strange, all of the light or shadows being accentuated. The blue of the sea seemed deep and beautiful, the glittering foam along the wave tops making sparks of light almost blinding in their intensity. The shadows on deck, where the men stood in readiness, were thick and dark.

But I had no time for sightseeing right now. Powering quickly away from our vessel, I flew out over the waves toward the oncoming brig. Soon it came into clear view, so that I could count the cannons along the side. There were ten of them; much more than a normal merchant would be carrying. And there were men on the deck, standing ready just as our men were. They were armed with various weapons and dressed in good, clean clothes, with the officer in charge wearing a uniform. With a sinking feeling I looked up at the flag. It was a white stag on a green background, antlers bristling upwards. The ship was a Sellander warship, patrolling the coast. What with the war starting back up between Fraistia and Durny, and Selland beginning to take the Durny side while Thwate took the other, patrols were much more common. Not that it was impossible for us to take on an armed brig with the *Seashooter*, but the cost would be higher and the return much less than a merchant would have given us. The men would not be as pleased with a haul of weaponry and provisions as they would have been with a merchant's wares.

Winging my way swiftly back to our ship, I came back to myself with an abrupt shift of vision and turned immediately to Leighton, "Hey, cap, I think you'd better take another look at that ship in your spyglass. I don't think that it is the brig you were hoping it was."

"What do you mean, sirrah?" The captain returned with a scowl, "The map said that it would be the ship *Feline*."

"Well, the map was wrong," I took the helm from him, pointing out across the water with my free hand, "That is a war ship, not a merchant."

Snatching up his telescope from where it had been set on the deck nearby, the captain fitted it to his eye. He stared for a long moment before letting out a grumbling noise somewhere between a snort and a gasp, "Hum, you're right."

I could not help rolling my eyes a little at this as he went on, "Well, it's still a ship smaller than us, and one which we can attack. We'll carry on with the plan; no change of action."

"Shall I tell the men, Captain?" I asked, trying to remember how many people I had informed that it was a merchant. At least two, if not more. I did not want to look like the sort of mate who would lie to make the crew happier for a short amount of time and then disappoint them with the truth.

"They'll find out soon enough," He shrugged carelessly, moving back to take the wheel, "Just tell Caraway to prepare for heavier fighting, Sarkin, and warn Dolgan. That should do the trick."

I shot one more glance at the oncoming ship, which was very close now, before jumping down from the raised platform of the helm and diving back down the hatch to the gun deck. The gunner was easy to spot, standing near the center of the line of cannons, issuing orders to the young powder monkeys. I caught his attention and he came over so that I could quietly tell him about the unexpected change in ships. As soon as he understood, I scrambled back up on deck and did the same for the second mate.

"A bit of a mistake with the captain's new map, ay?" Caraway said with a grim twist of his mouth. He was a serious, stolid sort of man, but he often had an uncanny sense for what the captain was thinking.

"Yes, the map couldn't change the wind." I returned with a small shrug, "But our plan is still the same."

The second mate nodded and we both turned to look over our dragon-like seashooter figurehead at the on coming ship. It was painted black with cream lines, and the name was done in gold along one side. With my limited skills at reading, I could just make out that it said *'Slnd Shark.'*

The first four letters designated it as one of Selland's royal war ships. It was smaller then our ship, almost half the length, but it was well armed and seemed to be just as conscious of our presence as we were of its own. That was the one problem with being painted bright red, with shimmering scales on your front: it did not make very good camouflage.

The tenseness mounted in the air as the two ships drew closer, our opponent tacking and weaving to catch the light sea wind while we ran before a heavier breeze coming over the land. Soon we were within hailing distance, upon which a voice shouted from the brig, "Ahoy *Seashooter*, slack sail and state your business."

It had a ring of distrust and command to it, as if the captain already guessed what we were. Which would not be difficult, if he had taken a close look at our decks.

"Slack sail yourself, you blathering oaf!" Our commander returned in fine style, using the speaking funnel which he always kept tied to the helm with a short length of string, "And surrender if you don't want to be destroyed!"

There were a few venomous but indistinct replies to this, while neither ship furled sail. We came at each other like rearing stallions, passing at a short distance to exchange full broadsides. Iron balls whistled through the rigging, one striking a yardarm and snapping it off like a brittle twig. Men rushed to chop away the fallen rigging, while others fired shots at the enemy with their long range weapons. Cannons, muskets and rifles roared out across the water and spray swept the deck from the cannon shots that missed to hit only the sea. I let off a few pistol shots across the water as we passed at close range, then hurried aft to look back at our enemy as she fell astern. One of her masts had been hit and fallen completely away into the water when they cut it free. But now she was turning into the wind, where as we would have to tack to get anything if we turned around. Remembering a trick which I had used before in fights to gain an advantage, I slipped through the door in my mind as our ship came about. There, I swept over above the *Shark* and looked down on the helm, seeking the man who was at the wheel. To my disappointment, it was not her captain. But my trick would still work, even if it was a little less effective in the long run.

Gathering my mental power together, I blew on the pale gray light that was his mind. With a sudden flicker it went out and the man fell to the deck limply. Other lights of various colors could be seen moving about on the deck, or bobbing toward the helm. The minds of enemy men. But it would take far too much energy to kill or even knock out all of the men on deck with my mind. If I tried, it would leave me helpless for any other fighting or gathering loot. Instead, I returned quickly to the regular world and watched as the *Shark* heeled strangely about near an arm of the coast due to the loss of her helmsman. She was soon righted as another man jumped to the wheel, but it had lost her both headway and maneuvering room. As she tried to collect herself for another assault, our ship tacked about and we were on her. Shouting orders to the crew, the captain executed an expert move and brought our ship up beside her opponent. At that close range, neither of us dared fire a cannon shot. But bullets from hand guns rang back and forth, accompanied by the cries of injured men. A seaman dropped beside me, shot in the leg just above the knee. I bent over him to help, but he waved me off with a gasp, "I'll be fine, sir. Don't bother."

Taking him at his word, I made sure he had a weapon at hand before moving off to help with the grappling hooks. These were thrown over to grip the rails or rigging of the *Shark*, after which they were tightened to pull us close together in a deadly lock. Then the real fighting began, as men poured off of the *Seashooter* onto the brig's deck. I led three men myself, over the rails and into the enemy ship. A sailor jumped in front of me and I hacked him down with a slash from my sword. My companions finished him off as we turned toward the main hatchway and began to battle our way across the deck. Clashing, smashing sounds enveloped us, with choking smoke floating in the air like a wraith. Soon, my companions and me became separated, as I chased a man down a hatchway onto the deck below. This was the crew's sleeping quarters, a dimly lit place since all of the lanterns had gone out with the shock of our ships coming together. The man I was chasing appeared to be some sort of officer by his clothing, and in the craze of battle I saw him only as a great prize. He stopped at the bunks, having no further place to go, and spun around to face me. His sword had been lost in the fighting above and now he only had a long dagger with him. I had my silver sword in my hand, more than twice as long and deadly sharp at the point. Coming closer to him, I stopped for just a minute as we gazed at each other eye to eye. Deciding to give him another chance, I growled quietly, "Surrender and I'll spare you."

He just bared his teeth in a crazy grin, reaching down to drag something out of the bunk behind him. It was a boy, not more then twelve years old, who kicked and struggled, shouting for the man to let him go. The officer put a knife to his throat instead, stilling his struggle. Surprised at this strange action, I took another look at my prey and realized that his uniform was not that of the ship, or even of the Selland navy at all. It was black with silver buttons and had a twisted insignia done in blue on the front.

"I won't let you go! I'm taking you with me, you brat," The strange man said, holding the boy up as a shield between us. I considered simply ramming my sword through both of them, killing them in one powerful blow. But seeing the boy hanging there with fear and pleading written on his face, I knew that I could not hurt him just to destroy at a single man. Though the life of a pirate is rough and we often must kill to survive, our main goal is to get the treasure, not so much kill the men. If we could get a ship or goods without a fight, we were always satisfied. Killing this one man and boy was not going to get us the ship. But neither could I just turn and walk away, when he might stab me in the back.

Quickly, I dropped my sword as if in defeat and raised that hand as if to show that I would not fight. The man slacked off a little on his grip of the boy, glancing over his shoulder with gleaming eyes. In that moment I drew my favorite pistol with my left hand and shot the strange officer directly through the forehead. It went off with the deafening blast of powder in a confined area. He slowly crumpled to the ground, blade dropping from his slackened fingers. The boy fell beside him, pulling free of his arms to crouch on the floor looking up at me. One of his hands wrapped around the dead man's dagger as if he meant mischief, but I gave him a level look to stop him, "Don't think of it."

Confusion flitted across his face as I stooped carefully to pick up my sword, never taking my eyes off of him. He was dressed as a regular farm boy or apprentice, with large ill-fit boots, cotton top and rough leggings. But on his forehead was burned a brand, still red and angry with newness. It was the same as the mark on the dead man's shirt.

"Why was he going to kill you?" I gave a light kick to the body, indicating who I meant and my contempt for him at the same time.

"I—I don't know," The boy stood up, cautiously tucking the plundered knife in his belt, "He has told me before that I was bound to his master now and had no other life...perhaps he did not want you to capture me."

His words raised more questions than they answered, but I just shook my head and turned toward the hatch topside, fairly sure that the boy would not stab me now that we had talked, "Stay here. Don't come up into the fighting. I'll want to speak to you later."

Without waiting for a reply I swung up onto the deck and looked around me. The fighting had slackened off and I could see that the men of the *Shark* were beginning to surrender, either in groups or singly. Many corpses and injured men lay on the deck, though our opponents had decided to give up before too many sacrificed themselves to pride. Heroism is usually an unpaid job.

The second mate came across the deck to me, calling for crew members to take the injured away as he came, "Our captain is setting the terms with theirs in his cabin. He wants you to be there."

"Alright," I glanced around once more, before noticing the line of blood on Caraway's arm, "Were you hurt badly?"

"No, it's just a scratch." He brushed impatiently at the wound, "Any orders, sir?"

"Just get things cleaned up and remind the men that all the loot is share and share alike." I told him, watching some of our crew drag a chest up from the hold with silk clothing spilling out of it along the way, "Oh, and there is a boy in the forecastle down there. Bring him over to our ship and take good care of him. I want to talk to him once the terms are settled."

"Aye, aye." The second mate saluted with a slightly mystified expression as I strode away toward our captain's cabin, breaking an already cracked piece of railing from the *Shark* on the way to get across more easily.

Chapter 2: The Mark of the Master

The captain of the *Shark* was a short, red-faced man with jowls like a bull dog and eyes like a rat. These orbs were continually darting around the room as he discussed terms with Leighton, seeming to search for illegal goods hanging on the walls or hidden under our captain's berth. His voice was in odd contrast to his figure, being a thin, high tone that seemed to come more from his nose than his mouth.

"So you see, captain, I really can not let you just take anything you want to. It belongs to the men and I can't tell them—"

Leighton cut him off with a heavy snort, "Humph, I believe that you can and more then likely do, tell them to do whatever you wish, sir. And they will carry it out, too. Besides, I am not giving you a choice between giving up their goods or not: your only choice is whether we take what we want while you live, or if we kill you and your whole crew first. So, will you agree to terms?"

Cuttle, as the other captain's most unfitting name was, gasped and squirmed in his chair for a few minutes with half-formed threats and wheedling noises bubbling between his lips. Finally he bobbed his head a few times with an almost reflexive jerk, saying, "Very well. I agree to your terms. You promise that I and my remaining men will not be harmed?"

"Yes, that is the deal," Leighton grabbed his hand to shake on it then stood up, wiping that hand openly on the side of his pants, "Get your men on to the deck, Captain Cuttle, and make sure that none of them try to do my people any harm. You know what would happen if even one of my men was hurt!"

"Yes, yes," Cuttle pulled himself out of the chair which he had been sitting in, following our captain outside. During the whole meeting I had been standing quietly to one side. Now I stepped forward and laid a hand on the shoulder of the *Shark*'s commander, stopping him with the words, "Just a minute. I want to ask you something."

"Well?" He eyed me as if I had been a stain of tar which had reared it's head to speak to him, "What is it?"

I met his eyes without backing down, "There was a boy in the forecastle of your ship, a lad of about twelve. He was with a man wearing a black uniform. Were either of them part of your crew?"

"No, neither of them," I could see now, by how he answered, that the only reason Cuttle was trying to avoid me was that he was actually frightened of me, "We found them adrift in a small boat, trying to get to shore. They begged passage to Littleton and as we were already heading in that direction I agreed to take them on. Is that all you wanted?"

I ignored the blustering sneer in his words and let him shake my hand off of his shoulder. "Yes, for now."

"Thank you for your time," I added as he started to walk away, hiding a heaping spoonful of cold politeness in the words. He left with a swift backwards glance, as if suspecting me of considering stabbing him in the back. I watched after him with a small half-smile of contempt, waiting until he was out of sight before moving out on to the deck. With a sharp glance, I made sure that the transfer of goods and injured men was going smoothly. Though Edna had taught me some of her healing ways and herbs, I would not want to be a full-time doctor on our ship. We had a sawbones aboard who was very good at his trade, though so rough that the men always claimed that they would rather take the injury than the cure. Today many of them did not have a choice.

Seeing someone being carried on a wooden plank across to our ship, I strode over to look at him. A young man with black hair and a distinct, mocking face, he lay pale and lifeless now. He had often been the quickest up the mast when rigging was changed and I had heard him spoken of well by the others of the crew.

"Dead?" I asked, though I already knew.

"Yep, Phillip is destined for the deep now," One of the men carrying him rejoined sadly, "Where shall we lay him for now, chief?"

"Over there, by the far rail," I pointed out a section where two empty barrels had been left when we weighed anchor, "Lay him across the barrels. He was a brave man and he will have a good burial when we set sail away from the coast."

Trying to console his friends with this promise, I watched them walk slowly across the deck. It was one of the more unpleasant things I had learned about having a larger crew: there was more of them to die.

With a shake of my head, I wondered where Caraway would have taken the boy whom I had found in the other ship. Probably not to the men's quarters, where the injured would be taken. And not in the captain's cabin, where I had my bunk, because that was where I had just left. Of obvious options, this only left the galley, as they were not on the deck. As if to confirm my suspicions, the second mate came striding out of that space and started crossing back toward the *Shark*.

"The boy is in the cook house," He told me in passing, "I'm off to find the captain. Anything else you need?"

"No, go on," I waved him off and went on to the galley. With the cooking fire burnt low and no lanterns lit, it was dim inside. The walls were stained with smoke and the port hole was so covered in dusty grease that you could not see out of it clearly. Chirn was not very keen on the cleaning up part of cooking and of course Bowen could not see how bad the window had become. With a mental shrug, I let my eyes adjust while looking around the place. The boy was sitting on a low stool by the table in the center, which was usually used for cooking purposes rather than eating. He sat at it with a round roll of bread in front of him and a cup of something warm in his hands. Bowen was nearby, nodding quietly as the boy spoke levelly; "They killed everything, even the cow. My parents were the first to go, then my two sisters. I was the only thing on the farm that they left alive."

A shiver ran down my back as he went on, not so much because of what he was describing, but because of the odd, cold way in which he spoke. It was as if he was telling a tale which had happened to someone else, long ago, and yet it was charged with a deadly quietness of purpose, "I was taken away to a holding place then. They branded me there, before sending me on with a man in a boat. We went down the coast until we met the *Shark*. You know how that ended."

Here he paused for a long moment, crumbling a little of his bread between his fingers without even noticing what he was doing. After a moment he added in an undertone, "They won't be able to run far enough once I start after them."

"There is a lot of space in this world to run," Bowen remarked quietly in return, "I know. But Sarkin is here now, if you want to tell him about it."

I had felt the tiny brush of his magic against my mind, alerting him to my presence. It was how he kept in touch with who was around him. I came in to sit on a chair across from the boy, walking quietly as if he was a wild animal that might be frightened away. He glanced up at me stealthily with a bowed head and was silent. I crossed my legs, unsure of how to start the conversation. I had already heard enough to guess what had happened to him, but why it had happened was still a mystery. Finally, after sitting in uneasy silence for a few minutes, I asked the boy abruptly, "What is your name?"

"Krift," He muttered, sipping at his drink.

Straightening my legs, I leaned on the table with one elbow, repeating, "Krift. An interesting name. What does that mark on your forehead mean, Krift? It is the same as was on that man's uniform."

The boy shot a glance at Bowen, before looking up to meet my gaze, "They never really explained it. The men who captured me...they said that it was the mark of the master and now my life was his."

The brand was impressed in a strange, twisted shape reminiscent of a bird's head, but with three lines slashing down across it like triple claw marks. My eyes went to it for a long moment, before I shook my head, "So your people were killed, your farm destroyed and you were captured to be brought before some sort of master whom would demand the service of your life. Do you have any idea why?"

"It...it has to do with the drawing of fire," The boy stumbled over the words, having entirely lost the cold, confident tone which he had been speaking in earlier. Now he seemed uncertain, hunching his shoulders as if in discomfort. I did not want to put him in a bad spot, as it seemed he had been through quite a lot already. But I was frankly curious and wanted to know what he had been talking about. His last words had been fairly mystifying, "The drawing of fire? What do you mean?"

Setting down his cup, the boy stood and pushed back his chair, "I'll show you."

There was once again the edge of coldness in his voice and an expression on his face that I did not quite understand. It had elements of concentration and oddly even a touch of shyness. But mainly it was an expression of grudging revelation, as if he did not want to show us what he was about to do, but was being forced to. It was not until he began the demonstration that I understood the look on his face.

First he crossed his arms and stood with his eyes closed as if deep in thought. Quite suddenly he snapped his eyes open and spread his arms wide. On the tip of each pointer finger glowed a small, fiery dot, bright in the dim air of the galley. Moving slowly now, gaze fixed and unseeing, he drew his hands together in a downward arc. Behind them a trail of fire was left in the air, a burning line of brilliant orange.

A gasp escaped me unconsciously as the lines lingered in the air behind his fingers. Working a little quicker now, he brought them straight up to a point above his head, leaving rods of fire behind. Quicker and quicker his fingers went, sideways, up, down and in all directions. Behind them burned the fiery lines, creating an image in the air. When it was finished, he dropped his hands to his side and stepped back. Floating weightlessly in the middle of the galley was an airy ship, made of silent fire. Every detail of rigging and sail was drawn there in glowing outline. Krift and I both looked at it, my feeling being one of wonder, where as his expression showed only a brooding satisfaction with a job well done.

Slowly, like a rainbow, the image faded away. I blinked, seeing the ship still burning on my eyelids, "I see. The drawing of fire."

But I did not really see, or understand, how he had done it. The fire was not mind magic such as Bowen and I used, nor did it look like the mirror illusions that the wizard Drisilibrin had once shown me. The fire had flicked and glowed like any candle flame, but silently, without the rippling noise of true fire. Yet there had been faint waves of heat coming off of the image; I had felt them on my face.

"That is the drawing of fire." Krift affirmed softly, moving back to sit in his seat with his head bowed, "That's why those men wanted me. I heard them speaking once, when they thought I was asleep. They said that the master was collecting all the people who have strange talent that he can find, and keeping them as his servants."

I nodded slowly, though he was not looking my way any longer. So, someone was collecting people that had unexplained powers, and using them to aid him in his ambitions. He had ordered their families killed so that there would be no one to look for them and probably told the messengers to kill the talented people too, if they resisted. That was why the uniformed man on the *Shark* had tried to do away with Krift.

As if hearing the direction of my thoughts, the boy looked up at that moment to say, "You saved my life... I must thank you. But what are you going to do with me now?"

Sensing the he feared we would force him to use his odd talents for us now, I simply shrugged, "What do you want to do? You could go back aboard the *Shark,* if you wanted and return with those men to the nearest port. If you have any other relatives, you could find them from there."

"I have an aunt, up in Clydesfort," Krift tapped his piece of bread against the top of the table, his tone reluctant, "She might take me in."

"Or," I went on thoughtfully, "You could sign up on our ship as a cabin boy or powder monkey for the time being. Then, when we sail up north towards Clydesfort you could drop in on your aunt and see if she was willing to take you in. It's hard work, and dangerous, being a pirate. But it's probably better than wandering across Selland on your own. And you would earn the usual wages of a pirate: a share of all the treasure taken in."

"You would let me join your crew?" Krift narrowed his eyes at me across the table, "Why? Because I have special powers and you want to use them?"

"Well, I don't really see how drawing glowing pictures can be useful to a pirate, except as entertainment when the days get long. Though I am personally interested in how you do them," I gave him a grin, folding my hands behind my head more comfortably, "It's probably just because I'm a softhearted fool that I make the offer. And a curious fool, too. So, do you want the job, or not?"

He hesitated, looking for a minute to Bowen, who sat silently nearby. The blind man gave him no encouragement, but his stillness had a quiet assurance to it that could be felt in the air.

"Alright," Krift nodded, making his decision, "I'll sign on. Are you the captain?"

"Nah, I'm just his right-hand man." I stood up, gesturing for the boy to follow me out of the room, "We'll have to go find the captain."

With a hand on the hilt of my sword I walked out of the galley, the boy following after with his cup and roll of bread in his hands.

ON THE WAY ACROSS THE deck of the *Seashooter* we ran in to Chirn, walking toward the room we had just left with a fishing pole swung dolefully over one shoulder.

"Chief," He said, stopping us with an upraised hand, "I couldn't get a fish with the ship moving around so much! And it's too late to try any longer. What am I going to do for the captain's dinner?"

I sighed and looked up at the sun, which was starting to come down toward the horizon, "Look, Chirn, there is probably going to be fresh supplies aboard this brig we just captured. There might even be fresh beef, as it is a war ship. So I'm sure the captain and crew will want the things from it cooked up, instead of fish. We've been having fish for at least a week now and everyone is ready for a change."

"Oh!" He looked over at the ship which we were grappled to, as if he had hardly noticed it was there before, "I suppose so. Thanks, Sarkin. I'll put this away and see what has come over."

He hurried off to put the fishing pole away, while I hurried my young friend in the opposite direction to find the captain, hoping to avoid another food conversation with the cook. We found Leighton in the hold of the *Shark*, directing some of our men in choosing items to plunder. So close to the shore we did not need their water barrels, but food was always useful and their spare sails could be packed into our ship in case of any emergency. Also, there was a casket of gold coins locked up and fastened with chains. This was for their captain to use in buying supplies, or anything else they needed if they sailed away from the coast of Selland. Leighton had ordered this opened with the key and Caraway was counting out the coins which they had found inside.

Also the ship's powder and balls were appropriated, while the cannons were spiked so that they could not be fired. From the crew's quarters and the officer's cabin, various smaller loot had already been taken away. The fine clothes of Selland sailors were always welcome among the men. Our captain had also found a locker containing a variety of drinks, to be distributed that evening at his discretion. Other than that, there were bits of money, hand held weapons and the shot for them, blankets from the beds, a few pots from their galley, maps and charts for our captain, and everything else that could be stripped from another ship. It was not as rich a haul as could have been taken from a merchant, so a few grumbles were heard among the men. But generally they were too content at getting any prize at all, to be complaining that it was not a trading vessel.

The crew of the prize ship watched the looting with expressions ranging from sullen to downright depressed. We had left them the clothes they stood up in, and enough supplies to get back to the nearest port in their ship. But they still had many possessions stolen and were not at all happy to have been bested in the fight. The feeling on our side was that it was just tough luck for them; you shouldn't join the navy if you did not want to face pirates now and then.

When I came up to the captain, he was watching everything with his hands behind his back and a content expression on his face, "Well, Sarkin, what do you think?"

"Everything seems to be going fine, captain." I replied, then could not help adding to needle him a little, "Though the *Feline* still has not appeared."

"Humph," Leighton waved a hand in the air, "Don't be so greedy, m'lad. I'm sure the map will be right next time. Now, what did you want?"

With a repressed smile at his vexation, I went on to give him a brief outline of Krift's history as far as I had heard it, before giving a request for him to be signed on as a crew member. The captain agreed to have him and it was soon worked out that Krift would be the first cabin boy we had ever had aboard the *Seashooter*. This was a position much more favorable for him than that of one of the young men who brought powder up for the cannons, as it was both an easier and safer job. More importantly, he would be directly under the eye of the captain and myself, so that we could make sure his talent for fire-drawings was kept quiet for the time being. Without knowing more about it and the reasons he had been captured, it was not safe to tell everyone. Even a well meaning crew member can be a little slack-jawed after some time ashore with a full pocket.

Like most ships, we had a small pile of papers aboard called the 'articles.' These laid forth our few rules, as well as marking down who was the officers at the time, and having the signature or symbol of every man aboard in them. When someone dies, we crossed them off the list. When another person joined the ship, they were added to the list.

Later that evening, while the crew were enjoying the meat and drink while admiring or trading their newly gained goods, Krift signed himself on to the ship in the official articles. He put his full name down, not just the crude symbol which many of the fully grown men used for lack of book learning (including myself). After that he was the official cabin boy of the *Seashooter*, and the captain sent him off on his first mission; to fetch Bowen from the galley, as well as our dinners. The boy nodded seriously, hurrying out of the cabin with an air of importance, as if there was no one else on board who could have brought the requested objects so well as himself.

I sat on my bunk in the cabin, fiddling with the dented gold band which I always wore on one arm. As the former first mate's berth had been, mine lay on the right side of the room as you came in. Straight across from me was the captain's bed, strewn with various articles of clothing, coin and paper which he had taken for his own use from the *Shark*. In between the two sleeping places there was a thick, heavy oak table with a metal brazier built into the center of it. Because of the cool fall evenings this had a few hot coals glowing in it, dangerously close to the ship's articles which lay on the tabletop with a quill across them. Against the back wall stood two tall lockers and a rack of weapons, these things being for the use of both the captain and myself equally.

From the roof above hung a lantern, casting a slowly wavering glow in the room. We had put back out to sea, leaving the stripped ship to find it's own way home. with all sails set, we made good time heading north east with the wind.

The captain moved to brush the papers aside on the table, laying a rolled-up map in their place. I thought at first that he was going to make a show of consulting his shipping chart for where our next prize would be. But instead he untied a piece of twine holding the paper in it's shape and said, "Now, Sarkin, I want you to cast your eyes on this bit of information. It was found in the cabin of the *Shark* by Glimpy."

I scooted to the edge of my bunk and leaned over the table as he unrolled the paper. It was a little yellowed with age, but did not crack too badly as he spread it out. Right down the center of the paper ran a thick line of ink, almost as broad as my little finger. This was decorated with a coiling dragon of red, the wingless sort with lizard-like legs and a large head. On the left side of the line was what looked like a mixed handful of words spread out haphazardly, here and there on the paper with no obvious pattern. Across from them, on the right side of the line, lay a few amorphous shapes like clouds, or islands on a map without names indicated on them.

"It looks like they split up the names and the places," I remarked, "Putting one on each side of the line. See, this larger mass looks a little like a shoreline, so this string of names over here is probably towns along the coast."

"Yes, very good." The captain nodded, "That's what I thought, too. But look here, this tiny island has an X marked on it in red. It might be the hiding place of some sort of treasure. But it will be a problem, always having to line up the islands and the words on the two sides of the map. And there is something else wrong, too. This shoreline is along the right-hand side of the island map, but the string of names is on the *left* side of the word page. So it must be a mirror image."

I frowned at the paper, about to say that we should copy one side on to the other, when another voice spoke, "May I suggest that you fold the paper in half and look through it while holding it near a light?"

We both turned with a jerk to see that Bowen had come quietly in and was standing near the captain's shoulder. Beyond him, Krift was just coming in the door carrying two plates heaped with steak and boiled potatoes.

"You should not sneak up on us like that, sah." The captain waved a finger at Bowen, who smiled quietly in return, "Sorry, captain. But I heard you talking and did not want to disturb you."

Krift lay the plates on the table, while I picked up the map to fold it carefully in half. Following Bowen's suggestion, I held it up and looked through it at the light. The paper was thin, so that the dark ink showed through quite clearly. Now the names matched up to the islands and the line of towns sat neatly along the coast. Of course, if I moved my fingers at all then the paper went into waves and the words no longer matched up. But with a steady hand it was easy enough to read.

"Here, try it." I handed the map to Leighton, and he looked at it for a long moment. Then he set it on the table, "Clever, but not clever enough for our Wiseman here. Very good, Bowen. Now, what do you make of this?"

He read off the names along the coast, describing to the blind man where the island with the mark lay. He ended by saying, "It looks to be just across from a place called Petal point, up north along the coast. A very small island, too; it doesn't show on most maps."

The former first mate made a small, thoughtful noise and replied, "Yes, didn't we sail up that way searching for seal hunters once, captain? I seem to remember seeing Petal point as a rocky arm sticking out into the sea, with seals laying on the shore."

Leighton nodded in agreement, remembering, "Yes, so do I. But we have not been up along the coast that far in a long while. The closest we have been lately is that trip to Cribbar reef."

Feeling the old excitement at the thought of hidden treasures, or anything interesting to be found that was of worth, I asked, "So, are we going to follow this map? It looks pretty old, but it might still lead to something."

"Hmm...perhaps." The captain held the folded paper back up to study by the light of the lantern. Krift, whom I had forgotten about, but was still standing next to the table, leaned forward to look over his shoulder at it. After a moment he remarked quietly, "It looks like the island is past Clydesfort. If we went that way, I could see if my aunt would take me in."

The captain looked over his shoulder at the boy with a faintly startled expression, as if he had forgotten about him as well, "Yes, yes, that's true. Well, I'll think about it. For now why don't you find a bunk in the forecastle with the men, Krift, and get some sleep. Just remember to be here early in the morning, preferably with breakfast."

"Yes, sir," Krift walked toward the door, stopped once to look back at us as he went on outside. Once he was gone I finally turned to my food and began eating. Good roast beef and boiled potatoes disappeared while the other two discussed the map, the boy and various incidents in the day. Slowly the conversation turned to the mark on the boy's forehead and his story of men taking away talented people to work for a secret master. Bowen told us that the boy had mentioned to him earlier something which the man with him had carried, a small object that could fit in his pocket, and which the boy had at one point taken from him secretly. He had not told Bowen what this item was, or why he had taken it, but the mention of it caused some speculation between the captain and me. I thought it must have been money, while the captain thought that it had to have been some personal item which the man in uniform had stolen from Krift first.

But without calling him back up from his bunk we could not answer the question. Instead, we drifted into discussing the war between Fraistia and Durny. This was fueled by the fact that our captain had heard from captain Cuttle that someone had kidnapped the king of Durny, and was probably holding him for ransom. It was just a rumor, and Cuttle had not spoken of it as a certainty. But if the king had been kidnapped, it would give Fraistia and Thwate a good advantage over the allied pair of Selland and Durny.

Except for the raising the number of war patrols along the coast, and in fact all throughout the Middle isles, this would probably not affect us very much. After listening to the conversation for a little while I decided to get some sleep. I would have to be up on watch later in the night, so I did not want to stay up talking too long now.

As I drifted off to sleep the image of a flaming ship reoccurred in my mind, and I wondered once again what sort of magic the boy must have to make such a thing. I would have to look into it further in the morning.

Chapter 3: Ice on the Mind

The day dawned cool and clear, with a light wind pushing us on toward the northeast. Krift had brought us breakfast early in the morning, careful not to spill the pitcher of hot tea as he balanced it on a tray. Now that we were big-time pirates, with a frigate and crew of over a hundred, the captain bought tea for himself and had it regularly. Chirn also drank it, secretly, as he made the captain breakfast, and Bowen would have some when it was very cold out. I always preferred apple cider or some other mulled fruit drink if I wanted something hot, so did not partake in his morning tea.

Another thing I did not partake in was the consulting of the captain's special chart, by which he hoped to predict which ships would be in the area at what times. It had not worked the first time and I saw no reason it should any other time. So, instead of wasting my time with it, I waited until Krift was done putting our cabin in order, and then followed him outside.

"Hey, Krift, would you like me to show you around the ship?" I asked, falling in step beside him. He gave me a sideways glance as if suspicious, which was penetrating of him, before answering slowly, "Alright…as long as there is nothing else I need to do first."

"There isn't," I assured him, and immediately began pointing out all of the masts, sails and lines while telling him their names. Once we had completed a circuit of the main deck, I took him below to look at the cannons and from there down into lower hold. Eventually we finished a tour of almost the entire ship, Krift listening quietly and intently to everything I told him. It was enjoyable for me as well, since I never disliked showing off knowledge of my own ship.

After the tour we wound up sitting in the prow of the ship, looking back across the deck toward the cabin. The sails above luffed lightly in the wind, shaking shadows across the deck behind them. We sat quietly for a few minutes enjoying the scene, before Krift asked, "So what is your goal? What is the point of this whole ship, other than sailing around looking for treasure? You explained to me everything else, but I still don't understand that."

I looked over at him for a long moment, trying to formulate an answer. His dark blue eyes were firmly on me, curious and unwavering.

"Well, I can only speak for myself," I replied after a little consideration, "as everyone here probably has a different reason for staying on as pirates. Some have run away from things in their past life: debts, crimes, shrewish wives. Others are looking for adventure, or to get rich. I have never been very ambitious. Money is nice and adventure exciting. But piracy is in my blood, since the captain is my grandfather and all of his family were pirates before him."

I gestured toward where the captain stood, overseeing the preparations for the dead man's funeral. After watching for a moment I went on, "As for goals, well, we are always on the lookout for bigger and better ships, or just enough treasure to outfit this one nicely. Personally, I am always trying to become a better pirate and learn something new. Like when Bowen taught me mind magic, then I found that I had a door in my mind."

"A door in your mind?" Krift gave me a funny look, asking just the question which I had hoped he would, "What do you mean?"

With a smile, I explained, "Anyone can use regular mind magic, if they are properly taught. It's just channeling the energy of your mind to do things like contact people from long distances, or hypnotize them. But one day during an anchorage in the port of

Welmur I found out that I had something few other people do. It's a part of my mind that I can go to, and use to slip into a different view of the world. It's like a door, so when I go through it my mind is free to wander outside of myself. There, I can see the light of other people's minds, and even enter them to see the regular world from their eyes."

With a sideways glance, I made sure that Krift was still following my narrative as I went on:

"At first, it scared me a little, and at one time it got me in a lot of trouble. But by now I have become used to it and know how to practice mind magic without scuttling myself," I shrugged, glancing at him again as I finally came around to what I had wanted to ask him all morning, "So, how did you come to use your drawing with fire at first? Were you taught, or did you just discover it?"

The boy turned away from me, hunching his shoulders, "I have always been able to do it. At first it was a secret, but eventually I let people see me drawing with fire. What a stupid idea!"

The cold, distant tone had come back into his voice again as he turned back to look at me with an icy glare, "You told me your goals, now I'll tell you mine. I am going to make the one who ordered my people killed pay for doing it, and pay a high price, too. It might not be any time soon, but it will happen some time. It will happen!"

He jumped to his feet, down onto the deck. Without a backwards glance, he ran away toward the galley, leaving me behind. A little shaken by his fiery determination, I slowly shook my head. Even in my wish to 'get even' with Skon Yew, I had never been so deadly focused or so wrapped up in my plans of revenge.

But, I reminded myself, he was younger than me, and had seen his whole family killed in front of him. I had run away from my own family when I was his age and had not even thought of them much between then and now.

Getting up, I stretched in a leisurely fashion before going to join the captain for the funeral, still wondering what places Krift's determination would take him.

LATER THAT DAY THE captain decided to set out in search of the island that was shown on the map he had purloined from the *Shark*. His plan was made official and the ship's coarse was altered just a little so that we were heading almost straight north instead of north-east. This meant we were not running directly before the wind, in which we lost a little speed. But we would have hit into the upper Middle islands if we continued straight ahead and it was easier to sail against the wind a little than to be always dodging islands day and night. Now we were heading up the open sea between the coast of Selland and the isles, with only waves and sky visible on either side of us.

Krift had recovered from his outburst earlier and was now helping Bowen repair a piece of sail which had ripped a week before in a strong gale. I was carving on a small billet of oak nearby, turning it into the handle for a dagger which had broken in a fight some time before. Everything was quiet in the captain's cabin, as he was out taking a trick at the wheel.

I had just cut a small flake of wood off of one side of the billet, nicking myself in the process, when a cry went up outside, "Sail ho!"

I stuck my cut finger against my shirt, dropping the wood as well as the knife onto my bed. As I hurried out into the open, I called up to the watch in the crow's nest, "Whereaway, lookout?"

"Off to starboard, sir. She's facing away from us, but...she seems to just be drifting," The lookout replied, leaning perilously over the rail of the little crows nest with a hand shielding his eyes. I turned to the right and strode over to the rail at the side of the ship, joining other members of the crew who had already congregated there.

Ahead of us, and far off to the starboard, a ship could be seen drifting on the water. She was a large one, probably a merchant because of the lack of gun decks, but as the lookout had pointed out she was just drifting. If the ship had been sailing in the direction it was facing, it would have either outdistanced us or kept nearly at the same place, as it was catching the same wind. But we were definitely catching up on it, faster than the difference in ships or loads could account for.

As we drew even, the captain called out, "Slack sail! We'll go about to hail her."

The crowd about me dispersed as every man jumped for the rigging, following the captain's orders. I came after them, enjoying the thrill of crawling out along the yardarms to fasten and unfasten the ropes. A quick scrambled down again came afterwards, hands brushing on familiar rough wood and line until I was standing on the deck once again, staring off toward the drifting ship. As we came about it drew nearer, the speed of the *Seashooter* carefully harnessed so that we would not outrun it, or plow it under.

As we approached the merchantman it became clear that one of the masts had been knocked down on the ship, falling half way off of the deck but still tangled in the rigging. This made the hulk list dangerously to one side, shifting in every lap of the waves. The other mast had ripped and torn sails hanging from it, billowing out while letting every wind pass through them. The sides of the ship did not look to be holed, though, or harmed in any way. In fact the hull looked to be in very good condition, as if the ship had not been drifting by itself for very long. It was painted a dull, palm-frond green, with black letters on it's side which made out it's name.

"The *Highwind*." Our captain remarked from his spot at the helm, "Yes, the chart said that it should be in this direction, but it was supposed to be much further on. I wonder what happened to it."

We pulled up beside it, the men running once again to adjust the sails, and then let them all loose so that we slowed to a stop beside the drifter. I stayed on deck, watching the other ship carefully. As of yet there had been no sign or movement from its decks, nor any noise but the sound of the wind slapping in the tattered sails.

"Ho the ship!" Leighton cried through his speaking funnel, "is anyone aboard?"

There was no answer, but suddenly the wind shifted just a little and we all caught a horrible scent blowing off of it's decks. It was the smell of death, dark and disturbing.

"Maybe another outfit got here first," One of the men muttered, suggesting that it had been pirates that wrecked the merchant. Some of the others agreed, while different members of the crew put forward their own theories. But we could not really know the truth until someone went aboard her.

I turned from staring at the large ship to look up at the captain, "Should we send a boarding crew, cap? Or do you think it isn't worth it?"

"Hmm, well. It could be a trap." The captain scanned the horizon all around, before sending up a call to make sure that the watch in the lookout was still doing his job. The sea was all clear around us, not another speck to be seen on the waves and no land to hide behind in sight. While everyone was scanning the ocean I took the opportunity to slip briefly through the door in my mind. Looking at the ship in that world, I could not see evidence of anyone living on deck. But there was just one faint glow from down inside its hold.

Moving forward in my mind, I went right through the ship's walls and searched it's lowest hold. Shadows lay thickly in the enclosed space. Up ahead something pale glimmered dimly. There, laying on a heap of old sailcloth, was a man dressed as a sailor. He looked just as limp and dead as a man could be, but there was still a faint glow of light around his mind. He was alive.

"It doesn't look like a trap," I told the captain, who nodded his personal agreement. With a wave of his hand, he took in a small portion of the crew, "Alright, Sarkin. Take those men there in a boat and go across. But be careful, go heavily armed."

This last command was somewhat of a lost order on me, as I never went anywhere any other way. But I made sure that the chosen men had their weapons with them, as others of the crew lowered the boat over the side. Then we climbed down into it, carrying a rope ladder and some smaller lines to use in getting aboard the *Highwind*. The boat tipped in the blue water as I scrambled down into it, settling myself in the prow. The others came down afterward and once they were settled I began calling steerage instructions. Sparkling droplets splashed up under the dipping blades of the oarsmen. The water was fairly smooth and still, the distance short between the two ships. But as we drew closer to the *Highwind* it's shadow fell over us and the smell from aboard her grew stronger. The men slowed a little to cast worried glances up at it's lightly ornamented side, so that I had to encourage them to continue, "Come on you soft soldiers, pull harder on those oars. We haven't got all day. Nothing up there is going to eat you."

"How does he know that?" I heard one of the men mutter to his fellow, but I simply pretended not to hear. There just might be something up there that would eat us, but as we had to go aboard anyway it would not help us to worry about it now.

Soon the little boat was drawn up and fastened on to the closer side of the ship: its port side, which was not the one with the broken mast hanging over it. I sent one of the men up the side to fasten the rope ladder onto the rail, before we all followed him up it.

The first thing that met our eyes was a dead man laying on the deck. He seemed to have been crushed by some great weight falling across his middle, though now there was no object on or near him that could have done it. His face was frozen in an expression of horror and even to hardened pirates like us there was something terrible in this drifting ship with wrecked mast, with a flattened body laying on the deck to greet us. Glancing around, we spotted other bodies too; some pinned by the mast, others looking to have been stabbed with giant spears, or simply clubbed to death.

"Do you think it could have been islanders, sir?" One of the men suggested, bending over a corpse that had been run through the middle with some sharp instrument of death.

"The Middle islanders do not usually sail this far from land to do their raiding." I returned, walking over to peer at a navel cutlass that was laying on deck, "and none of the weapons here look like what they would carry. In fact, all of the weapons I see are ones the men of this ship probably carried. There is not a dropped club or broken spear to be seen."

After this speech I straightened up and shook my head. There was something which struck me as uncanny about this drifting ship, but I was not sure exactly what it was. The ripped sail flapped dismally above, and the timbers creaked softly as if murmuring to themselves. No other sound was heard aboard the *Highwind*.

Remembering the man I had seen down below, I said to my crewmen, "Three of you continue to search the deck. Two others check the cabins and forecastle. You, follow me into the hold."

The man I pointed out was a tall, stout fellow with arms like an oak's limb and a jaw which seemed capable of crushing stones. His name was Stan, and the weapon he carried over one shoulder was a large, heavy boarding ax. With this large helper in tow, I found my way to the aft hatch and began to climb down. It was dark within the innards of the ship, the wooden walls absorbing all of the light. But I had brought an oil lantern from the boat, lighting it now to show us the way. It's glow bounced off of the wide ribs of the ship, making shadows flicker at the edge of my vision. It gleamed off of the stacked crates lining each side and the barrels lashed neatly in a row. I walked slowly forward in the direction which the living man lay, keeping a sharp eye out for any human movements. Once, I stopped with an upraised hand to halt my follower, thinking I had heard someone's voice murmuring beyond a crate. But it was only the men on deck calling to each other above our heads.

"A little spooky down here, isn't it?" Stan remarked in a whisper as we continued on.

"Yes, though no corpses yet. The fighting was mostly topside," I returned, walking as quietly as I could. But the planks still creaked under our combined weight, adding to the mysterious sounds of the ship. Finally we came to a loose pile of sails, both drawing in our breaths suddenly at the sight of a man laying on them. But he was quite still and, though there was no sign of injury on him, he did not even appear to be breathing. Wondering if he had expired since I saw him through the door in my mind, I moved forward and lay a hand lightly on his throat. Faint beneath the skin, there was a pulse of life.

"He's alive," I told Stan, moving my hand to grasp the inert man's wrist, "But very cold...strangely cold."

I added the last words in a tone of surprise, withdrawing one hand to rub it with the other. His skin had been so cold that it had chilled my fingers at a touch. Yet I could not see anywhere on him a fresh mark or even bruise to indicate how he had been injured. Once again, there was something strange and inexplicable about what was going on aboard this ship.

"What's wrong with the fellow?" Stan asked, looming over our find.

I shook my head again "I don't know. There is something strange going on here." Immediately afterwards I turned as a voice called us from above, answering, "We're coming!"

Before adding to my companion, "Here, wrap him up in this piece of sail and we'll carry him back to the boat. Maybe the sawbones can awaken him and we can find out what happened here."

"I'll get him, chief." Stan wrapped his strong arms around the bundle of man and canvass, picking him up as if he had only been a billet of firewood, "You can go see what the others need."

With a nod, I led the way quickly back to the hatch. There I helped him get the unconscious form up onto deck, before leaving them to join Glimpy, who was beckoning to me from the cabin door. Glimpy was a skinny old man with one squinty eye and a mouth full of rotten teeth, but he was as tough as a leather whip and often the sharpest when it came to finding things.

"What is it?" I asked him, as he waved for me to come into the captain's cabin.

"Heh, hold your horses and I'll show yer," He told me disrespectfully, skipping across the cabin and pushing the younger man who was with him out of the way. This cabin was set up with nice furniture and a rich carpet on the floor. Two bunks occupied one wall, while the third was against the back. On one of the stacked berths lay the body of a boy almost half my age, stabbed in the heart with a long dagger. The bed below him was empty, though the blankets were riffled and torn as if it had been searched. But the third bed was the one my attention was being drawn to with a wave of Glimpy's withered old hand, "Now, cast yer eyes on that, chief."

I moved forward to sweep my eyes over the berth. It was a simple ship's bed with drawers built in to it and a rough woolen blanket of dark blue thrown over the top. But the pillow was a pale lavender silk affair (which seemed a little flashy to me) and showed drops of dark red sprinkled across the top of it clearly. At first, I was inclined to ask why Glimpy had brought me here just to see the captain's blood on a silk pillow. But then it occurred to me that the drops had not soaked into the cloth, as I would expect them to. Instead, they stood up in perfect little domes, like jewels. Reaching out, I touched one of the drops, feeling it cold and hard under my fingertip. Slowly, it melted away to soak into the pillow as it should have. With a frown, I exclaimed, "They're all frozen!"

"Yep." Glimpy chuckled mirthlessly, "Now yer see what I mean. The weather ain't been cold enough in this part of the sea lately for it to freeze and it ain't cold enough now for them to stay frozen. Yet frozen they are, or I'm a toothless jackal!"

I forbore from remarking that that was just about what he was, instead picking up the pillow and shaking it lightly. The frozen drops of blood clung on, without moving at all or melting away.

"I'll take this back with us to show to Captain Leighton. Let's get the others and clear off this ship. I don't like its feel," I told the crewmen, turning back toward the door. Behind me, Glimpy snorted softly, "Nobody would like it's feel. There's been witchcraft aboard this ship, or I'm a squished iguana."

Ignoring the fitness of this remark as well, I led out the way to find the rest of our crew.

DESPITE THE LARGE CARGO it held, no one was sent to get anything from the drifting ship. As soon as we came back in the boat the sails were set northward and we left the other vessel far behind. Even across the intervening water, the crew had felt the strangeness and fear that was aboard that ship. None of us wanted anything more to do with it. The *Highwind* was left to drift with the wind and waves, so that any other pirate could have her if they wanted. They were welcome to it.

After having shown the captain the silk pillow, and told him about what we had found on the ship, I went down to see if our sawbones had made any progress with the unconscious seaman. We had no specific sickbay aboard our ship, as they did in some large warships. Instead, the men were always treated in their bunks and the doctor simply kept his things in the hold. The sawbones was a small, thin man with bright, piercing eyes and a habit of wearing all black, which had won him the nickname of Vulture. And even though he had come with a regular handle, that nickname had taken its place entirely. I climbed down into the crew's quarters to find Vulture standing over one of the lower bunks, tapping a hand impatiently on his thigh. He was not known for his patience, despite the fact that he was a doctor.

"Any improvement?" I came up and looked over his shoulder, seeing the crewman from the *Highwind* still laying with his eyes closed and a bluish tinge to his face.

"No." The sawbones told me shortly, "I can find nothing wrong with him except for that he is cold. And nothing I do seems to warm him."

"Have you tried forcing hot brandy and ginger down his throat?" I asked, remembering our old cook Edna telling me that ginger was a warming herb.

"Yes, and chafing his arms and legs with a rough cloth, and putting hot water bottles in bed with him," Vulture replied, adding with a shrug, "Nothing is working, though I am waiting now to see if the water bottles will improve his condition with time. Oh, and there is one more thing."

He moved over to pull the man's arm from the blankets and turn his hand palm upward, "I found this on his hand. Perhaps it has something to do with his malady."

I bent over the hand, letting out a small gasp. There were lines of light blue and white on the man's hand, glinting icily. They made a shape on his palm, a clear mark of shimmering frozen water. It was the same mark as had been branded on Krift's forehead; a bird's head with three slashing lines striking down over it.

"Go find the cabin boy and bring him here," I ordered the doctor, who gave me a stiff glare before hopping off to do as he was bid. Once he was gone, I looked around to see who was nearby. Most of the crew was out, only one of the men who had been injured in the fighting being asleep in his bunk. Not believing that he would awake any time soon, I sat down on the floor beside the cold man's bunk and closed my eyes. I wanted to see what the mark looked like through the door in my mind and if there was anything wrong with his mind. As I traveled through my mind to the door, I wondered briefly if this man was one of the talented ones that the 'master' was looking for, branded with ice as Krift had been with fire. He could also be only a victim of whatever calamity had befallen the rest of the crew, including the captain who had left frozen blood behind on his silk pillow.

In coming through the mental door I saw the crew's quarters in different shades, all the shadows deeper and richer, while the rays of light glowed in unearthly brightness. The mark on the man's hand glowed as well, but in a deep blue color like frozen fire. It flickered and bent with a wind which I could not feel, appearing to have a life of its own. Moving through the silence of the inverse world, I drifted closer to look at the light of his mind. It was dark green in color, a rich, forest hue. But it was very dim, and on closer inspection I noticed something else. Around his mind, containing the light and dimming it, was a net of the same icy blue as the mark on his hand. It did not glow quite as brightly, instead appearing cold and hard like strands of frosted steel. Tentatively, I let my mind brush up against the net, trying to find a way in through the cracks. A sense of burning cold ran all throughout my mind, forcing me to recoil immediately. Instinctively, I withdrew back into the regular world, shivering to the core of my thoughts. No wonder the man was cold and did not move: that net had been as sharp as a winter's frost during Midwatch in the crow's nest, with a north wind to accompany it.

Rubbing my hands together as if to warm them, I shivered again and had to clamp my teeth together to keep them from clicking. There is something about chattering teeth which always annoys me, so I kept my mouth tight shut as the chilled feeling slowly wore away. I was just beginning to consider going back through the door in my mind to see if I could do anything for the patient, when the sound of footsteps rang on the ladder and the sawbones returned. With him was Krift, a puzzled and worried expression on his face.

"You wanted me, Sarkin sir?" He asked as they came to stand beside me.

"Yes," I stood up, holding the man's hand open so that the boy could see it, "First, what do you make of that?"

His face tightened, thick eyebrows coming down in a weighty frown, "It's the mark of the master."

Then he came closer and ran a finger over the lines, adding, "And...It's made of ice, in the same way as I would draw with fire."

Krift looked up at me sharply, expression hard, "someone has hurt him with the ice. It's—it's frozen him inside. That's why he doesn't move: he's frozen."

Though I knew from my own examination that it was true, I asked, "How do you know that?"

This made his gaze fall, while he bit his lower lip for a full minute before answering, "I can do the same with fire, except for that it makes the very opposite happen. Whoever has it on them feels as if they are being burnt...they can't sit still with burning up inside."

I nodded slowly, seeing the frightening image in my mind of being eaten alive with fire from the inside out, "I see. Well, do you know of a way we can cure this man? I need to talk to him, ask him why this 'master' person ruined his ship and did this to him."

"Well..." The boy hesitated, shifting his gaze all around. He was always awkward about admitting to anything, unless it was his desire for revenge, "I think that I could help him, maybe. But I am not sure."

"Would it hurt him to try?" I asked, then shook my head, realizing it was a silly question, "It doesn't matter. He will die if we don't find a cure. Do you have any objections, Vulture?"

The last words were directed to the sawbones. He gave me a long, bright look before saying, "If it has to do with magic, it's entirely out of my realm. Do as you will."

He shrugged one skinny shoulder and stepped back, waiting to see what we would do. Though we had not wanted anyone else to know of Krift's powers, I decided that the doctor would have to be taken into our confidence.

I nodded to Krift encouragingly, "Do whatever you think will save him. I'm going to use my own magic to watch his mind meanwhile. Don't be afraid, just do whatever you think will work."

The boy said, "okay" In a small voice, crossing his arms over his chest in preparation as he had before. I waited a moment, curious to see what he would do. After preparing himself, Krift reached out with one hand and grasped the frozen man's palm, holding it open. Carefully, he brought the finger of his other hand forward, glowing bright orange at the tip. With utmost concentration, he began tracing the icy mark with his burning touch. The mark began to disappear behind his finger, fading away into normal skin that was just a bit more red in color than the surrounding hand. But the boy did not burn his patient, or leave any fire drawn behind on the skin.

Pulling my gaze away from the spectacle by force, I slipped back through the door in my mind to watch him from that point of view. The first thing I noticed in coming through the door was the color of Krift's mind, which held a surprising combination of colors I had never seen before. It was dark, almost black, fading gradually into a brilliant, glowing ember shade near the center of his mind. I had never before seen a person's light that naturally had more then one color in it: everyone else I had seen before had only one, single hue to their personality.

After watching it for a minute, I remembered what I had come here to see and turned to look at the patient's mind. There was no change. It was still encased in a net of shimmering ice. But Krift was not yet done with his job, so it might take a few minutes longer to notice the change. Turning my inhuman gaze to see what he was doing, I saw the glowing flame on his hand burning bright in the inverse world, meeting up against the glow of the frozen mark. But the mark was slowly getting smaller, it's power fading away.

Soon the whole symbol was gone, leaving the hand free and clear. With hope brimming, I looked toward his mind again. But there was no change to be seen: It was still encased in ice. He had not been cured.

I noticed Krift stand up to frown at our patient thoughtfully. After a moment he turned toward where I was standing and tried to say something to me. Quickly, I darted back into the regular world, shaking my head, "Sorry, I didn't hear that. What did you say?"

"It didn't work," Krift told me, looking both nervous and frustrated, "I thought that removing the seal would make him thaw, but there is something deeper still holding him."

"There is a net around his mind," I explained, describing to him what it looked like, "Can you trace it like you did the mark, and free him?"

"Without seeing it? I don't know." The boy stood still, deep in thought. Then he looked up at me with the spark of an idea in his eyes, "But you can see it, looking through that door in your mind. So if you could bring me through the door, or somehow show me the net while you are there, then I would be able to thaw it."

He was excited, clasping his hands behind his back expectantly as he waited for an answer. Now I was put in the spot of having to use my magic in a new way and I was the one to hesitate. I had never even thought of trying to bring someone else through the door in my mind with me, so that they could see the inverse world. It did not sound possible. After thinking about if for a few minutes I came up with an easier way, "Alright, look. You get ready to trace the lines, Krift, and I will go through the door in my mind. Then I'm going to sink into your thought just a little bit: you'll feel it, but it won't hurt you. There I'll project into your mind the image of *his* mind and you can use it to follow the lines. Just close your eyes and trust the image that you will see. Okay?"

"Okay." He nodded, closing his eyes. I sat on the floor beside him to do the same, taking a deep breath. I had done many small tricks with magic before, slowly learning how it could be useful in a pirate's life. But things always came up that I had never done before, and this was one of them. To put a picture in the mind of someone else, a picture of something that was happening in the real world, I would have to have a strong link with their thoughts, but not so strong that I could not see what was around me.

Trying to remember everything that my various teachers in magic had ever told me, I slipped once again through the door and focused my vizion on the net of ice. Then, always keeping it in view, I drifted slowly over until my light was fading into Krift's. Slowly, our thoughts mingled until I was in just the position of mixed mental view which we had decided on.

"Now!" I whispered in the boy's mind, projecting what I was seeing into it as clearly as I could. Our thoughts had mixed so far at that point, that I could feel the motion on the outskirts of my mind as he raised his hand and began tracing the lines. But I had to be careful not to actually see from his point of view, or else we would both lose the vision of the frozen net of icy lines.

Like a spider unweaving its own web, the boy's finger traced the lines, burning them away into nothing. He worked quickly and steadily, while I poured all of my concentration into holding the image of the net in place. The trapped light behind the net glowed brighter and brighter as it was unbound, until the last line was erased and it burned free.

Feeling the weariness which always came with using magic, I shook free of Krift's mind and slipped back into the other world.

Chapter 4: Crushing Tentacles

The man we had set free immediately began shivering violently, clutching the woolen blanket to him with curled fingers. He moaned a little, incoherently, before his eyes snapped open to stare unseeingly at us. As I stood up one of his hands shot out to grasp my wrist in a tight grip.

"The griffin!" He exclaimed in a hoarse voice, pulling me closer without even seeming to notice that anyone was there, "It came down out of the sky, wrecking, stomping, destroying! Agh, the griffin..."

At his words a memory shot through my mind and I unwrapped his hand firmly to ask, "What griffin? What did it look like?"

"Huge!" He pulled his arm away, throwing it over his eyes as if to shield himself from the very thought of it, "It was black, and huge. I ran. The *thing* riding on it's back chased after me. It caught me! Oh no, It caught me!"

Our patient fell to moaning and shivering again, unable to yet face or explain what he had seen. One of the crew who was trying to sleep on a bunk nearby opened his eyes for a minute and grumbled, before turning over and falling back to sleep. Krift had stepped back, appearing to be startled at how our experiment had turned out. I looked over at the doctor, beckoning him closer, "It's back in your territory now, doc. See if you can get him warm and a little calmer. But first, let me have a word with you."

Stiffly, he let me lean closer to his ear, where I whispered sharply, "Don't tell anyone about what you saw this boy do. Or what the man said when he awoke. No one else in the crew is to know, except for me and the captain, whom I will tell myself. Got that?"

"Yes, I will be discreet." Vulture brushed me away and went to administer to the chilled, shocked man in the bunk. I drew Krift away, leading him up onto the deck. From there, we began walking slowly toward the cabin, while I told him, "That was good work, you freeing him from the ice. Don't worry about how he was acting a moment ago: he should recover soon enough. But, listen Krift, I don't want anyone except for Bowen and Leighton to know what went on down there, besides you, me and Vulture. The crew don't need to know of your powers and we should to learn more about this griffin before telling them about it."

He gave me a quick glance, guessing, "You know something about it already, don't you?"

I nodded shortly, "Yes, I think so. But what the thing was on it's back...I hope that I don't have a good guess."

As we entered the cabin door my thoughts went back to the great black griffin which Skon Yew had been the master of, the griffin which had once been known as 'Hope' on the island of the Shadow City, but which he had renamed Nightwing. When I had defeated the Dark Prince in a battle, his griffin had survived, picking up the prince's body and flying away with it, shrieking, into the air. Could it have lived on somewhere in the world, secretly, preparing for a vengeful war by collecting powerful people to use against it's old enemies?

And had Skon Yew somehow come back to life to ride it, either as a living being, or as a pale ghost?

Realizing that I was just standing with the door open, I motivated myself into the captain's cabin and sat on my bunk. Krift had come in as well, and was nervously rearranging some things left on the captain's bed. For a time we were quiet, while I thought these things over and he waited for me to speak. Eventually, I came to the rope-end of my thoughts and stood up, "Krift, go find Bowen and bring him here if you can. I will find the captain. They should both know what we heard."

"Yes, sir," Animated by having something to do, the boy shot off. I followed him, still wondering if I would ever be free of my old enemy. Whether it was Skon Yew on the griffin's back or not, it was still his original design that had turned it against us.

THE FOUR OF US TALKED long into the evening on that subject, but in the end the only conclusion we came to was that we would have to wait for the man we rescued to be able to tell us more, before we came to a conclusion. Though they shared my fears that the griffin could be Nightwing come back for revenge, both the captain and Bowen considered it unlikely that the ghost of Skon Yew was riding him. I thought it unlikely too, but I also knew that seemingly impossible things could, at times, happen.

"Don't worry about it too much, Sarkin," Leighton counseled, giving my shoulder a fatherly grip, "If that metallic bird-beast comes around, we'll just have to deal with him."

"You're right, captain," I nodded, trying to lay my anxiety aside, "Even if it is the same griffin, he is not unbeatable. I just wonder what could be riding on him that can freeze a man's mind like that."

Krift had not spoken much throughout the meeting, but now he said quietly, "It was probably someone he captured, like me, that can draw with ice instead of fire. In one way or another, it forced them to work for him."

"Yes, that is a good idea," Bowen returned, "It is like a story I heard once on Ullabar, about a water-monster who challenged Coyote to a duel..."

The captain and I waited for him to go on, as his stories were always an interesting distraction from the life and trials at sea. But he simply shrugged, adding, "I'll tell it to you sometime."

"Well, hmm, very well," Leighton pretended that he had not been hoping to hear the story just as much as the rest of us, straightening his maroon coat with a jerk, "Now, Krift, go tell Chirn to heat some grog for the crew: it feels like it's going to be cold tonight. Sarkin, I believe it's your turn to take a trick at the wheel. I will check the charts against our treasure map, to find the best route to the island."

"What about me, captain?" Bowen put in, with just a touch of a lazy drawl to needle him with.

"You, sah, can go sew on some sails, peel some potatoes, or do whatever it is you do around here," Leighton returned in a ruffled tone, knowing that he was being teased. I left with Krift, waiting until I was outside to snort in amusement. Sometimes the captain was like a bustling housewife, though I believe he fancied himself more like a strict officer at those times.

The night was cold outside, and I was glad that I had snatched my heavy cloak as I was going out the door. It had been given to me by the Magyan and was lined with fluffy wool inside to make it warmer. Swinging it around my shoulders, I headed up to the helm, replacing Ramses at the wheel. He rubbed his hands together and pointed up at the sky, "It is a clear night this evening, isn't it my friend? That always makes it colder."

I nodded, checking the direction on the compass nearby, which was lit with a lantern, "Yes, no frost yet, but winter is not far off."

A gust of wind flapped across the ship sideways, making it lurch sideways. When it leveled out, he returned, "Oh, winter will wait a little longer before setting in. I hope we are out of northern latitudes by then."

"I hope so, too," Cold weather always made the old scar on my leg ache, though I would never have admitted it to anyone on the ship.

Ramses moved off, leaving me to hold the wheel and watch the first stars coming out in the darkened sky. Everything was comparatively quiet across the ship, though I heard the men on watch in the prow talking in muffled voices to each other. Below me, on the deck, light from the cabin spilled out in thin lines across the planking. I stood feeling every bump and dip of the waves through the ship, knowing them all as signs of good sailing.

When I finished my trick at the wheel, I went back to the cabin to turn in, wrapping my cape around me as a blanket instead of going through all the work of taking it off. I slept solidly until the early morning, feeling subconsciously all through the night the smooth riding of the ship. But just as I was beginning to awake there was a bump that was different. The ship did not fall as far as it should have, or perhaps it simply grated off of something that should not have been there. Either way I felt the motion come up through the floorboards; a sort of shiver or lurch. Without warning the ship came to a stop.

It was not drifting gradually as it would if the sails were slacked off, but with a sudden violence which almost threw me out of bed. One of the crew called out near the bow, yelling something I did not catch. Jumping up, I hurried outside, blinking in the morning light. The masts were bending ominously in the breeze, sails straining.

The first thought that came to my mind as I stood looking across the deck was that we had struck ground. But we were far out in the ocean, between the continent and the islands, and there was no known land-forms in this area. My second thought was that we had hit into a smaller ship, running it under. But that would have made a bigger impact and would not have caused the ship to stop so suddenly.

It was more as if something had grabbed hold of us and was keeping the *Seashooter* from moving. Captain Leighton came out of the door behind me, asking, "What is going on, Sarkin?"

"I don't know," With a mental note that I would find out, I darted across the ship toward where some of the crew were leaning over the rail, looking down into the water. When I was a little more than half way across, the scene in front of me changed abruptly. What appeared to be a long, waving serpent shot up above the prow, waving over the men's heads. Swiftly it coiled down and wrapped around the head of one of them, jerking him screaming up into the air. It was not until then that I realized that it was not a snake at all, it was a huge tentacle.

With a glance I saw that other tentacles were reaching over the side of the ship, grasping the rails or slithering like oozing snakes across the deck. We had been wrapped in the arms of some giant sea monster.

Reaching the front of the ship, I drew my sword and hacked at one of the tentacles coming over the rail, slicing down into it with a sickening *'squish!'*

The crew were trying to pull our captured member back aboard, fighting with the arm that held him. One of them used a cutlass to slash at the tentacle, forcing it to let go. I slashed at another slimy limb, before drawing a pistol to fire at one reaching toward another man. It writhed and withdrew, as the ship heaved beneath us with the monster's wrath.

Men were pouring up out of the forward hatch, shouts echoing across the ship;

"It's a squid!"

"Or an octopus!"

"Watch it, the arms are stronger than anchor chain."

"Hack them off, crew! Don't let them grab you!"

All around me the fight went on against the invading tentacles, men hacking and slashing at every arm in view. The ship creaked and groaned, crushed by the giant's grip. I felt something begin to slime up around my ankle and looked down to see an arm wrapping itself around my leg. Before I could react, it jerked suddenly and threw me off my feet. My sword flew out of my hands, landing with a clatter on the deck. My face smashed into the planking, sending pain shooting up from my nose. I scrabbled to regain my feet, or just turn over and face the thing wrapping around me. It pulled me steadily toward the edge of the ship. Splinters bit into my fingernails as I attempted to slow it, before I finally felt someone's hands grasping my arm and pulling me back away from the rail.

"Cut it off of him!" The captain's voice cried out above me. There was the hissing thud of a sword falling and the tentacle went slack. I scrambled upright with Leighton's help, shaking my head to clear it.

"Thanks," With a gasp of gratefulness to my rescuers, I turned to see how the battle against the oozing limbs was faring at other places on the deck. All around, the men had fought the tentacles off until every one of them had retreated over the side, leaving wiggling tips and pieces behind. The grip on the *Seashooter* was released, letting it flop back down into the waves in a rain of spray.

"Are you alright, m'boy?" The captain asked as I wiped a hand across my face to have it come away with a stain of blood. Being slammed on the deck had done a good job to my nose.

"Just fine," I told him, "It's only a nosebleed."

Silence had fallen over the ship as we waited to see if the creature was permanently frightened off, or if it would return. I moved closer to the edge of the deck, peering over into the dark blue waters. They heaved strangely, roiling as if being brought to a boil. Something moved right beneath us: a half-seen shape of slimy skin and flexible muscles. The water around it seemed murky and gray, as it shifted just below the surface. Then it faded away, deeper into the sea.

"Do you think it's coming back?" One of the crew asked me in a frightened tone. It was the man who had been picked up by a tentacle, his hair smeared and crazy but his head otherwise unhurt.

"We'll just have to see." Was my uncertain reply, as we all stood watching for any other signs from below.

By now the ship had started moving again, sails filling with the stiff breeze. But it had not yet come up to full speed when there was a ruffle in the water in front of it, and a huge shape lifted itself up out of the sea. Pendulous bulges of reddish skin, thick-lidded, squinting eyes the size of a dinner plate, large suckered tentacles, it was our sea monster: an extremely large octopus.

Waving it's eight injured arms in the air, it regaurded us malevolently over the length of it's mantle. Blue blood ran down from the dismembered ends of the octopus's tentacles, dripping into the sea. All of the arms slammed down, spraying water up around it in glittering droplets. With a strangely graceful undulation, the sea creature shot itself back down into the ocean, disappearing beneath the waves. Weapons held in hands, stained with slime and discolored blood, our men stood waiting apprehensively.

With a shock the ship rocked up on it's side as the monster breached beside us, sending waves sweeping across the deck. Everyone was flung to their knees, or stumbled back with arms flailing. I fell back against the rail, watching the enormous head rise up beside us. A deep, gurgling noise issued from it's beak, echoing across the waves. I stared at the wrinkles running across it's skin and the dull, empty eyes in its head, feeling almost hypnotized by it's sheer size and strength.

Then I saw two of it's arms reach out and begin to wrap themselves around the mainmast, pulling the ship over to the port.

Coming to my senses, I yelled at the top of my voice to be heard over the sound of water and creaking wood, "Chop it away! It'll break the mast, chop them away!"

Propelling myself at a running stagger down the tilted deck, I grabbed on to a dangling line and used it to keep from sliding too far toward the octopus. Some of the men joined me, swarming up the angled stick of the mast with blades held at ready. Below us others of the crew fired off muskets at the creature's face, or cried out in fear as they slipped down the deck in it's direction.

I reached the encircling arms first, drawing one of my long daggers to stab it repeatedly, the knife sliding in to it's hilt with a squelch each time. My sword I had not yet recovered and wondered if I ever would see it again with how the ship had been pitched about in the last few moments. Beside me, Glimpy clung on to a rope and started whacking at the same tentacle with a giant hunting knife, chuckling madly, "Chop 'er away, sir, aye, aye!"

The sea monster let out a squeal as two more men joined us, stabbing at the thick appendage. Unlike when we had been fighting it before, this was not just the tip of it's limbs; it was a stronger part of the tentacle near the center.

There was a jerk across the whole ship, shaking men free of their places to fall into the waves or the octopus's grip, and two more of it's arms came up to grab on to our mast. With a resounding crack, the wood gave away, making the mast slew sideways in it's rigging. Glimpy screamed and dropped away beside me, his knife glittering as it followed him. I clung grimly to a ratline, my head ringing with the cracks and creaks of the ship under assault. The mast jarred as it came to a stop, cradled in the torn ropes which hung over the side. Spars were broken off of the other two masts, leaving ragged stumps. After a moment I heard the captain issued a command below, "Fire!"

With a hollow boom like breakers on a rocky coast in a storm, the port cannons went off. The ship shuddered, a smell of gunpowder and charred flesh rise up into the air beneath me. The octopus let out a horrible, bugling, screeching noise before slowly sinking away out of sight, arms dragging and flailing like wet lines let loose from a windless.

By now I was hanging on the bottom edge of the mast, out over the water, dizzy and half-stunned from being swung around and slapped with sails. I noticed vaguely that some of the men around me had also hung on, while others, like Glimpy, had fallen off into the waves. Now that the octopus had let us go, the ship was only listing a little to port from the weight of the wood which I clung to.

"Are you alright, sir?" One of the men near me gasped as he went by, scuttling along from rope to rope toward the ship.

"I'll make it," I told him, forcing myself to start moving. Carefully, inch by inch, I worked my way back along the mast, through the tangled rigging and sails, to the deck of the ship. Feeling entirely worn out, and yet wound tight from the action, I dropped to the comparatively safe and solid footing of the ship. It felt wonderful to leave off clinging to the lines for a few moments. My fingers felt as if they had rusted at the knuckles, I had been clinging so tightly to the ropes.

But there was work to be done, and I only had time to let my breathing steady before turning to help others get off the broken mast, fish seamen up out of the sea, and generally try to reorganize the ship. The monster had been struck by at least two of the cannons balls which the captain had ordered fired at him, and had slipped away into the water. Thankfully, we never saw him again.

A FEW WEEKS LATER ALL of the damage which the giant octopus had done was repaired, except for that we had lost two men to it's ravages. Though he had been flung off of the mast, Glimpy was not one of them, and I was glad to see the sharp old timer still prying into everything aboard ship a few days later. The two lost men had disappeared entirely, not even their bodies could be found later.

A new mast had been fitted from a tree cut on a nearby island and the carpenter had been working overtime to get everything fixed up on board. I helped him when I could, nailing new rails on the side and caulking the small cracks which had opened up in the hull. Finally, everything was done, bruises were healed, and the ship felt like it was back to normal. But, remembering the time which we had been attacked by a sea serpent in the *Blue Bucket*, the captain had forbidden Bowen from ever even mentioning a water monster in an Ullabarian tale while at sea. Both times he had before, something had come up to answer him.

Now we were approaching the seaside town of Clydesfort, a small settlement in the rough, rocky land of northern Selland. This was about opposite of Cribbar reef along the coast, but by some trick of wind and waves it was not nearly as tropical in climate. Though the weather at this latitude was often warm, the mainland did not sport the palm trees, bright sand and clear waters of the Middle islands. Instead, it had gravelly beaches, steep hills and scattered groves of Scarlet pines, with their distinctive multi-colored needles.

Clydesfort was built on a jutting piece of land sticking off into the sea, with a shallow, long bay on its northern side. The houses set among the gray rocks of the land gleamed white as we approached. Little fishing boats pulled in and out of a harbor, sails striped with bright colors across their creamy white background. Today the sky was slightly overcast, gleams of sun poking through now and then to glint off of buildings on shore. I stood feeling the wind on the raised platform near the helm, with Krift standing beside me.

"Have you ever met your aunt before?" I asked him, shading my eyes with one hand against a sudden sun-glare as the clouds parted above us.

"No," Krift shook his head, "My father always said that he meant to take us to see her, as she had been his favorite sister. But you know how those things go; always a wish until they are too far past to do any good."

"Yes, I know how that sort of thing goes," I replied, remembering the time long ago when my mother had promised us all summer to take us to her favorite swimming place along a nearby stream and never found the time to do it. By the next summer, I had run away to sea.

"But most people try their best, and what gets left out is usually not the important things."

"I just hope she likes boys," Krift muttered, meaning his aunt.

With a shrug, I said, "If not, you can always come back here. In fact, I'll come ashore and try to help you find this old dame, okay? That way you know that we won't leave you in a lurch."

"Thanks, Sarkin." One of his few, fleeting smiles went across his face, lighting it wonderfully. I reminded him with mock solemnity that I was 'sir' or 'chief' to him aboard ship, but all the time I was wondering if he would always be such a serious companion. Not that there was anything really surly about his outlook, but I hoped that his bit of time aboard the *Seashooter* had shown him some of the ups of life, and not only the downs.

Soon we had sailed as close to the shallow water of this part of the coast as we dared, so I had to jump down to issue orders for the furling of sails, as well as the lowering of anchors. The men all jumped to it smartly, looking forward to some leave on shore after the often-monotonous weeks at sea. In a surprisingly short amount of time we were sitting quietly at anchor beside the very tip of the point, dropping the ship's boats off to carry us ashore. The captain's gig was lowered off near the front of the ship and he climbed into it with me, Krift, Bowen and a number of the crew as rowers.

Not all of the crew were going to land, of course; only about half of them could leave the ship, in case a wind or a warship sprung up and it's anchorage required changing. The shore leave had been decided by ballot, except for that Caraway had been asked to stay board to supervise. The men left behind would spend their time either resting or working on any small things which needed fixing before we got back off to sea. The ones going ashore would spend the time as they wished until evening, as the captain was going to be in the town all that time picking up a little supplies and listening to the news.

Krift sat in the center of the boat, looking curiously around at the houses on the point and the little boats on the water. I sat not far behind, helping at one of the oars, while Leighton called out directions from the stern. The gray waves lapped at the side of the boat, seeming somehow thicker than the water not far off in the deep ocean.

The thin clouds still moved overhead. I pulled steadily, so used to the motion that I did not even have to think about it. Instead, my thoughts drifted a little back in time to the day when Vulture had declared the man rescued from the *Highwind* well enough to speak to us. I had gone down to the crew's quarters with Bowen and the captain, where the man had been sitting up in his bunk, reading from a worn Bible kept in the forecastle. He was a tall man with reddish-brown hair and a thick, plain face toughened by his time at sea. Obviously, he had been an active, stolid sailor with a quiet disposition. But now he was nervous and generally shook-up, clutching the book and biting his lower lip when we asked him what his name was and what had happened to him.

With a lot of coaxing, we had eventually got him to tell the bit of story he knew. His name was Wallace, and he came from the port of Welmur lower down along this coast. He had shipped on a few vessels before, and was on his second trip with the *Highwind*, leaving his home port of Welmur for the new colony on Bree island, up north. The ship's cargo was repackaged Durny wine, woolen blankets, farming tools and all the other items which would be needed on a new colony.

Everything had been going regularly, when one clear morning a dark dot appeared in the sky, circling overhead. The captain of the ship, Bogan by name, had a reputation for being a hard sleeper and had not awoken when the first mate called out, "A griffin! It's a griffin!"

Wallace had been working with some of the other men, scraping the deck with a holystone. They dropped their job at the cry, jumping to see the strange sight. A great, black griffin, with wings of metallic feathers, had come swooping down, snapping off one of the masts with a swipe of his front leg and slamming itself heavily to the deck. Something, a being which Wallace would not name or describe, had been riding on its back. This being had made strange symbols of glittering ice in the air, before leaping off of the griffin with a long dagger in its hands.

Then everything had descended into chaos and Wallace's description went vague. There had been a battle between the men and the griffin, during which Wallace had become frightened after seeing it stick its beak right through the first mate. He had run below, into the hold, trying to hide. But the unnamed thing had followed him, catching him at the pile of old sails. It had touched him on the hand and head, sending a lighting bolt of cold power through him. After that he could only remember a long nightmare of cold and ice, before we had awoken him.

No matter how we pressed him, we could not extract any more of the story. Both Bowen and I agreed silently that it would be unwise and unkind to use mind magic to find out more, as it was some sort of deep magic which had harmed him before. So we had left him. Since then, he had not changed for the better, though he had began to come out on deck on fair days and even help with the simpler tasks.

Suddenly my mind was brought back to the present as Captain Leighton ordered 'back water' and we came to rest beside the Clydesfort docks. Jumping out onto the wooden planking, I tied the boat up and helped Bowen onto the dock. He was still agile and quick-witted, but without eyesight he might have misplaced a step. Krift scrambled up beside us, brushing his hair out of his eyes. The captain warned us not to be gone too long, before the boy followed me up the dusty street into town.

Chapter 5: Mistress Painter

The problem was how to find out where Krift's aunt lived. He told me that her name was Matilda, and that she was supposed to live in a house with a view of the sea. But almost all of the houses in sight would have a view of the sea, being perched on the point of land above it, or set along the upper edge of the sand which bordered it. So, after looking up and down for a few minutes, I decided to find a good, respectable inn and go in to inquire if anyone knew of a lady named Matilda living nearby. As it was not a large city, there was a good chance of someone knowing who we were speaking about. And if there was more then one Matilda about, we would just have to take our chances with the first we heard of. If she was the wrong one then we would move on to the next.

Leading the way through the fishing district, with it's boatshops, sailmakers, netweavers and small, cozy establishments, I soon brought us up a low hill into the middle-class part of the town. Here everything was bustle and movement, with people going briskly about on the streets and horses clopping through now and then on their way through. Clydesfort had once been only a military outpost on a lonely road stretching up from southern Selland, and had slowly grown into a comfortable town. With the war going on, dispatch carriers came through more often than before on their way toward the forts and shipping ports even further north, making the trade in inns and stopping places better.

After a little poking around, we found a large, clean inn set on a slab of stone overlooking the bay. It had flowers growing around it, a lawn with benches set in it, and whitewashed posts at the corners of the veranda porch. Altogether, an auspicious place to find a single aunt of modestly comfortable means. Though it was not generally the sort of place a pirate would frequent. I just hoped that no one had recognized our ship as a known raider and was spreading the word abroad to catch any man who looked like he had come from it.

"The Happy Seahorse," Krift read from a sign next to the road, which had a picture of the grinning animal on it. He glanced up at me after a moment, "Do you think she would come here?"

"Maybe. We'll just have to find out." I shrugged, leading the way up a narrow gravel walk onto the porch. The door was wedged open with an old boot, letting out the sounds of clinking glasses and chattering voices inside which showed that it was not empty, even in the middle of the day. Krift followed close behind me as I walked in, seeming to be nervous about meeting regular landlubbers after being at sea for a few weeks.

The room was tall and airy, joisted with great honey-gold beams only lightly stained with the smoke of the winter's fire. The walls were hung with nets, ship's wheels and other nautical pieces, in between a few large paintings of seascapes. It was obvious that this establishment wanted to feel as much like the seaside as possible, which struck me as a little ironic, when the sea was just outside for anyone to look at.

Round tables were set here and there about the room, a few of them holding customers who were eating and drinking cheerfully. Against one wall was the bar, with a small, shriveled looking man operating it. I made my way over to him, avoiding walking down the center of the aisles by going quietly around the edge of the room. There was no point in attracting undue attention.

"Excuse me," With an effort, I remembered how to be polite in my address, "but do you know of a woman called Matilda living around here; a stout, hearty woman with dark hair?"

The description I had already begged from Krift, in hopes that it would aid our quest.

"Heh, what's that?" the barkeep came over and put a hand to his ear, obviously a little hard of hearing. Which was odd, considering that he had some of the biggest ears I had ever seen.

"A woman. Named Matilda." I repeated, raising my voice. But before I could go on I felt a light touch on my arm and turned to meet a pair of seagreen eyes under faintly curly light-brown hair.

"I know Matilda," The barmaid told me, setting her empty tray on the counter while looking me up and down a little doubtfully, "What do you want with her?"

I tried to make my expression reassuring, wondering if the scars on my arms and face told against me very much, "This boy here is her nephew. Krift is his name. He is looking to stay with his aunt, here in Clydesfort, because of a family tragedy."

Vague was best, and if it was worded right the barmaid might feel some pity on the boy. She looked at him closely for a minute, luckily his hair had grown out over the branding mark, and then said, "Yes, he does look rather like her. Well, she used to come here every four or five days, though I haven't seen her yet this week."

"Do you know where she lives?" I pressed hopefully, putting a hand on the boy's shoulder to steady him.

"Well, I think—" She began, only to be was cut off as a stooped, rough-looking fellow with stringy dark hair who came up beside her and asked for another drink.

"Just a minute sir, and I'll bring you one," She promised, before turning back to talk to me as if to resume her explanation. But the customer would not be put off, grabbing her arm tightly and giving it a shake.

"I want another beer!" He declared in a harsh, slurred voice, obviously having had one to many already, "and if you don't get me one, I'll start to get unpleasant!"

His fingers bit into her arm, making her let out a small squeak of pain. Frustrated at being interrupted when we were just getting to the point, my temper snapped. Drawing a pistol from my belt, I whipped it up and pointed it at his head. One finger clicked back the locking mechanism.

"Let go of her." I ordered quietly, waving the gun a little so that I knew he could see it, "We are trying to talk and I don't like being interrupted."

His weaselly face stared at me blankly for a moment, as everything around us seemed to go quiet. Then his mouth gaped open and he released the girl's arm to go stumbling and staggering with wide eyes out of the door. It was then I realized that most of the people in the establishment were looking at me.

"So much for not attracting attention," I muttered to myself, putting the pistol carefully away in my belt. The barmaid was looking a little pale and had stepped back a pace. But she spoke bravely, "Thank you sir. I...we don't usually have ruffians like that in here."

"Of course not," I gave her a bitter half-smile, which went roguish when she returned it, "But could you please finish what you were saying?"

"Yes," she nodded, regaining her color, "Matilda lives at the end of this road, I believe, up at the point of the land. I think her house is two-stories, and made of native stone, but I am not exactly sure. Does that help?"

I nodded, "thank you."

Without another word I flicked her a coin and turned to hurry the boy out, tired of being stared at by everyone in the place.

"Remind me not to go in places like that, Krift. They are too rough for my tastes," I told the boy in an undertone as we got outside, feeling grim again. If anyone happened to be looking for pirates, I had just made myself a prime suspect. It was the curse of being a Sellander: our hot tempers sometimes came to the fore at the worst of times.

But at least we had a clue as to where Krift's aunt lived. After walking quickly down the little gravel walk, I turned on to the main cobbled street and headed left. This would take us further along the road, out toward the tip of the point. A mixture of houses, stores and large boulders went by on either side of us, the first two objects slowly petering out as the point got narrower. Soon there was only larger houses, perched here and there in the rocks, with seashell gardens and iron-rail fencing around them. The road had become slightly narrower too, having a border of small, tough shrubs with silvery leaves. The seabird's cries were sharper here and the wind from the bay swept gently over the rise to sing among the stones. We came to the end of the path, where it ran around in a loop, to make turning around with a carriage easier. There was an old barrel, cut in half, set in the center of the loop with flowers growing out of it. Beyond that was the gate leading to the house, a tall, whitewashed affair of cobbles and beams.

The gate was open carelessly, creaking in the breeze. We walked up to it and stood looking passed it toward the entrance of the house. That door was open as well, hanging forlornly between the shadows of the inside and the gray sunlight of outside. there was dust and sand blown partway into the door: even from this distance I could make out footprints scuffed in it. An air of abandonment and disuse hung over the whole place, somehow amplified by the fact that there was a clothes line just in view around the side of the house, with very dry looking clothes flapping from it.

"Maybe this isn't the right place." I suggested after we had stared at it for a time, saying nothing.

Silently, Krift shook his head and pointed at a white piece of board affixed to one of the gateposts. It had faded purple butterflies painted on it, encircling letters chiseled deeply into the wood. I could see that the first symbol was an M, and asked grimly, "Does that say 'Matilda?'"

Krift nodded, his face hardening into a strained expression. I let out a silent, mental sigh, "Well, let's go see what's in the house. Maybe there is a clue as to where she went. But be careful. Someone has been in there since it was abandoned."

Pulling a dagger from my belt I gave it to him, as he had no other weapon, before we went quietly up to the entrance of the house. All was silent inside, only the noise of the insistent little wind running through it and fluttering curtains audible from the doorway. With a whispered reminder to Krift to be careful, I stepped inside. Our own footprints were left in the dust behind us.

There was a long entrance hallway here, shadowed and echoing. A light sifting of dust covered its floor, gritty and smudged by passing feet. Some of the prints I saw looked only like those of birds and squirrels, but others were undoubtedly human.

We crept passed a few staring paintings of stiff-looking family members hanging on the wall, then came to the end of the hallway. I poked my head through the door there, peering into a comfortably-furnished sitting room furnished with high-backed chairs and overstuffed couches. There was no one there, but two doors led off of it, one to the right and one straight ahead. The door ahead of us was cracked open just a little, and I thought I heard a faint humming noise drift in from beyond it. With a pistol in my hand, I gestured at the door, walking stealthily across to it. Once there, I used the muzzle of the gun to swing the door open.

Inside was a mostly bare room, with a pale, planked floor and a window facing toward the south. Grayish overcast light was coming in the window, through the thin white curtains, and pouring across a table which stood in the center of the room. The top of the table and the floor around it were splattered with bright colors. Thick, oozing paint which dripped languidly from the top of the table to spatter down below.

Sitting with crossed legs in the puddles of multi-colored paint was a young girl, perhaps a few years younger then Krift. She had almost unnaturally long, black hair, falling straight down to where it pooled around her on the floor. Her smock was bright white and there were many sparkling silver bangles running up each of her arms. Both her hair and clothes were blotched with colorful paint, while she was doodling in the paint on the floor with one finger. Now and then, she would hum a few soft bars of song as if to herself.

After just standing looking in for a minute, I moved across the floor and looked down at what she was painting, drawn on by curiosity and almost a feeling of hypnotism. On the floor, vague and shadowy, was the image of a woman with dark hair, looking back over her shoulder as if in fear. The girl dabbled with her smeared finger, adding a hat of bright red to the woman's head.

"Who is she?" I asked, looking into the girl's face. It was a rather plain face, with a wide mouth and bulging cheeks like a frog. But her eyes were large and long-lashed, having some sparkling quality to them which reminded me of crystals.

A smiled curled across that plain face.

"A woman." The girl said unhelpfully.

"But what woman?" I pressed, ignoring Krift as he tugged on my sleeve and said something which I did not hear.

"One I don't want to tell you about," The girl replied, blinking slowly. I noticed then that there was something else odd about her eyes: no matter what expression the rest of her face held, they were as blank and empty as a dry pail. Prickled by her refusal to answer, I frowned, "But it could be important. I want you to tell me her name."

The smile grew, spreading the wide mouth to its fullest, "You're bothering me. Lomp, Doomcop, deal with him."

Her tone had not changed, but I sensed it when two men stepped out from beside the door and stood one on each side of me. At the same time Krift jerked me backward by one arm, "Sarkin, move!"

A pair of large, curved swords slashed down where I had been standing just the moment before. The spell which the girl had cast was broken, and I realized that we had become entangled in a trap. Two hefty, tall men stood in the room now, armed with heavy scimitars. They had already tried to take off my head once, and if it hadn't been for Krift they would have succeeded.

But my gun was still in my hand. Raising it as they advanced, I threatened; "Don't move, or I'll blow your heads off. Just stop right there."

They hesitated only a moment, then came on. Pushing Krift behind me, I cried, "Run!" While firing my pistol at the one on the right. In the heat of the moment, I had not aimed carefully and it only struck him in the arm. With a roar, he dropped his sword and they both charged me. Whipping out a dagger, I used it to block the other ones' sword, then making a slash at his side. It missed, and the one I had shot grabbed me by the shoulder with his uninjured hand. With a jerk, he pulled me off balance, swinging wildly to stab at his hand. Meanwhile the other giant was snatching at my legs, so I kicked at his face whenever it came into view. But both of the men were amazingly strong and the one I had both stabbed and shot did not seem to mind it very much at all. Before I knew what was happening they had both picked me up off the floor and tossed me like a sack of grain against the far wall.

I did not know what had happened to either Krift or the strange little girl. When I hit the wall it was mostly with my head and everything went dark and dizzy. I felt it vaguely as the giants pounced on me again, slamming me against the wall until darkness was complete.

"SARKIN...SARKIN?" SOMEONE was holding my hand, or clutching it rather, and repeating my name in a frightened tone. Thinking that I was being called for a night watch, which I did not feel at all like taking, I mumbled, "Aw, let me sleep."

"You're awake!" The voice sounded relieved now, so I cracked open one eye with the words, "Not that I wanted to be. Why—?"

Then I saw Krift sitting beside me, his face pale with worry, and I remembered everything that had happened, "Oh, yes. All that."

I propped myself up on one elbow, pulling my hand away from him. Now that I was fully awake my head felt, to put it lightly, quite a bit worse for wear, and I had the bad feeling in my stomach that we were in a fix.

"Are you going to be alright, Sarkin?" My companion asked anxiously, as I peered slowly around the room.

"Of course. Eventually," I told him, taking in a nice bedroom with red carpets, a white porcelain washbasin and stern iron bars in the one small window. The bed I was laying on was of the fancy, four-poster variety, with a canopy of pale lavender overhead. The blankets were of some rich cloth, which felt smooth and soft when I crumpled one hand into them. The light in the room was provided by a few glass globe lanterns hanging on the walls: outside the barred window it was dark.

"Where is this place?" I asked, turning my gaze back to the boy, who sat perched on the edge of the bed, watching me.

"Still my aunt's house," He shrugged, waving a hand at the window, "This is her bedroom, I think. She was always worried about assassins breaking in to kill her while she slept."

I looked at him hard to make sure he wasn't joking, then sat all the way up and swung my feet passed him to the floor. I had, of course, been stripped of all weapons, but at least they left me my clothes and shoes, "Who is that strange girl, and what does she want with us?"

"She's one of the master's talents." Krift's voice rang hollow as he drew his knees up and hugged them, "Her and her servants are from the far-away land of Yanganni. I heard them say that, and they called her 'Mistress Painter.'"

"Hmm. A painter. From Yanganni." I stood up, resting a hand against the wall until I found my balance again. Though I had heard of that land before, it was only in wisps and rumors. They said that it was beyond Thwate to the east, a land of strange animals and stranger people, where they threw their children to the beasts as sacrifices if the year's harvest did not go well. I wished that the girl had met that fate long ago.

"Do you know what she wants of us?" I asked, moving over to look out between the bars of the window. It was a dark night, thick clouds hiding any moon that would have been showing.

The boy nodded, gulping, "She said that she was going to turn me over to the master, keeping you as a pet for herself. She said that the master lets her keep such things, after he makes sure that they are harmless. In the morning, he'll be here." Realizing that he was trying hard to hold back tears at the thought of recapture, I moved over and lay a hand on his shoulder, "Don't worry, Krift. We'll find a way out of here. This isn't the first time I've been locked up somewhere, nor the worst. This odd little girl and her thugs won't get the best of us so easily."

He nodded hopefully, "But how will we escape?"

I went over to inspect the door to the room. it was firmly locked on the outside and made of thick timbers. "We'll think of a way. We are both magicians as well as pirates, aren't we?"

I gave him a reassuring glance over my shoulder. He nodded again, "You can contact Bowen with your mind magic, can't you? Then they would know where we are."

"That's a good idea," With a quick agreement, I wondered why the idea had not come to me before. Perhaps it was because I had been dead to the world up until a few minutes ago. Going to sit beside Krift on the bed, I told him to keep a watch on the door and tap me if anyone came. Closing my eyes, I began spreading out the mental fibers of my mind, forming them into a long rope reaching out to the blind man where ever he might be. This was mind magic as he had taught it to me, using the lines of your subconscious without having to go through a mental door. It was much easier to use and quicker to communicate with, than the species I usually worked with. It took only a few moments before I felt Bowen's mind, though it was further away than I had expected. As soon as we were in contact he felt my presence and sent a message, *Sarkin! We had just about given you up for dead. I tried to contact you earlier, but only got a fuzzy feeling that you were there. What has happened to you?"*

"A lot," I told him, before going over a brief outline of what had happened to Krift and me since entering his aunt Matilda's house. Like always, speaking through mind magic made it feel like I was standing right beside him and I could almost feel the ship rocking under his feet. When I was done explaining what had happened, I asked, *"Do you think you could have the captain send a few men up here to help us get out of this joint? I don't know how many 'pets' Mistress Painter may have in store."*

There was a brief pause on the other end of the mental line, before Bowen replied slowly, *"I'm afraid not, Sark. Somehow word got around in the town that there were ruffians flashing guns in the bar room around here, and the constables added that with the red ship in the harbor. It wasn't long after the captain and I got back aboard that we saw a pair of large Selland war ships making for us. We had to cut cable and run."*

It was an effort to keep the bitter color of my thoughts from coming through, as I realized who the ruffian with the gun had been. And I had a good bet what sort of weaselly-faced pig had squealed on me, too.

"Alright, Bowen, we'll just get out of here ourselves. Is the Seashooter *safe now, or are the Sellanders still after you?"* I flashed back, after I had got my feelings under control.

"We're safe." I could sense the content in his voice with those words, *"The warships were too slow to catch us, with a fine breeze and our fast rig. Besides, they had no real proof of what we are. Now we're hiding out behind a few small islands miles offshore. They won't find us."*

"Good," I sent back, *"But where can we meet up with you?"*

"Can you make it to Petal point?" Bowen asked, after another pause of a few minutes, probably used to consult the captain, *"We can send a boat ashore at the cliffs there, every night next week until you appear."*

"That will have to do." I knew that Krift and I could get horses and a carriage of some sort in this town, which would take us to the point in a week if we had good luck. Once we had escaped this strange house, of course. I cut the communication off with the ship after replying, before turning to Krift to explain about the war ships and our plight.

"So, we must be at Petal point by the end of the week. And we will have no help escaping. But I have an idea. Can you make your fire actually burn things?"

"Like wood?" With an intelligent glance around the room, he nodded, "Yes, I can make it burn things. Shall I cut a hole through the door?"

"No, there might be a guard." I lowered my voice, pointing at the bars of the window, "Can you burn the sockets holding those in?

They are wood, and if they were charred enough I could probably wrench the metal out."

Instead of answering, he jumped to his feet and moved over to he window. After completing the little ritual of crossing his arms and concentrating, he moved his glowing fingers over to touch the wood around the iron bars. it crackled as he touched it, and I had a pause of fear wondering if he could keep the house from catching on fire. but all that was to be seen under his careful hand was a soft flicker, like a candle being shielded from a breeze.

"there." he let out an audible breath as he came to the end of both the top and the bottom of the bars, "they should come out pretty easy now."

to demonstrate, he reached up and grabbed one of them. with a crunch like biting into the crust of newbaked bread, the iron rod came free from it's sockets. crumbles of blackened wood fell to the floor below it, and just a little ash blew away.

"Good job." I told him, stepping up to help pull all of the bars out. With a few cracks and crunches, the window was clear. It was just large enough for me to fit out of without trouble, and the glass panes swung outward in a frame so that we did not need to break them. The only problem was that we were on the second story and it was jagged rocks below us. Turning to look around the room for something to use as a rope to let ourselves down with, my eyes lit on the expensive blankets of the bed.

"Well, it works in fireside stories. And it seems practical enough," I muttered to myself, striding over to pull off the blankets and sheets, before knotting them together in a loose rope. Krift stood back as I tied one end around the bedpost, pitching the other out of the window. When I leaned out to see how far it had reached, the end appeared to be dangling about six feet off of the ground: close enough to escape on with ease.

"I'll go down first," I told the boy, jerking on it lightly to make sure that the end tied to the bed was well secured. It repaid me now for all the work I had done around the rigging on sailing ships for so long, both climbing and tying off ropes, "You follow me after I whistle, or if someone tries to get in the door."

Krift nodded, "Be careful of guards, Sarkin. There might be one patrolling around the house."

"Right." I pulled myself up to the window, slithered out and grabbed on to the rope. Going hand over hand, I lowered myself rapidly down, grimacing as I stretched the bruises gained from being beat against the wall. Once I reached the bottom I let out a low whistle, holding the rope steady with one hand. The boy came out of the window and started down the rope slowly, as I glanced around to make sure that we were alone. The night was dark, especially after having been in a lighted room. As far as I could see, we just had a few rocks and a line of shrubs as company.

Panting, Krift dropped down beside me to ask, "What about the rope, should we just leave it like that, showing how we escaped?"

"No way to get it down." I shrugged, letting go of the knotted blanket, "and no reason too, either. It won't matter how we escaped if we can get out of here fast enough."

Agreeing, the boy fell in behind me as I led the way around the house, out of the hanging gate. There was no lights on in the building except for the one in the room we had just left, and I heard no noise but the wind in the rocks. I was left with the feeling that the escape had been too swift, too easy: but I wasn't about to go back and ask Mistress Painter why she hadn't posted a better guard. Perhaps she had hoped that I would be unconscious longer, or had not known what resources we possessed. Then again, maybe she had just been young and foolish. Either way, the 'Master' would not be pleased when he showed up in the morning and found us gone. Which was a good reason to make as much time as possible that night.

The difficulty we had was that all of the places that you could hire a carriage were closed to all but official business at this time of night, and we could not simply walk all the way to Petal point in a week's time. So we decided to hike out of the housing district and wait for morning, when Krift could go in to town and hire a carriage on pretense of being a journeying carpenter's apprentice. It could easily pick me up at an arranged location. He would be the least likely of the two of us to be recognized by anyone and we could disguise him just a little to help with the illusion.

We had been out of town and walking west for a little while, my head beginning to ache again from the pounding it had received, when Krift asked me quietly, "One thing has been bothering me Sarkin...What do you think happened to my aunt?"

I considered this for a moment, stopping under the shade of a few trees not far from a small dirt road, "I don't know. Either she escaped, and that girl-thing is waiting for her to return...Or they killed her and were waiting for you to show up." There was a long pause as Krift came to a stop beside me, head bowed in thought. Eventually he spoke, "I don't think they were waiting for me. That girl was magic, she had a talent like I do. but she wasn't the sort of person you would leave to keep a trap. I think my aunt must have run, and that girl happened to take a liking to living in her house."

"That's a good possibility. Perhaps your aunt was the woman she painted looking back, afraid," I checked to make sure that nothing else was hiding out in the shadows beneath the oak trees, then found a leafy hollow between their roots to lay in. I felt entirely worn out and there was no point in going further without a carriage. Flopping down with my hands behind my head, I added sleepily, "Luckily, the griffin probably won't risk searching the whole town for you tomorrow. Too many people would see him. And if we can get you in and out quickly, we should be far from here in a fast carriage before he even shows up."

I heard the boy crunching into a comfortable position not far away, before he replied anxiously, "I hope you are right. If that griffin were ever to find me...I just don't know what I would do."

"Well, I guess I would have to rescue you," I told him, half asleep by now and barely paying attention to what I said. In fact, it did not even strike me at the moment that this was the second time I had been traveling through a land trying to keep a young person from the griffin's claws.

Chapter 6: The Griffin Returns

The next morning I gave Krift my shirt and had him belt it on like a tunic. Then I peeled a few little curls of inner wood from a tree, and stuck them firmly in his thick hair. I wished that I had some tools or papers to stick in his belt, as I had always had in mine when I had been a carpenter's apprentice. But the disguise would just have to do as it was, so I sent him off with a few coins in his pocket to secure our transport. Meanwhile, I moved my carcas around to the north, where the wide road to Petal point left the town. Here I set up shop and began the tedious procedure of waiting.

It was early in the morning, the sun just barely glancing over the horizon at this part of the world. A horse trotted by once carrying a silent rider, which making me jump a little. But mostly the road was clear and even the town was fairly quiet. Finally, a small, red carriage pattered down the road and the horses were drawn to a stop nearby. Krift jumped out to beckon me in, ignorant of the fact that an apprentice would usually ride up on the seat beside the driver, not inside like a master. But as he was not really my apprentice, we both clambered in to the spoke-wheeled vehicle and gave the driver the order to go.

Though I could remember riding in one when I was much younger, it had been quite some time since I rode in a carriage. The jolting felt rough and uneasy compared to the slow swing of our ship, and I found myself clinging with one hand to the velveteen handle on the side of the bench seat. The boy sat beside me, leaning toward the window so that he could peer out of the curtain whenever it flapped open because of the jolting. He seemed much more at ease in a wheeled vehicle then I felt, which made me grit my teeth and force myself to let go of the handle.

With a quick glance outside, I saw the land rolling by smoothly in shades of grass green, Scarlet pine and sea gray. The sun was out again today, throwing glowing beams across the rough pastures we were passing on one side and the rocky shore on the other. All the time my ears were alert for the noises of pursuit behind us, but they did not come. By noon we had passed through another small town, where we stopped briefly to get some bread, cheese and a bottle of light ale. We ate it on the move, keeping the wheels turning. The country on the far side of the town got steadily rougher and less inhabited until we were moving through steep hills of rock and scrubby pines. By that time it was nearing evening.

Now that we were away from prying eyes, both Krift and I peeled back the curtains to get a better view outside. The road had moved away from the seashore, so that the sight of it was shut out by the hills. Here and there we would pass tiny lakes of fresh water, or a running creek splashing between the rocks on a hillside. The air was cool, pleasant to breath or feel on your face, and if I had been more accustomed to the sensations of riding in a carriage I might have enjoyed the journey quite a lot. As it was, the motion of the cart and the bump on my head combined to make me feel a little ill, despite my experience at sea.

That evening we stopped at a small wayside inn, getting something to eat as well as fresh horses and driver. As soon as they were ready we went onward, not stopping until morning found us in a tiny village on the shores of one of the larger blue lakes. Here we got out to rest and walk around for half an hour, before getting back in the carriage and moving on. Things went on this way for most of a week, until I was both used to and heartily tired of traveling by wheels and horses. When we finally got out at the little town of Petals, at the base of Petal point, I was very anxious about how our ship was getting on and hoped to never again be in a situation where I had to ride a carriage to get from one place to another.

Petal point is a large, curving spike of land sticking out into the ocean more than three quarters of the way up Selland. Its name comes from the fact that on a map, its shape resembles a narrow petal or young leaf. Just north of it is a second point, curling out in the opposite direction, which had the far more prosaic name of William's point. Between the two I knew there was a small, shallow inlet of the sea full of rocks and stones, curling up into the mainland. The captain had once pointed this out to me on a map, explaining that there was a legend of a ship having got stuck in this inlet one stormy night, and crushed on the rocks. Because of that, the northern side of Petal point was supposed to be haunted.

Luckily, we were making our way up the southern slope of the point, where there was not said to be any danger of ghosts. In fact, the worn little trail we followed was supposed to lead to a monastery, set out on the point where the monks would not be bothered by the worldly laws of the township.

"How far do we have to go before we find the boat?" Krift asked me, trotting along beside the path in the short, wiry grass.

"Almost to the tip, I think." I replied, my thoughts brought back to the present, "the coachman said that there was a staircase built into the side of the cliff below the monastery, where you could go down to a bit of beach that was less rocky than the rest. That is probably where the captain will send the boat to land."

"I see." Krift went back to looking around himself as we traveled, taking in the rough but not unpleasant scenery. Directly around us was a small highland of short, springy grass just turning yellow because it was fall. Low hills topped with rocky outcroppings and a few stunted Scarlet pines occupied the same space. To the right of the trail about a dozen feet the ground fell away into steep hills and cliffs of broken rock, gray and sharp in the sunlight. Beyond that was the sea, white-capped and strong as it threw itself endlessly against the gravel beaches.

The noise of the wind and the sea were constantly around us now, loud and spirited. It made me feel good to be out of the rolling, confined space of a carriage. Walking free with those familiar sounds around me was a vibrant pleasure. And the feeling of the warm sun on my hair was pleasant as well; for the wind was just cool enough up here to make the sun enjoyable.

Seabirds wheeled and called out over the deeps, flashing white as they argued over the fish which washed ashore. It seemed that no living person could be out in this wild place except for ourselves, until we rounded a small hill and saw the monastery. It was a large, low building, set out on an open cliff above the sea. A stone wall ran all the way around it, built of the native material, and the tops of fruit trees could be seen waving their branches on the other side of this wall. The buildings inside the wall were made of stone as well, re-enforced with imported timbers which were worn to a pale color by the sun and salt spray. Sticking up far above the angled roofs of thatch we could see a bell tower, with a bell hanging silent and dark within it.

Both Krift and I stopped to admire the sight of the monastery on the edge of the sea for a long moment. It was impenetrably solid and yet so free that it reminded me of a good ship riding the waves. It was a few minutes before we noticed a man with a shepherd's crook leaning against a tree not a dozen yards from us. He was dressed in the plain brown habit of a monk, with a wooden cross hanging from a string around his neck. His hair was cut in the odd way which they favored, a tonsure, and his face below it held an expression of deep peace.

"A beautiful view, isn't it?" He remarked, leaning his crook against the tree to walk closer to us, so as to be heard over the wind and waves, "The monastery of St. John is, I think, in the most beautiful place in the world."

"It is a nice view." I replied politely, not wanting to start the conversation off by contradicting him, though I could think of a few places I liked the looks of even more.

"By the way, have you seen a boat come ashore below here, anytime in the last few days?"

"Yes, there is one there now," he nodded, gesturing out toward the cliff, "Some of the brothers went down to see if all is well, as sometimes a ship will anchor here to bring an injured man to us for healing, or to refill their supplies of water. The men in the boat said that they were waiting for one of their own, who had accidentally been left behind at the last port. Are you that man?"

"Yes." Wondering what that monk must really think of us, if he guessed what we were, I added, "Did they say anything else? Tell any news from the ship?"

"No, they were mostly quiet." The monk gave me a small half-smile, and a one-shouldered shrug, "pirates usually do not tell much of themselves. But I pray you, use the stairs to get down to the beach; it is the easiest way. And may the one true God be with you."

With these words he turned and walked away, whistling to a dog which lay under the tree and picking up his crook as he went. They were soon out of sight around a hill, going after the sheep which I had never seen. I stared after him for a minute, before shaking my head, "Well, he saw right through us. Come on, Krift, let's get back to the ship before all of Selland knows what we are doing."

He nodded, following as I walked passed one wall of the monastery to the edge of the cliff. Here, a steep staircase of wood and cable had been built as a way to the wide, sandy beach below. Looking down from the top of the stairs, I could make out the shape of a boat pulled up on the shore, and the forms of a few men lounging around it. Nearby they had built a campfire, which spiralled smoke lazily up into the air. Rising with it, I thought I could detect the scent of roasting fish or clam shells.

"You go in front," I told Krift, unsure if he would be afraid of the drop, "I'll walk right behind to steady you incase you slip."

"I'll be fine," he assured me, eyeing the stairs with a mixture of adventure and determination. With a steady stride he began the steep descent, and we were almost to the bottom when a shout went up from the men lounging at the boat, "Look, it's the chief!"

One of them hurried over to greet us, while the others went to picking things hastily out of the fire. The one who came to us was Ramses, a wide smile hiding in his pointed beard.

"Ah, my friends, you have made it," he said in a pleased tone, "now we may leave this beach. The captain will be very glad to see both of you; he was worried when you did not come back to the ship at Clydesfort."

"Yeah." I grinned, feeling a sharp sense of homecoming, "we were pretty worried about ourselves too. But how is everything on the *Seashooter*? No trouble while I was away?"

Ramses shook his head, "No, everything went smoothly. Though there is one little thing you might want to look in to...Chirn has a new knife, a big one."

"What do you mean?" I asked, following him toward where the boat was drawn up on the sand. But he would not tell me anything more than that the cook had a new knife, and I might want to see it. Puzzling over what he could mean, I climbed into the boat as it was heaved out into the water, and we were soon speeding back to the ship. It could be seen from the beach, a bright red shape with sails furled, resting out on the open sea. The waves made it bob gently, like a hand beckoning me home.

It did not take long for us to get there, so that we were soon being hauled aboard to be greeted heartily by the captain and questioned endlessly about our adventures.

We gave away only the roughest outline to all of the crew, before being closeted privately with the captain and Bowen in the cabin to tell the whole story. It was a sobering one: both of them expressed how glad they were that we both got back intact. We all agreed that we would have to be more careful in the future, especially when Krift went ashore for any reason. And, as his aunt had not been found at Clydesfort, he would have to stay on as our cabin boy.

When all this was over I finally got the chance to make my way to the galley to look into the knife Ramses had mentioned. Swinging open the door quietly, I saw that Chirn's back was to me as he cutting something on the counter. Seizing the opportunity, I came silently up behind him to peer over at what he was doing. A chunk of meat lay on the wooden counter, being butchered into smaller pieces for dinner. Beside it lay a few old kitchen knives, nothing special. But in Chirn's hand was a long, shining blade which he was using to hack through a tough joint, holding it in both hands like a sword. In fact, it was a sword, one that I recognized immediately, "that's my sword!"

With a lunge, I brushed him aside and snatched the blade from him, feeling a burst of anger. I had thought that the blade was missing after the fight with the octopus, lost forever in the sea. Now I came back to find him here, using it as a lowborn knife in the kitchen.

"What were you doing with my sword?" I growled at the cook, wiping some of the sticky meat juices off with the palm of my hand.

"Um...well, cutting up dinner with it," Chirn looked terrified, realizing that he had been caught, "I didn't know that it was yours, Sarkin! I just thought that it was the blade of someone else, lost in the fight."

"Right, the blade of someone else." I scowled at him. "Who else has a blade like this? You know that almost every other blade on board is some form of cutlass, or saber. Who else has a silver sword with fancy lines engraved on it? Where did you find it, Chirn?"

"I found it washed up against the galley door, jammed in a crack," He twisted his fingers together, whining, "I thought that it was lost and...well, I needed something to cut big pieces of meat with. It was handy, so I used it."

"I always knew I should have had you keel-hauled from the beginning," I sighed, looking from Chirn's pitiful face to the blade of my sword. As the first mate, I had the right to run him through right now, if I felt like it. But really, Chirn was such an idiot that you couldn't help having pity on him now and again. Especially since he was usually a good cook, if nothing else.

"Alright, listen up," I poked him in the chest with a finger, putting on a stern face, "I'll let you go this once. But if you ever even touch this sword again, it's the sharks for you!"

The picture of humble gratitude, Chirn nodded, though I guessed that he would stick his tongue out at my back as soon as I was gone. He had that particular make of mind that could be easily cowed, and just as easily forget it in self-pride the next moment.

I left the galley without looking back, thrusting the sword in my otherwise empty belt. It was frustrating to have had all of my weapons stolen, for though I had some other daggers and pistols in the cabin to replace them with, I had none as special to me as the ones the queen of Grackland had given.

BY NOW, WE WERE ONLY a short haul from the island which the captain's folded treasure map indicated. Late afternoon of the same day, we had anchored off the shore of it and put a boat over the side to see what was there. The island was a small one, only about as long as our ship and roughly round in shape. It was made up of a spiky outcropping of rock, a sandy beach and about a half-acre of sandy dirt with weeds growing in it. There was no trees on the island, but there was a lot of birds nesting in the rocks. The noise of them was so loud that we had to almost shout to be heard, once we landed on the island.

It was the captain, me and six other men who landed, carrying picks, shovels and the map with us. The X marked on the map had no exact co-ordinates, being sprawled indiscriminately over one section of the island. Luckily, this was the part in the dirt instead of rocks, or else we might have needed gunpowder to find it.

As it was, Leighton decided on digging at a point in the grass where the mark looked like it crossed the strongest on the map. There, he set us all to work. Meanwhile, he wondered about looking at the map and speculating on other points at a slight distance that we could try, if this hole did not work out.

I used a shovel to dig with, jamming it into the dirt that one of the other men loosened with a pick. Under the strain of work, the sun which had felt pleasant earlier became uncomfortably hot. After digging for about fifteen minutes straight, I stopped to wipe the sweat off of my forehead and survey our work. The hole was going along pretty good, starting to get fairly damp along the sides, but it had not yet brought up anything worthwhile.

With a grunt I bent back to the work, encouraging the men with a few words of mixed urging and praise. We went on for another fifteen minutes, then began to hit hard lava-rock in a solid cap. With this we decided to move to another location. No one would have dug up that cap of cooled lava, buried something under it and put it back again. It could easily be the foundation of the whole island. Buried treasure could be difficult to find and sometimes you never did locate it. That was either because the map was a dud, the treasure was already gone, or it had been hidden in such a way that we simply missed it.

We had just flung a few shovelfuls of dirt out of the second hole when the captain called out from a a couple yards away, "Sarkin, hold up a minute! What do you think of those clouds?"

I straightened up once again, this time brushing a loose strand of hair out of my eyes. Looking up where he was pointing, I saw a billowing pile of dark clouds beginning to rise over the northern horizon. Below the clouds I could just make out a few sparks of bright light; lightening so far away that the thunder had not yet reached us. A few minutes later there was a tiny rumbling in the distance.

"Looks like a storm, captain." I noticed that the air had gone very still, almost stifling, "probably with some wind, later on tonight."

"That's what I thought." Leighton nodded with mixed satisfaction and apprehension. "It looks like we'll have to shelter under the lee of Petal point, later on. For now, you keep four men digging, while the other two can row me to the ship and bring the boat back. That way I can start preparing the ship for the storm. Then when it starts getting either too dark or too stormy, you can row back aboard and we will be all set to run for it."

The captain was still hoping to get a treasure out of this island, though we had not hit anything yet. With a little hope left myself, I agreed to keep digging, and bent back to it as he left with two of the men. They soon returned to help us, and in another half hour we once again hit bedrock.

"Let's knock off a few minutes." I suggested, seeing that everyone was tired, "have a drink and maybe something to eat. Then we can get back to work on a new hole."

As all of the men set down their tools, or stuck them upright in the soft dirt, I walked over to pull a flagon and some jerky from the boat. The sea birds had quieted by now, seeming to sense that the storm was coming this way, hunkering down to avoid it. Silence and still air hung over the whole place. Which made it all the more startling when there was a sudden screech in the air almost directly above us, a loud noise like a nail over iron. I ducked in immediate reaction, almost dropping the flagon. The beat of giant wings passed over the island, and one of the men called out in fear. Twisting my head to look up, I saw a shape which I had hoped to never see again: the great black griffin, Nightwing.

He swooped through the air, diving down towards our ship with a clacking of his metallic wings against the spars. I gasped as he folded his wings and fell towards the deck. On his back rode a figure with long, pale hair streaming out behind it. There was a lurch as Nightwing landed on the *Seashooter*. Rigging was torn out, and the whole ship tilted to one side with frightening suddenness. I clutched the bottle so hard in my hand that it almost shattered, staring with eyes and mouth wide open like a puffer fish.

Gathering my wits, I dropped the things to the ground, as cries and screams began to ring out on my ship.

"Quick, into the boat!" I shouted at the men on the island, who stood staring with varying expressions of fear and awe. I heard one of the sails on the ship get torn asunder a second later.

Five of my little crew ran down to grab the boat with me, shoving it into the waves. The sixth would not come when we called to him, backing up against the rocks and shivering like a freezing dog. With a curse flung back on him as a coward, I jumped into the boat and grabbed an oar, along with my more loyal companions. I did not know what we were going to do to stop the griffin, chop him with a sword, or shoot at him with guns. My mind raced through the possibilities as I rowed with all my might. Anything to get him to leave, though I knew he was made of metal so that blades would have little effect on him. In the back of all of our minds was what he had done to the *Highwind*. It did not matter that we had no idea of what to do once we got there: the important thing was to get there and do something.

When we were half way to the ship the griffin let out another scream, this one louder than any before. It seemed to contain both triumph and frustration, shooting through my head like a glowing bar of steel so that I flinched and paused with the oar raised.

The great beast's wings pumped, knocking men flying out of the ship on either side. Guns were going off on board, ricocheting harmlessly off of the griffin's metal hide. He rose into the air, tearing down a yard arm as he shoved off. A human scream echoed his inhuman one, freezing my head when a moment before it had been on fire. I recognized that voice. It was Krift and he was calling my name.

Clutched in Nightwing's front talons, he was dragged up into the air kicking and struggling, calling out for me to help him. Feeling anger and terror mount to my head like a potent brew, I jumped up in the boat and whipped out a pistol. I was trying to take aim when I remembered that there was a better, surer weapon in my reach. Closing my eyes, I flung my mind through the air, shooting it through the silence of the inverse world. I went right for the griffin, seeing his head turn toward me with it's one gleaming eye. The other was put out, shattered from a fortunate shot which Ramses had fired many years ago.

I was almost to it, intent on using my arcane skill to stop him, when suddenly my mind was brought to a shuddering halt. Some invisible barrier was protecting both the griffin and the boy he carried. I slammed into it at full speed and was knocked by it back into the regular world with a ringing noise echoing in my mind. Shocked by the barrier, which had been like nothing I had ever felt before, I stumbled and almost fell out of the tipping boat. One of the men steadied me, pulling me down onto a bench so that I would not fall.

"Krift!" I shouted after the quickly-disappearing form of the griffin, though he probably could not hear me by now, "Krift! I'll get you back somehow!"

They disappeared toward the south, Nightwing having come and gone so swiftly that I could barely believe he had been here at all. I stared for a long moment, blinking at the sky. Full of bitterness, I eventually bowed my head and picked up the oar, starting to row on toward the ship. We picked up the swimming men who had been knocked out of the ship on our way, saying nothing in the bitter silence which had descended on us all. The refugees sat and shivered, both from mental shock and the cold of the ocean water. Pirates fall overboard sometimes, but it is rare that we are knocked out of our ships by giant, metal griffins. A roll of thunder went by overhead, as the clouds advanced ever closer.

Grimly, we pulled up to the side of the *Seashooter* and climbed swiftly aboard. Ropes hung down from the masts and strips of torn sail with it. The yard arm had gone overboard and was slowly drifting away. The crew were picking themselves up from where they had been knocked over, or clutching at wounds gained from huge claws and beak. One was dead, stabbed through as if with a giant spear. All in all, we had gotten off lightly compared to the *Highwind*, but I was yet to hear the worst news.

"*Sarkin.*" It was a communication from Bowen, sent through mind magic, "*I need your help, in the galley. It's...it's the captain.*"

Feeling like the world might end any moment now, I gritted my teeth and hurried over to the galley door. On the way, Caraway stepped in front of me and said, "Sir, about the—"

"Do whatever you think best." I told him abruptly, cutting off the question. He looked a little startled, but there was no time for reassurance. I pushed passed him to stride into the kitchen. It took a moment for my eyes to adjust, before I began to understand the scene. Bowen knelt beside a chair, holding the captain into it, where he slumped as limply as a jellyfish. Chirn stood against the counter, grasping two knives, a rolling pin and a spatula as if he could defend himself better the more weapons he had. Laying at his feet, stretched full length on the floor, was a figure with long, pale hair. To my surprise, it appeared to be a young lady dressed in blue clothes, with a lightly bleeding wound on her head.

Unable to account for her, I turned to the captain and went to my knees beside him with Bowen, "Is he injured? What's wrong?"

There was no sign of a wound on him, no stain of blood anywhere visible on his clothes. But when I reached out a hand I felt how cold he was and a shiver went through me.

"That thing." Bowen said quietly, with a blind gesture in the girl's direction, "Got to him."

He grasped the captain's hand and turned it up so that I could see the palm. On it, shimmering frostily, was the 'Mark of the Master'.

"He's frozen," I whispered, beginning to understand what that meant, "and the griffin kidnapped Krift."

My gaze swung over to the girl laying on the ground and I stood up. So, she was the thing which Wallace would not speak of, the thing who had frozen our captain. But I knew we could not kill her now: there was a chance that she could undo her own spell and perhaps show us to the griffin's hiding place if she was kept alive.

Seeing the direction of my gaze, Chirn put in proudly, "I'm the one who knocked her out. The captain had been down here to warn us that a storm was approaching, so we should stow everything away. Then we heard that terrible flying creature scream and he went to the door to see what it was. Just a moment later he stepped backwards in surprise and that girl jumped into the room. She touched him on the head and hand with a glowing finger, before he fell down. So I hit her with this pin."

He waved the rolling pin in the air, accidentily dropping one of the knives with a clatter. The girl began to stir a little at the noise, reaching up to touch her head with a low moan. Quickly, I stepped out to pick up a loose piece of rope from the deck, returning to put a sack which used to hold potatoes over her hands and lash it securely there. Obviously she had to touch someone to hurt them. I was not going to have her freezing any more of us with her icy magic.

Her eyes opened, a sharp, pale blue. They contained a clear anger and frustration at having been captured. She began to roll back and forth, struggling with the bond on her hands and kicking viciously at me with her feet. I drew my sword, stilling her with it's point, "Now, tell me who you are."

"Kangren gui!" she spat out, followed by a stream of more foreign words in a sharp tone of voice. To my surprise I recognized the language, though it had a different accent to it than I was used to. It was Gracklandic, and her words were mostly curses. Bringing to mind the language I had learned in my stay there, I spoke to her firmly, "Stop. Tell me your name, and where you come from."

Her almost white hair was partially wrapped around her face from her struggles, and she flicked her head once to get it out of her eyes. They met mine with the same fierceness as before, but now I noticed a strange emptiness in them, as there had been in the expression of Mistress Painter.

"My name is Karen and I come from the far northeastern Grackland." Her words could have been ice themselves, they were so cold and brittle. "You dog! untie me or the master will hang your innards from the top of your ship's mast, and give me your fingers as a necklace!"

What a pleasant prisoner we had been given. But her threats meant little to me, as the griffin would already hate me enough for killing Skon Yew so that one more incentive would hardly matter. It had just been his bad luck that in stealing Krift from us, he had left me a captive in return.

"I wouldn't speak like that in your position," I told her, which might not have been the strict truth, "we can do what ever we like to you now, and I assure you that the crew will not be happy to hear about what you did to the captain. It is your innards on the mast you should be worrying about, not mine."

"I am not afraid. The master will make you pay sooner or later, now that he has the fiery one." Karen gave a shrug, as best as she could while laying on the floor with her hands in a sack.

"But he doesn't have you," I pointed out, hoping that she would explain further why Krift was so important to Nightwing. But she did not deign to make any reply, closing both her mouth and her eyes as if I did not even exist.

"What does she say?" Bowen asked then, reminding me that the conversation had not been understood by either him or Chirn.

"That her name is Karen, and she comes from Grackland," I explained wearily, putting my sword up and turning away from her, "other than that, she has just made it clear that she is very stubborn, and not a little brave."

Though how much of the bravery was her own, and how much due to the influence of the griffin was not easy to discerne. I was starting to get an inkling that these people that Nightwing captured were somehow under his control, either through hypnotism or some other means of bending their minds to his will. I would have to look into the idea soon.

"Can she unfreeze the captain, if we untie her?" Bowen asked, still holding Leighton to the chair so that he would not fall down.

"I'll try to find out." Crouching next to the girl so that I could read her expression better, I spoke in Gracklandic, "I know that you can hear me, so listen: if you do as we say and don't make trouble, I will not let any harm come to you. But you have to try to help us. First, unfreeze the captain. Take your spell off of him so that he isn't trapped in ice any longer."

She kept her eyes closed, answering, "No. I could not take the ice away even if I wished, and I do not want to. No matter what you do to me, I will not help you."

She fell silent again after this speech and would not speak any more no matter how I pressed her. Finally, I gave up trying to talk peacefully and said, "alright, if you won't help us by yourself then I will make you."

I slipped through the door in my mind, into the frosty blue light of hers.

Chapter 7: The Crew is Persuaded

The first thing I noticed was that there was something wrong with her mind. Not that her personality had a glaring defect, or that she was naturally stupid; on the contrary, something was repressing a part of her mentality or altering it. I only went far enough in to feel around me the basic shape of her thoughts and see all around the bright, pale blue that was her color. From it I got a strong feeling of repulsion towards me and an anger that was partially linked to the feeling of something being wrong with her mind.

As for the repulsion, that was natural. It was frightening to feel someone in your mind, poking about and changing things. I had felt it before myself, so that nowit gave me just a touch of guilt to force my way into her mind. But it was necessary. I needed to find out if she had been telling the truth about being unable to help the captain, to glean any bits of information about where the griffin was hiding, and find out if she was under some sort of deep hypnotism imposed by the griffin.

First things first. Pushing away my feelings of guilt, I propelled myself deeper into her mind. For a few minutes I slipped into seeing things from her point of view. Everything here was dark. Her eyes were closed, but her ears were open. I heard Bowen addressing something to Chirn, but I could not quite make out the words. A feeling of frustration and bitten-down fear gripped me. Remembering myself, quite literally, I slid away from the outer parts of her conscious, deeper into the realm of memory. Here I watched from Karen's eyes as the griffin swooped down onto the *Seashooter* and lashed out at the crew. I realized dimly that he was making a distraction to inable the girl to slip aboard being seen. Using a gap in the fighting, she went stealthily away to the galley, with the thought in mind that she was supposed to find the 'fiery one'. Krift.

But she found the captain instead, freezing him with a touch before being knocked out herself. Quickly, I moved the memories forward, coming to the part where she was telling me that she could not have healed the captain if she had wanted to. Sadly, I found that she had been telling the absolute truth: she could freeze a person with a few touches, but she could not undo the spell even if she wanted to.

Leaving memories behind, I decided to try and track down the feeling of strangeness, of something wrong, that haunted her subconscious mind. It sounds odd, I know, to speak of someone's mind like a hunting ground and everything in it fair game. In the years I had been learning the skill, mind magic had never ceased to seem a little strange, and often very hard to understand or explain. But I had slowly become used to practice it, so that it was like learning to tie a complicated knot; at first you struggle, and have to carefully remember every step of the instructions. But eventually you can do it was barely a thought and it is only how it is used that you have to be thinking about.

Anyway, I was eventually able to find out what was making the discord in her mind. It was a carefully made, web-like repression, stretching over all parts of her conscious. It hid many things, sinking parts of her thoughts right out of sight, and letting just a few others shine brightly in her mind. The strongest change was a forced obedience to and respect for the griffin. He became a perfect master, almost a god, in her thoughts, ever watching and ever on the side of right. She would not have disobeyed him to save her life. To her that act would have been trading all that was right for everything that was wrong.

This was tied directly into her mind, affixed there by strong bonds of honor. But there was also a line attached to her thoughts which led out and away somewhere, just as there had been on mine when the dark bird had stolen my memories. In fact, it seemed that some of her memories had been repressed, so that she could not remember much about her life before serving Nightwing.

Most of the anger I had held against Karen had faded away by now, turning in to a feeling of sympathy and horror at what the griffin had done. I could not bare to imagine that this might be what was happening to Krift right now, his mind twisted and changed to suit Nightwing's purposes. I hoped that his will would be strong enough to resist it for a long time, until I could catch up with him.

Determined now to free this young lady if I could, my mind began to follow the line out from hers, away across the sea. I went quickly, not paying attention to the scenery as my thoughts flew along the invisible beam. Southward was the direction, down the coast of Selland toward a point unknown. But before I reached where the beam was coming from, I hit my own mental limits. Wishing that I had previously stretched them further with more practice, I stared off toward the south, where the line still stretched in front of me. Somewhere down there, just on the horizon, a bright light glowed. It was the color of a winter sunset, burning orange and brilliant. Looking at it gave me a bad feeling, making my head seem to ache even though I was far from it. That light was somebody's mind and it was a mind stronger and more bright than any I had seen before.

Whether it was the griffin himself, or a person that worked for him, I could not tell. But I knew that it was the one twisting talented people's wills to work for Nightwing.

Unable to go any further, I returned to Karen's blue light and tried to work the hypnotism free from that end. I was able to loosen it just a little, dim the view of the griffin and free some of her older memories. But mostly I could do nothing at the moment: whoever had a hold on her had sunk it in too tight, and it was only by destroying him or forcing him to release her that she could be made entirely free.

WEARY FROM WORKING so long through the door in my mind, I came back to the ship with a sigh. I could feel a familiar woolen blanket thrown over me, and the long rolling of the ship in a rough sea. Opening my eyes, I found that someone had put me in my bunk. I was not in the galley any longer. With a tilt of my head I looked across the room and saw the captain tucked in his bunk as well, still cold and unconscious. In the center of the cabin Bowen sat on a chair, repairing a hammock that had become frayed on one end. Near me was set another chair, with Karen tied to it securely, but not cruelly tight. She looked to be asleep, and there was a light bandage around her head where she had been struck. Someone had been thoughtful enough to preserve her life while I looked through her mind.

"Bowen, we have to get Krift back." I told him, pulling myself up to a sitting position in the bunk. "This girl cannot undo the spell on the captain."

He left his broken hammock to come sit beside me, nodding, "I was worried that she might have spoken the truth. What else did you find?"

"Someone has twisted her mind. She is not acting under her own will." I shook my head, clenching a fist in the blanket. "The one who did it is too far away for me to reach, through the door and I could not help her much from here."

I looked up at Bowen, who was still nodding slowly, "How is everything aboard the ship? Are we safe from the storm?"

"Yes, Caraway has taken care of everything. I explained what happened to the captain to him and he helped move you all to this room. Chirn still needed to work in the galley, so you had to be out of the way. The rest of the crew don't really know what has happened, though Caraway has tried to reassure them," my blind friend told me.

"He is a good man." I was pleased at how level-headed he had been, and the fact that we could trust him in any emergency, "I will have to thank him. And have the crew assembled to explain everything. It's going to be a hard job."

I sighed again and Bowen advised, "Save it for the morning. It is storming out there and at least half the crew is asleep. Nothing will change for tonight."

"What about Leighton?" I looked across at the captain on his bed, thinking of how good he had always been to me, "Will he live until we can get Krift back?"

My companion was silent for a long moment, before replying, "he has a strong will. With the right care, he might live for some time. But what he will be like when he is set free, I do not know."

We both thought to ourselves about the crewman from the *Highwind*, how the time with his mind frozen had effected him. Wallace was not absolutely mad, but it had left its mark on him. And he could not have been under the ice for more than a handful of hours. The captain might be there for days.

Dispirited, we both turned in to get a night's rest, Bowen going out to the galley, where he slept so that he could start the fire early in the morning, and I without stirring a foot from my bed. Though I was tired I did not sleep well, the address I would have to give the crew in the morning was weighing on my thoughts too heavily.

In the morning I arose stiffly, immediately meeting the eyes of our prisoner regarding me coldly. I held her gaze and we stared at each other for a time. Finally I stepped forward and said with a rough attempt at gentleness, "Don't worry: I won't let the crew hurt you. What you did is not your fault and you cannot be blamed for it. Later I will put you somewhere that you can move around a little, but for now you will be safest here."

She said nothing and I turned to leave with the feeling that her eyes followed me all of the way out, emptily hostile. On deck I found that it was an overcast, blustery day with a heavy moisture in the air, as well as beading along all of the lines, rails and spars of the ship. We were anchored under the shelter of Petal point, which broke some of the force of the wind. The cliffs rose up beside us on the starboard side, dark and forbidding. After a moment I noticed that Caraway stood near the helm, overlooking the ship with his hands clenched on the rails. I climbed to join him, seeing the worn look on his face as I stood beside him. He probably had not had much more sleep than me the night before, perhaps even less.

"Is everything alright, sir?" He turned at the sound of my footsteps, a questioning expression on his face.

"Better than anyone could hope for, under the circumstances," I nodded to him, gesturing across the deck at the repaired yardarm, replaced rigging and men working quietly near the bow. "You've done well. I couldn't wish for a better right-hand man."

A smile shifted his usually serious expression for a brief moment, "Thank you, chief. I've tried my best. But after that giant beast attacked...well, a lot of the men are still shaken."

Turning to face the rest of the ship with him, I agreed, "they will be. I am too. Bowen told you the full story of what happened to the captain?"

He nodded, "Yes. It's hard to believe, even after having seen some of the things that you can do, sir."

I remembered one time when I had used mind magic to shift away some clouds that had been overhanging us for days, and another when we had been under attack from a larger, rival pirate ship and I had killed their captain using the same. Caraway's mentioning it made me wonder what the crew thought of me and what stories they whispered in their quarters on a long night.

"Is there any way we can save captain Leighton, other than rescuing the cabin boy?" Caraway went on, grasping the railing tighter, until his knuckles turned white, "it seems a terrible way for a man to die, slowly like that, trapped in ice."

"No other way that I know of," my face felt go tight and straight with contained emotion as I made my reply, "but we'll find a way to rescue Krift and save the captain, before it is too late. We have to. He is our leader and...he's always been a good friend to me."

With a shake of my head, I peeled away from the rail, making towards the ladder, "Assemble the whole crew on deck, second mate. I need to talk to them, explain what is happening."

With a salute that I only saw out of the corner of my eye, he said, "Aye, aye sir. Right away."

While he went about his business, I moved to stand in front of the cabin door. For a bit of comfort I lay a hand on the hilt of my silver sword, trying to get my thoughts straight, the words which I wanted to speak clear in my head. Soon almost all of the crew we had, about two hundred men, were standing on the deck, or perching on the spars above, to hear what I had to say. My head was calm and cool, but my heart was beating hard as I looked over them. With the captain out of the picture, these were my responsibility, every one of them. My decisions would effect all of them, so that they would have to *want* to follow me in every order I gave. Because if they did not want to follow me, they would mutiny and put a new leader in my stead.

When the crew had settled into their places, I spoke in what I hoped was a calm, carrying voice, "Thank you for assembling so quickly, men. You must guess by now that something has happened to the captain. And you must want to know what it is."

There was a ripple in the crowd, everyone's faces expressing curiosity and intent. Leighton was a captain generally well liked among the crew. Everyone wanted to know if they were still sailing under him or not. With a few comments to that affect, they waited for me to tell them.

"Well, to get straight to the truth of the matter, he has been frozen in the same manner as Wallace was when we first brought him aboard from the *Highwind,*" I made the plunge, hoping I could keep the conversation in hand. Somewhere in the crowd, there was a low moan of fear.

"But there is more," my speech pressed on relentlessly, "there is something that most of you do not know. When Wallace was cured it was not only by the doctor's hand, nor by my own mind magic, that he was saved. Our cabin boy, Krift, has powers of his own. He had wanted them kept quiet, so that it caused to trouble, and that is why no one knew. But it is through him that we were able to save the man from the *Highwind* and it is only through him that we can save the captain."

The men started talking among themselves, waving their hands as they discussed this piece of news. Voices got loud and strident. It was starting to look like it would deteriorate into an argument, when one of them called out, "What sort of powers does this 'er lad have, 'zactly?"

I held up my hand to quiet them and through curiosity they obeyed, "He can draw patterns of fire in the air, or manipulate it to thaw a person frozen by a spell. He can even burn them with this magic fire if he wishes to. But as you probably know, there is a problem. Krift was stolen by the griffin, who has been capturing people with talents such as his to use for his own ends. To do this the griffin twists their minds, using magic to force them to his will.

They become tools, almost mindless so that he can order them to do whatever he wishes, and they will carry it out without ever realizing the wrongs they are doing. Such a person is the one who froze the captain, a young woman bent to the griffin's will and forced to carry out his wishes."

There was another space of arguments and conversations cropping up all throughout the crowd, as the crew tried to understand everything that was going on. Two of them called out again, the first asking, "How do you know all this?"

While the second pitched in with: "Is that great beast really the same griffin that worked for the Dark King, Skon Yew?"

"Yes," I chose to answer the later question first, as it was simpler, "it is the same griffin, called Nightwing. What he wants these people for is uncertain. He could simply want to control their power for the sake of itself, but I doubt it. It is more likely true that he wants to either use these people to conquer lands, or to wreak revenge on me, or the new Fraistian King, or anyone else that he blames for Skon Yew's death."

I looked around for a minute, seeing if there would be more questions. But everyone was muttering quietly to their neighbors, or waiting patiently for me to answer the first question.

I obliged slowly, "we do have one ace card in this whole twisted game. In stealing Krift, the griffin lost something of his own on our ship. The girl who is hypnotized to do his bidding. I have her captive now. She was caught in the very act of freezing our captain and tied up so that she could cause no more mischief. now—"

A roar of curses, growls and questions why I had not had her killed already, were flung at me from the crew. I held up my hand again, shouting to be heard over the roar, "listen to me! She is our one clue to finding the griffin, and Krift, which is the only way to save the captain!"

A few voices stopped, petering out as their owners began to understand. With Caraway's help, I was able to get them calmed down enough to continue listening to me, though they still muttered among themselves. Firmly, I went on, "the only way we will save the captain is by quickly finding Krift. Then Leighton can be freed and continue leading us as he always has! But to do that, we need to keep the girl alive. She should know where the griffin's lair is and be able to tell us the quickest way of getting there. Also, it is not her fault that the captain was frozen. She was forced to do it by Nightwing. We must let no harm come to her, so that she can lead us to Krift, who in turn will free the captain. Do you all understand that?"

I looked across the crew, having rammed the truth home to them as hard as I could. Just for good measure, I added, "And if any of you will for some reason want to imperil our captain's life, by trying to hurt the girl, than I will tell you now: the man who harms her in any way will be given fifty lashes at the mast. It does not matter if you were only trying to speed things, by getting the answers we seek out of her. The questioning will be left to me alone. Anyone who interferes will have to face me."

There was blank silence after this statement. I had made my point and carried my case. I was in charge now, until the captain was well again, the girl was not to be questioned by anyone except for me. This was not a ship where whippings were handed out lightly or often, but the crew knew that I would not hesitate if there was a cause.

Now it was time to stir them to action with trust. "So, men, we must all work hard and fast if we are to save the captain. As soon as this storm abates just a little, we will put up all sails and head south down the coast. Because that is the way the griffin flew and until I get more information, it is the direction we will go as well. Eat a good hot breakfast now, and prepare for weighing anchor as soon as possible."

With something to work toward and a warm breakfast promised right away, the men let out a feeble cheer and filed away. Soon I was left with just Caraway standing next to me, while a few of the men went about their duties on deck nearby.

"Good job, chief," The second mate told me, before moving off quietly about his own duties. I took a deep breath, letting it out slowly as I gripped my sword hilt tightly in my hand. I felt both shaken and a little elated. Everything was going right, I was in command. A thought that filled me full of pride while still touching me with a heavy responsibility. But the immediate weight on my mind now was the fact that captain Leighton was still frozen in an icy spell.

Turning back to go in to the cabin, my mind was trying to jump ahead to what I had to do next. Plot a course down the coast of Selland, hoping the storm would calm enough to leave the shelter of the point and yet that we would still have a strong wind from the north. Make sure that the captain was kept alive...there was many small responsibilities awaiting me. As I came into the cabin, I found Karen's pale eyes fixed on me, hard and yet a little questioning. She would have heard the noise outside and guessed that it had to do with herself. And yet she could not have understood the Sellish words spoken.

"You won't be hurt, as long as I can find out where the griffin has taken Krift." I told her in Gracklandic, moving passed her chair to open the locker in the back of the room and take out a chart of the coast. Going back, I unrolled it on the table in front of her to begin looking it over. "You know, it would make things easier for both of us if you told me where his lair is. I will find out one way or the other, by taking it from your mind if you do not tell me."

She just glared the daggers of ice at me which she could not use with her hands tied together. The door opened and Bowen came quietly in carrying a plate of food for me. I wondered if she was hungry, but it really was not safe to untie her hands at the moment. I would have to think of a place to keep her where she could not get out, and yet I could get in to talk to her without being frozen.

"Thanks," I said, as Bowen set my breakfast near the chart. He nodded, taking something out of a pocket and holding it out in my direction.

"Krift gave this to me a little before he was captured." The blind man explained, "It's something he stole from the man who was bringing him to the griffin. He was still worried that Nightwing would find him, so thought this would be safer with me."

It was a thin rectangle of what looked like dark, smooth metal. Almost as long as my hand and about as wide as four fingers, it was traced on top with glowing lines of vibrant green. I took it, marveling at the brightness of the lines and the smoothness of the material. Even more interesting to me, the etching depicted the shape of a classic lighthouse.

"What is it?" I asked, turning the object over to see nothing but blank metal on the opposite side, with a single line of green running from the top to the bottom.

Bowen shook his head, "I don't know, and neither did Krift. He only said that it seemed very important to the man keeping him, so he took it."

"We'll make a pirate out of him yet." I muttered, looking once again at the shape imprinted on the front of the thin slip of metal. There was nothing to show what lighthouse it was supposed to be, or if it was even a real one at all. I knew of two myself, on the coast of Selland. One far down to the south, near the town of Littleton, and the other just a short ways below Clydesfort. Other than that, there was at least three along the connected coasts of Fraistia, Grackland and Thwate.

"Is anything marked on it?" Bowen asked, reminding me that there was no way for him to know, if Krift had not told him, about the picture. The glowing green lines and the dark metal were entirely flush with each other, so it could not be felt. Carefully, I explained to him the layout of the slip and it's strangely contrasting colors.

"Perhaps it is supposed to be the Littleton lighthouse," he remarked after my explanation, "as that was where Krift's keeper wanted to get to. Or at least where he told the warship which picked them up he wanted to get to."

"That's right." I looked up in surprise, recollecting Captain Cuttle having told me something like that, "but what could this metal piece be for? Not just a reminder of their destination, surely?"

Bowen shrugged. "I don't know. But you had better keep it for me now. You might need it at some point."

Agreeing, I slipped it into my pocket and quickly ate the breakfast he had brought. As quietly as he had come, he left with the empty plate, leaving me alone in the room with a frozen captain and the girl who had done it. Karen had watched our whole exchange without a word, though I had noticed a slight interest in her expression when Bowen first gave me the bit of metal. Her quietness was a little unnerving, since I knew she must be hungry and uncomfortable in her bonds by now.

"I am going to find you a place to stay." I told her, as I could not leave her here in the cabin, where she could reach me in my sleep. With these words, I left the cabin to go down to the gun decks. Here some of the gun crew were busy cleaning and repairing a few of the cannon, using their free time to get everything perfectly in order. I walked past them with a nod, going to look in a few of the powder lockers and other little storage areas. There was no room in these to store a living girl, so I went further down into the hold. Here the ship's carpenter had his own place, a friendly little room with a chest of tools, wood shavings on the floor, and smaller pieces of wood hanging on the walls. The carpenter, on the other hand, was not very friendly. On the outside at least, being an older man with an inclination to be grouchy if disturbed for anything other than business about the ship. But I had long since learned how to get along with him, and sometimes we even had a good time talking over woodworking techniques together.

The trick was to get him engaged talking about his favorite subject, wood types, and then slip in to what ever it was you really wanted to talk to him about. As such, when he stopped sanding on a length of railing to snappishly ask me what I was doing, my reply was: "Oh, I was just hoping to find a bit of wood for carving a new wooden spoon. do you have a good oak billet for me, Grey?"

"Another one?" He spun on his tall stool around, regarding me with a sharp, squinting eye, "I just gave you one a few weeks ago for that knife handle, and now you want another."

"Yes, preferably not as splintery as the last." I replied easily, though there had been nothing wrong with the other piece of wood, "I don't want to be eating splinters with my soup this winter. How about this one here?"

There was a slightly flawed billet hanging on the wall nearby, which I lay my hand on as if about to take it down. But that move got Grey out of his chair in a moment, over to stop me. "Nay, nay, you don't want that one, it's warped! Here, look at this little bit of apple wood, it's a pretty one."

"I'm not sure it is big enough for what I had in mind, though. What about this piece over here?"

"It's too big, I'm saving it for a more worthy project!"

The dickering went back and forth like this for a little while, until I was settled on a choice of wood. By then I had smoothed his temper enough to ask a small favor of him. There was a little storage room adjoined to his carpentry shop, which could only be reached by first going through his workroom. It had a few beams in it at the moment, but those could be shifted to some other location easily. Then it would be just right for putting Karen in, as the door was stout, had a lock on the outside (sometimes Grey worried about people taking his wood without asking) and was not too stuffy or foul on the inside. It was dark, of course, and we could not afford to put a lantern in the girl's hands when she might decide to burn both the ship and herself up in a fanatical act of revenge. So I asked the carpenter to install a tiny window in the front, with a pane of glass in it so that she could not bother him about his work, and yet she would not be entirely in the shadows. With a minimum of expected grumbling, he agreed to do the window, while I shifted the beams.

It felt good to do a little plain, hard work, instead of the mental labor of keeping the crew in line and using mind magic. I felt better afterwards in more ways than one and thanked Grey as I went to fetch Karen. He just grunted after me, going back to his sanding with no care for what was to be stored in the room. It was another plus of keeping her there, that he would neither be afraid of her nor tempted to do a little questioning on the sly. For all I knew, he had not even heard the explanation I had given the crew earlier and did not care what had happened to the captain. All Grey ever worried about was his wood and how he was going to use it next.

My next challenge was how to get Karen from the cabin to the wood shop, into her room. I worried about it all the way back up, but my fears ended up unfounded. I simply untied her from the chair and marched her there, keeping her hands tied in the bag in front and a knife at her back. She made no resistance and sat on the floor without protest when we reached the improvised cell. I brought her a few bits of furniture too, some straw and blankets to sleep on, before cautiously untying the bag from around her hands. She seemed completely subdued, slumping against a center post in the room, watching me with the same cold silence. I brought down food and drink, setting them just inside the door carefully in case she made a dash at me. But the strange young woman did nothing, making me wonder if she would starve herself to death simply to spite me.

"Here, eat, drink." I spoke in Gracklandic, moving the bowl and pitcher closer to her, "there is nothing wrong with the food."

She still made no move and I gave up. She would eat when she felt the real edges of hunger, or else she was so stubborn that she would not. But either way, I would get the secret of the griffin's lair from her, even if it was to pry it from her dying mind.

Feeling oddly depressed by her lack of animation, I left the room and locked it behind me. I mounted the ladder to the deck, just in time to hear a voice call out, "Chief! The wind is going down. Shall we up anchor?"

Feeling how the wind was falling off and seeing that the storm was starting to break up, I hurried to the helm, giving my consent for the ship to be prepared for sailing. Shouting orders, directing the men, I took the wheel and we sailed briskly out of the lee of the point to catch the full brunt of the wind. With tight sails and singing rigging, we started to make our way down the coast of Selland.

Chapter 8: The Blazing Brig

Five days later the wind had veered to the north-west, slowly forcing us more and more to the east. We had to constantly be beating against it, or sail off course a little to catch it. Over the next few days it swung around even further to the west, and our progress was slowed all the more. Frustrated at our slow speed, I would often spend my time pacing up and down the deck, or uselessly repeating calculations with the captain's charts. A few times I tried to enter Leighton's mind through the net of ice, to give him some reassurance in his prison. But the strands of the net were too tight, and the holes too small. Every time I tried, I was repulsed and left shivering with the cold.

I also spent some time every day trying to talk to Karen, in an attempt to free her from her own mental trap. This was a slow, painstaking job, and I was never sure how she would receive me when I came. Some days the she would sit against the center post of her wooden cell, slumped and disinterested in all that was around her. She would not even seem to see me those days, staring off into space blankly with her hands in her lap. On those days, I would often take the opportunity to use a little mind magic on her, trying to free corners of her mind, or following the line from her mind as far south as I could go. As of yet, I had not been able to make it to the end.

On other days, the prisoner would be on her feet, stalking back and forth like a wildcat. Her fingers would be glowing blue and as soon as I entered she would jump at me, trying to freeze me as she had the captain. Those days I had to be quick, and keep my sword between us. Then there was not much else I could do except for leave her food, which she ate little of, and speak a few words before going away.

Quite often I was frustrated by her stubbornness and how well she resisted my efforts to free her. But after walking out and punching the walls a few times (much to Grey's silent amusement) I would remind myself that she could not help it, being influenced by outside forces. Then I would think of how hard Ramses had worked to get me back when I had lost my memory and wonder at how patient he had been.

Today the wind had slackened off as well as being around to the west, making it so that our speed felt like a snail's pace. It was another gray, overcast day and I was making my way down to speak to the prisoner. The ship's rocking was gentle, a sort of chugging along in the calm sea. The light in the carpenter's shop was bright and cheerful as I came in, throwing it's beams over the golden sawdust on the floor. Grey stood leaning over his bench, planing a board to be used as a table top in the crew's quarters. The wood curls came up from it in long, thin strips, catching the light and turning yellow. He turned to give me a scowl, to which I nodded amiably in return. We rarely spoke on my daily visits, which kept us from arguing on the days that there was not time enough to go through the process of haggling over wood first of all.

I went over to the door in the wall, holding a tray in one hand and the key in the other. Leaning forward, I looked in through the little port hole which had been set in the door and saw Karen sitting in the center of the room. A listless expression was on her face, while her hands hung limply in her lap. It was going to be a quiet day. Sticking the key in the small lock, I turned it and stepped inside. Unlike usual, the girl turned her head to look at me, eyes bright. My hand shot down to the hilt of my sword so hastily it still had the key in it. But when she turned her face away again without shifting position, I came cautiously forward. Near her on the floor, I set the tray, never taking my eyes off of her. If she was trying a new tactic to catch me, I would be ready for it.

But she only moved a thin arm over to pick up the hard little apple on the tray and hold it in her hands as if it would tell her fortune. I sat on the floor at a short distance, trying to read the expression on her face. She was turned partially away from me though, so I could not see what she was thinking.

"You should eat that." I told her in Gracklandic, more for something to say than anything else. It became difficult after a while to make conversation with someone who never spoke, "you look too thin, so you might get sick. It's always better to eat an apple then just sit staring at it."

The young woman threw another glance at me, still holding the apple, before turning quickly away. Wondering if she was starting to feel less hostile, I went on as if I had not seen, "you know, there's been times before that I would give my best dagger for even a small, hard apple like that. Once we went without fresh fruit for three weeks and everyone was starting to feel sick. You get scurvy without fresh food and that is never pleasant to see. Or so the captain's told me. He's usually too careful about the crew's food for it to come to that, so I haven't seen it."

"Would you stop talking about eating?"

To my great surprise, Karen spoke back to me, her tone low and harsh. Her hand on the apple clenched it even tighter, so that the fruit began to split open, "you are always talking to me, always so nice! Why are you so nice to me?"

She seemed almost to be sobbing now, while I sat stunned, staring with my eyes wide open. Perhaps my time had not been as wasted as I though it had been. She whipped around to glare at me, throwing the apple in halves across the floor. I scrabbled back a little, drawing my sword to lay it across my lap. But she did not seem to notice.

"Why have you kept me safe and brought me food to eat? I wanted to starve, die with my mouth shut, serving the master to the end. But instead you are nice to me! Why?"

Honestly, that was a hard question to answer. I did not really know what she was like, or if she had been a nice person before. As far as I could tell, she enjoyed working for the master and freezing people's minds so that they would die insane and imprisoned, all alone. There was really only one reason I could think of for having treated her as gently as I had.

"Once, my mind was tampered with as yours has been," I explained slowly, "not as deeply, perhaps, but all of my memories had been stolen entirely. My friends tried to help me, but I would not listen. I ran away. It was a long time before I recovered my memories. All that time one friend, at least, did not stop trying to help me. You are hypnotized, Karen, and it would be paying back a debt, in a sense, to set you free." Then I shrugged, grinning just a little, "besides all of that sentimental hogwash, you are my only link to finding Krift and saving the captain. I owe him a lot. There has never been anyone who yelled at me as effectively as Captain Leighton."

The girl had been facing me, listening with a frown the whole time. Afterwards she turned away to mutter fiercely, "the master would not tamper with my thoughts as you claim. Everything he does is right."

But she did not sound convinced and I had hope that she could eventually be brought to see reason.

With this thought in mind, I soon got up to leave her to her own conclusions. Locking the door behind me, I gave another passing nod to the carpenter and strolled off, whistling lightly under my breath. After climbing up on deck, I decided to take a turn around it to see how everything was going topside. Not only because I was in charge of the ship now and felt responsible, but because my conversation with Karen still whirled in my brain and needed thinking over.

On my way toward the bow, I heard a strange sound coming from beyond the forward mast. It was a solid, woody thump, repeated at steady intervals with the lighter tap of footsteps in between. Curious, I walked quietly forward to see what was going on.

A man was standing about a dozen steps from the mast, something held in one hand above his shoulder. With a flick of his wrist he flung it at the pole and there was a *thump* as it stuck in, point forward. Then he walked over to pull it out, before returning to his first position. The man was throwing a knife, I realized, and with a high degree of accuracy too. That explained the thumping noises and the footsteps.

My interest caught, I walked closer to watch him as he threw it again, sticking it into the mast at about head height. He had drawn a circle there with a piece of chalk, and there was a dot in the center as the bull's eye. The blade was stuck with it's tip just under an inch away from the dot in the center of the mark.

To my surprise I saw that it was Wallace who was practicing throwing knives, his expression calmer and more focused than usual. When he saw me, he turned with a nervous smile. "Oh, hello chief. Um...is everything alright?"

He was obviously worried that I would be angry at him for practicing instead of working at something, so I nodded pleasantly to reassure him, "yes, everything is fine. Where did you learn to throw knives like that?"

"A colonist from Ullabar taught me." Wallace shrugged, awkwardly tucking the knife in his belt, "he had taken passage on our ship and was bored on the long voyage back to Selland. So he showed me how, just to pass the time."

"Hmm." I walked up to look at the marks on the mast. They were all grouped fairly close to the center. "I used to fling my daggers at sea birds aboard the *Blue Bucket*, but I never could get them to hit point first. In fact, they rarely hit anything except the deck. Could you show me how to throw them like you do?"

"Well," Wallace took the knife back out, fidgeting with it in his hands, "I suppose so. It's...it's a little bit difficult at first. You have to know about how far you are standing from what you want to hit and judge the speed at which the knife spins too." He looked a little doubtful, "are you sure you want to learn all this?"

I nodded, walking the short distance over to where he had been standing earlier. Learning how to use a weapon in a new way was almost always worthwhile, besides the fact that throwing knives had always sounded interesting to me. I knew that there were special daggers made just for that use, but the knives both Wallace and I had were normal daggers, balanced more toward the hilt than the blade. It might be helpful to me at some point to know how to throw them with accuracy, and it would certainly get my mind off of my troubles and responsibility for a time.

Enjoying the feeling of learning something new, I stood and listened intently as Wallace showed me how to hold the knife and what motion to flick it with. He demonstrated a few times, before passing it over to me to try.

My first throw went wide of the mark, flying across the deck and almost hitting into a man as he climbed down from the crow's nest. With a startled glance our way, he hurried out of range, while I went over to pick the knife up. When I came back, I tried it again. After about nine tries I got it to stick into the mast without bouncing off, or sailing past on a journey down the deck. But it was not even in the chalk ring and I was beginning to tire of chasing after it.

"I have to go talk to the cook, now," I told Wallace, yanking the knife out of the wood. "But we can practice some other day, ay?"

"Yes, if you like, sir." He seemed pleased that I had appreciated his teaching enough to want more, walking away with a small smile on his face. With my thoughts full of whirling blades, I made my way to the galley, still whistling lightly to myself.

THE DAYS PASSED AS we drifted with maddening slowness down toward the southern tip of Selland. The captain was kept alive on a liquid diet, but he got thinner and more worn looking every day. I knew a person could not live for a long time like that, even with the best care that he could be given. In hopes of finding a cure I experimented almost recklessly with mind magic, often wearing myself out to the point where I had to rest in the cabin for the rest of the day. My experiments encompassed such things as transferring the energy of an actual burning fire, breaking the ice shield with a mental sledgehammer, trying to unravel it string by string and any other idea which came to my mind.

Nothing worked, so that I had to leave the captain to Vulture's care until we could find Krift. The fact that we were making such slow progress weighed heavily on all of the crew, sometimes I even heard grumblings starting to rise in hidden pockets among them. Superstitiously, they blamed Karen for the bad winds, saying that she was a Jonah on the ship, a person of bad luck. At times I heard rumors that they were even starting to blame me, because it was a poor leader who couldn't find a better wind for us to follow. I often thought of putting ashore and searching for Krift by land, but it would have required going directly against the wind to reach the coast of Selland, and we had drifted far to the east by now.

The two efforts I made in that time which were beginning to pay off were learning to throw knives and talking to the prisoner. She was beginning to speak to me now, often hesitantly, in only a few words at a time. But it was a breakthrough nonetheless, giving me some hope that she would eventually throw off her bondage to the master. She might even confide in me where his hiding place was, what it was like and what he was trying to do with the people he captured.

On a clear, windy day, with the wind still from the west, we were just passing a group of islands on our starboard side when a ship shot out from behind them and cut across the waves toward us. It was a small brig with a Neptune's head carved on the prow and a black flag at the mast. As it approached it could be seen to carry a heavy armament on the decks, along witha large crew bristling with weapons. I spotted all this through the captain's spyglass as it flew toward us and immediately shouted over my shoulder, "Caraway! Ready the men for action, tell Dolgan to load the starboard cannons. But don't fire until I say. I don't think these fellows know what they're up against."

After giving the commands I jammed my eye to the glass again, watching the other ship's progress. It came full on toward us for a little, before suddenly slowing and beginning to jink from one side to the other. I watched as some of the sail was taken in and could almost have chuckled aloud. This little ship was obviously a pirate that had mistaken us for a merchant at a distance, as we only ever flew the flag of Selland at our mast while traveling. But by now the captain of the brig had seen our gun ports and realized what we were; a pirate ourselves, with no country's warship titling before our name.

Now the brig was uneasy: had they just jumped into a trap, trying to spring one themselves? The *Seashooter* was superior in cannon, men and perhaps even speed. A rank of advantages which any pirate would fear.

Meanwhile, they had approached to a distance where running against the wind into the islands was not a practical choice, which left it up to me whether it was 'hail-fellow-well-met' or 'death to all rivals'.

They were slowly coasting towards us now, bristling with armament like a cat who sees a dog, trying to bluff it out. I called the second mate up to me, passing him the telescope, "Caraway, what's the ship's name?"

"The *Ogre*, sir." He replied after a moment of scanning the brig.

"Good. Keep an eye on them while I do the talking." I bent to pick up the speaking funnel beside me, which we always used for hailing a ship at a distance, "if they show any sign of continuing the attack, warn me."

He nodded and I put the megaphone to my mouth. It felt strange to be in this position, literally calling the shots, after Leighton had been the one in this place all the rest of my career.

"This is First Mate Sarkin, of the *Seashooter*, speaking," I called across the water, hoping that they were close enough to hear me clearly. I could just imagine a dull-looking officer putting a hand to his ear, and whispering to one of the men, 'Eh, what did he say?'

But my message continued evenly dispite my imagination, "State your business, and if you have none, clear out!"

We could not afford to have another pirate lurking around after us, hoping to either cripple us from behind or get in on any of our kills. We were not a crew who enjoyed feeding the crows on our pack's hunting.

There was a long pause, before a heavily-accented Fraistian voice shouted back, "We are looking for meat, sir S'arkin and if you want to make us clear out then you will have to use something stronger than words!"

I exchanged a bemused glance with the second mate. Were these people really so foolish as to invite us into a fight? Their captain, or spokesman at least, sounded like a braggart, but it was surprising that any free sailor would let their leader make such a precipitate decision.

"If you do not leave immediately, I will be forced to show you what we've got," I returned loudly, through the funnel, "It's your decision, and your doom."

Sprinkled with what I gathered were rude Fraistian expressions, his general reply was, "Then prepare for war!"

Immediately I threw down the megaphone and leaped for the wheel. Taking it from the previous helmsman, I spun our ship to be squarely side-on to the presumptive little brig. We were moving slowly now, sails flapping in the cross breeze, while our smaller opponent was racing before the wind. But we had the advantage of being broadside-on to them, for a ship's prow is usually very ill protected or armed compared to its sides.

In these few moments Caraway had jumped down to the deck to stand near the hatch which led to the gun decks below. He and I both shouted orders for the men to assemble on deck and prepare for repelling boarders. Then I gave the order to fire all starboard cannon, which the second mate relayed below.

There was a rippling roar as the right side of the ship exploded into smoke and sparks, lurching as all of the cannon fired almost simultaneously. The *Ogre* was raked by a full charge of rounds, as she sailed toward us at top speed. Orange sparks leaped up, twinkling around the helm. Her cabin collapsed in flames and there was screams from on board as the deck lit on fire. To my surprise and frustration, I realized that Dolgan had once again gone to using his favorite rounds: burning ones.

With her rigging on fire but the mast still intact, the ship came careening toward us. I spun the wheel, trying to swerve out of the way as the impromptu fire boat homed in on our side. Clenching my hands tightly to the wheel, I realized that the crazy Fraistians were aiming to crash right into us. Into the *Seashooter*, while they were on fire.

With the *Seashooter's* sails only half full, she was responding sluggishly. Using all of my strength I turned the ship to the port, hoping to catch the westward wind. Slowly, slowly she responded, the sails beginning to fill. But the wind was not going to be in time. There was a grinding, solid collision and the *Ogre* rammed directly into our side.

I was almost thrown to my knees, the wheel just saving me, while men across the deck were sent sprawling. Pulling myself up on the spokes I shouted at the top of my voice, "Repel the boarders! Cut away those burning lines!"

The brig's rigging was tangling with ours, sending flames licking onto our mast. Men scrambled to their feet as the crew of the *Ogre* started climbing over the rails, waving their weapons and screaming mad war cries. All the time our frigate was turning slowly to the east, dragging the other ship with her as a dead weight. The wood beneath me creaked and groaned as if it was being torturedby the stress put upon it. And the other ship was all ablaze like a bonfire.

Suddenly a flaming bit of wood fell from the *Ogre's* mast and hit the deck near me. I jumped for it, leaving the wheel free, to kicked it overboard with the toe of my boot. It crackled nastily at me as it left, as if it knew of my fear of fire. But that fear wasn't going to hold me back in the middle of a battle.

I turned back toward the deck and saw one detachment of my men fighting theirs on the deck, trying to keep them off while others climbed the rigging to hack away burning lines with glinting blades. The *Seashooter* was sailing unsteadily, weighed by the ship rammed onto it's side. Grabbing the helm I lashed it in place with a few turns of a rope which hung nearby for that purpose, before hurrying down to the deck below, jumping off of the ladder after using only a few rungs. Wherever we were sailing, we needed to keep the other crew off of our decks and try to stop our ship from burning to the water.

Grabbing a man who was hurrying past, I shouted at him to bring water from below, organize a bucket chain to put out the flames which were beginning to creep up on the railings. He nodded, eyes wide, and dashed off again. Meanwhile I spun around to see how the fighting was going, drawing my own sword from it's place at my side. Smoke and flickering lights filled the air, sparks and ashes fluttered to the deck around me. The invaders were successfully being repelled from getting a real hold on our ship, though they fought with the crazed abandon of desperation. I noticed in a brief moment of lucidity that they seemed skinny and underfed, fighting desperately rather than with any concerted strength.

A bullet whipped passed me, whispering savagely as it passed my head. Recalled out of my contemplation of the scene, I ran across the deck to join the fray, calling, "keep it up, men! They can't last forever!"

One of my crew fell, a saber in his thigh. Dragging him back I took his place, chopping away a hand which grappled onto the rail. There was a scream as the owner of the hand fell away, leaving a gap on the rail. Another man tried to take his place, but I scared him off with a jab toward his exposed face. He reeled off into the smudged air, disappearing towards the flames.

With a creaking tear, the *Ogre* began to pull away from our ship, disentangling itself from the cut rigging. Slipping out into the water, it dripped burning beams and men. With a jerk we were free, the burning brig listing madly away on it's own course.

Coughing on smoke, I turned as someone grabbed my shoulder, giving it a hurried shake. It was Glimpy, pointing aft with a horrified expression on his face. Following the direction of his finger, I saw a sight which filled me with a horror to match the crewman's. There was flame rippling in a sheet over the top of the galley, licking up it's walls from the side. It was just starting to eat into the cabin as well, catching the dry wood of the superstructure with rapacious ease.

"Fire!" I shouted hoarsely, and perhaps needlessly, "the galley's on fire!"

The timbers were soaked with the oil of cooking, making them begin to blaze upwards magnificently. Luckily, the captain was not in the cabin any more, having been moved to the doctor's quarters for more careful attention. But either Chirn or Bowen might still be trapped in the fire in the galley.

The last of the enemy borders had been repelled: with a surge, the men left the rail to face the new menace of the flames. Spurred by fear for my blind friend Bowen, I was in the lead. The fire had not yet reached the galley door, though the roof was all a crackling glow. Guessing that the handle would be hot, I kicked the door open with a few blows, sending a shaft of pain through the old wound in that leg. Smoke billowed out of the open doorway. I heard someone coughing and hacking inside.

"Bowen!" I called, squinting against the fumes and stepping inside.

"Sarkin..." His voice came back weakly from the other side. Bowing my head, I hurried inside, bumping against the table and feeling my way around it. The air was so thick that I could barely see and breathing was an action easier to do without. Holding my breath, I ducked down to where the air was a little clearer and saw Bowen feeling his way toward me across the floor. Confused by the smoke and noise, he had been unable to find his way out when the fire started. Blind, there was no way to use the door as a landmark from a distance. In a short dash I was by his side, flinching as a chunk of blackened, burning wood fell from the roof to land beside me. More would be coming soon as the room collapsed.

It took all of my will power not to run right back out of the burning room. My instincts were telling me to forget everything, dash out of that nightmare blaze and leave it behind. But I would not leave Bowen in there with it. Forcing myself to be calm, I grabbed his arm and pulled him to his feet, dragging him around the table toward the open door. Unable to hold my breath any longer, I sucked in a lungful of smoke and fumes. Choking and coughing, we stumbled outside together, falling to the deck by the mizzenmast.

I gasped in the fresher air, coughing out all the burnt wood I had accidentally consumed. Once I could think of anything but being able to breath, I turned to Bowen, who was wheezing hoarsely beside me. Making a fist, I thumped him on the back until he was gasping steadily instead.

"You alright, matey?" I asked between rough breaths, worried for him.

He nodded, sitting doubled over with a hand on his forehead. "'I think so..."

Reassured, I looked across at the cabin structure. The galley was a complete loss, falling in and burning even as the men hauled up barrels of seawater to dump on it. The cabin fared a little better, charred and missing most of one wall, with the roof creaking on burnt timbers. But it had not yet entirely caved in.

Forcing myself to my feet, I joined the men throwing buckets of water over the cabin in an attempt to save it, and over the ruins of the galley to keep the sparks from spreading any further. Step by step we fought the blaze back, working until we staggered blindly with the buckets and hauled on the barrel's ropes without even thinking. Finally, hands feeling burned and eyes puffy, we stopped to look around us. The fire had been put out across the whole deck, prevented from spreading below. One side of the *Seashooter* was charred along a section of the hull, painted soot black by the burning brig which had rested there. Some of the rigging and spars had been charred as well, hanging black on the masts. The cabin and galley were unusable, made of ash, charcoal and burnt timbers. The injured men, both from the fight and the fire, were being tended on deck by Vulture. Though some looked gravely wounded, I did not see any dead, so that was something to be thankful for.

I looked around me, taking it all in, then moved to peer over the starboard side. There was a ragged gap in the hull of the ship, punched in from where the brig had hit. The crack was probably leaking water into the hold, but not enough to worry me yet. I wondered if anyone at all had survived on that ill-fated pirate ship. They must have been starving to have attempted such a foolish attack at all. A sad fate to come to, especially on the sea. Their doom had been a terrible one, but the fire had not been their fault.

"Stan." I spotted the tall, strong man standing nearby, gazing around him with bewilderment at the ruins on deck, "go get Dolgan and bring him up here. If he resists, just drag him."

He nodded with a tiny salute, hurrying off below decks. I looked at the galley once again and stepped over to ask Bowen, "was Chirn in there when it started to go?"

"No." The blind man had recovered a little and was sitting up straight against the mast, "he went out to help with the fighting, or so he said."

"Well, at least we did not lose a cook." I glanced around and finally spotted him standing with a large kitchen knife in his hand, looking over the side as if he still expected someone to come crawling up from below. But I had no time to think about the cook at that moment, for Stan returned, hauling the gunner by the back of his shirt. The gunner knew what was coming: his hands were trembling, and his face crumpled in fear.

"Dolgan." I turned to look at him squarely, as Stan set him on the deck in front of me. He seemed barely able to keep his feet and did not meet my eyes, "I have warned you about using heated shot and fire rounds without permission, haven't I?"

He shot a terrified glance at me "Y-yes. But I thought that under the circumstances—"

"You didn't think very much!" My anger at what he had caused towered upwards and I slashed a hand through the air to show him what he had done.

"Under the circumstances it was the worst thing you could have decided to do! Look at this, look at all this. You satisfy your vanity by seeing ships burn, but you have no sense of when it is right." I looked at him coldly, as he stammered and tried to answer me. But I cut him off again, "it is no wonder, now, why you had to leave the army in such a hurry. I don't have to tell you that you are no longer our gunner, do I?"

"No, sir."

"And I don't have to tell you that you are no longer one of the crew, do I?"

"No, sir."

"But." I looked at him hard, putting my hands behind my back while pacing back and forth in an unconscious imitation of Leighton. "What do I have to tell you now?"

His face was as chalky as a student's undone lessons as he replied, "punishment. What my punishment is."

I nodded, coming to a stop. I looked across the deck, at the crew watching in intent silence, "what do you think his punishment should be?"

There were growls from all quarters, suggesting shoving him weighted into the ocean, dragging him behind for the sharks, forcing him to get in a burning boat off of the side, and other just punishments of that sort. But I had seen enough ruin for one day and decided on a much simpler, slightly kinder, retribution.

"No, he has served as one of us for a time, so we will spare him being burnt alive. But he has, through his decisions, let the stores in the galley be burnt and endangered the supplies in the hold. So he will be set adrift on the sea, in the gig, with no food whatsoever, only one noggin of water."

I stepped toward Dolgan as I finished so that he would know I was speaking to him as well, "he may row where he pleases and land on any island he wants. But if he attempts to come back aboard our ship, he will be shot. Do you understand, former gunner?"

The last words were addressed only to the miscreant, who mumbled without spirit, "yes, sir."

He was taken to the gig, set in it, and lowered over the side by many willing hands. Our ship drifted slowly on, helm burnt down and sails hanging. Without direction, catching the wind as it could, it creaked through the water.

Chapter 9: A Floating Hulk

As soon as possible I went down to the hold, to see what sort of damage had been done there. I soon found that the dent in the side was leaking worse than my calculations had feared, water pooling in the low points up passed my ankle. Sloshing through it, I came to the carpenter's shop in the prow. It was a little higher than the hold here, with the keel turning upwards, so the water was not quite as deep. Opening the door, I poked my head in. Gray was dragging out tools from his chest, sticking them in his belt or pockets.

"We got some damage on the hull out here," I told him, absently watching the chips of wood floating around the floor, "you had better hurry."

"And you had better get someone clearing away this water!" He snapped in return, slamming the chest and snatching up a bucket of tar from his bench.

"Yes, I will." My eyes snapped up to look at the prisoner's door, "but I wanted to ask if you wanted someone to help you, and perhaps to check on the prisoner."

"She's fine." The carpenter grumbled, pushing passed me out into the hold. "And of course I will need some help, you don't expect me to put the ship back together by myself, do you?"

Ignoring his first remark, I went to peer in the little port hole window of the cell door. Karen stood in the corner of her room, watching the water seep in with an expression of fear. I opened the door to tell her briefly in her language, "don't worry, the battle is over. We will stop the leak."

I closed and locked the door again immediately, before wading out across the hold to the ladder leading up.

"Hey, send down some men to help Gray with the hole!" I shouted, getting someone's attention. He looked down the hatch as I continued, "and get together a crew to man the chain pumps. It's filling up down here."

"Aye, sir." The crewman moved away and I turned back to look at the water in the hold. The chain pumps were a system for emptying the bilges, where water collected in the bottom of the ship. They were a pair of long, wooden tubes made of elm trunks, with a chain running up one of them and down the other. All along the chain was set little scoops of metal and rubber, which drew the water up one of the tubes when a windless was worked on the deck. There was one of these pumps on each side of the ship, port and starboard, used for bailing out the water in the bilges. It naturally leaked in through the boards at an almost imperceptible rate all the time, filling them with a sludgy slime. But when there was a leak, they filled quickly. As I stood and watched, the chains began to rattle and the water to get churned up in the bilges. The pumps had been rigged and the men were working them.

Splashing further back in the hold, I came to where the casks and chests of supplies where lashed. Some of them had broken loose and were floating about in the water. One or two had even been smashed open, spilling hard breads and salted meat into the seawater. I fished up all of the meat I could, figuring it could not have been harmed by a little more brine. But the bread was a complete loss, soaked with foul water, bound to go moldy.

Stacking the meat on top of an upright barrel, I grabbed a few of the smaller chests and heaved them up out of the water onto the higher ground of other barrels. Hopefully, they were sealed well enough that whatever was in them would not go bad too quickly. Using a piece of rope laying nearby, I tied them loosely into place, promising myself that I would see them checked and stowed better later on.

Slowly, the water at my feet was going down, though more was still leaking in where Grey and his crew tried to temporarily plug the leak. We would not be able to fully repair the side of the ship until it could be beached somewhere quiet; until then the pumps would have to be manned every day to keep the water level low.

Leaving the food supplies for later, I climbed out onto the upper deck. The evening was drawing on, sun setting somewhere a little right of forward. Perversely, the wind was swinging around to the north-east now that we were injured and lacking means of easily steering the ship. With ropes rigged to the rudder, the helmsmen were slowly bringing the ship around, but it was much more difficult to steer this way and took careful setting of the sails to match it.

Both on the starboard and port, near the ruins of the cabins aft, was set up a windless, which was a capstan holding wooden poles at waist height for the men to push on. Everyone was tired, having fought fire, foes and now water all day long. Choosing carefully among the men, I told one of the weariest to go below and took his place at the bar. With the rough pole gripped in my hands I shoved, joining the others in the endless procession of going around the windless. Usually when the anchor was being taken in, or any other hard hauling was being done, a chant of some sort would be sung for us to work to, helping to keep time. But no one felt like singing today: everyone was far too worn out. On all of us weighed the knowledge that the ship was far off course, the captain might die before we could get to where we wanted to go and that the pumping would have to go on.

After shoving the bars around into the dark blue of twilight the water was finally drained out of the hold and we could stop pumping for the night. With a sigh of weariness, I straightened up and stretched my arms above my head. After a moment I let them fall, walking slowly over to what was left of the cabin. The framework of the walls still stood and part of the sheathing as well. But it was so crispy that I opened the door with caution, moving through it only with a feeling of anxiety. Looking up, I saw the places that the roof had been scorched through, leaving little holes with starlight on the other side. I decided to sleep outside that night. Too weary to even get something to eat, I dragged my thin cushion and bed coverings off of my berth and took them outside. Luckily they were still intact. On the deck I flopped the cushion down, then dropped myself on top of it. The blankets were damp from water being splashed across the room to put out the fire, but I did not care. My eyes were shut and my mind asleep before I even had time to think about it.

The next morning I arose stiff and a little chilled, but feeling deeply rested. The wind was still steady from the north-north east and our ship, almost feeling like a hulk in it's crippled state, sailed slowly on before it. It ruffled my hair as I stood and looked out across the pale blue water, forming endless little waves across the sea. On our port side, we passed a medium-sized island, bright green palm fronds waving in the early morning sun. We had gone so far south that we were in the lower section of the Middle islands, where we might even come to the lands in which the people were burned black and often turned cannibal, if we kept going in this direction.

I shook my head at these thoughts, turning away from the view. Today we would have to rig up a more stable helm of some sort, as well as a temporary cookhouse where the galley had once stood. Right now, Chirn was standing out in the open, using the cauldron to cook porridge over a fire in the old galley's fireplace, which had been cleared of rubble for this purpose. Smelling the food cooking, I suddenly remembered my prisoner and the fact that I had not brought anything to her the night before. With a swift kick to shove my bed up against the cabin wall, out of the way, I went over to the cauldron to ask the cook, "did any bowls survive?"

"Yes, about four of them." Chirn picked up a stack from the ground, showing them to me, "I say 'about' four, because this one is burned on one side. But it will still work if you hold it at an angle."

He demonstrated, tipping it on it's side. I saw that there was also a handful of spoons and other utensils piled near him and guessed that he had been scavenging since before dawn. Chirn did, occasionally, do the right thing.

"That's fine." I said, looking into the pot of boiling oatmeal and raisins, "would you fill a bowl of this for the prisoner, then put some in the broken bowl for me? Thanks. And where can I find a cup or glass of any sort?"

wiping the steam from the pot out of my eyes, I looked where he pointed and saw a few glasses laying in the ashes nearby. I picked one up to wipe the grit out with the edge of my shirt, then went to fill it with water at the drinking barrel. Chirn dipped out steaming glop, pale and flecked with purple, from the cauldron. It did not look like much, but I knew that he would have sweetened it with brown sugar. After a damp morning spent on the deck, anything warm to eat would be good. Taking the bowls and a pair of spoons, I hurried down into the hold, over to the carpenter's shop. Gray was still asleep, snoring loudly on his raised bunk in the corner. He had worked hard the day before and earned a long rest. Leaving him for the moment, I juggled the bowls and cup to unlock the prisoner's door, before pushing it open. Inside, Karen sat on the floor, a blanket pulled around her shoulders while her arms hugged her knees. As always, she was turned a little away from me and I could not see her face.

"Sorry I didn't come last night," I told her, closing the door behind me, "things were pretty bad after that fight."

She made no response, so I walked across the room and tapped her lightly on the shoulder. Karen jerked a little, surprised at the touch, and tilted her head up to look at me. I could see now that her face had tear lines on it, as if she had been crying. But now she just stared up at me for a long moment, eyes dry and pale, before asking abruptly, "aren't you afraid?"

"Of a crying girl?" I replied, in no mood to debate whether I was afraid or not. Pushing the bowl of porridge and cup of water down into her hands, I stepped back to my usual place by the door and sat down. The floor was a little damp from yesterday's flood, but not unbearably so.

Karen poked at the food in her bowl, "you can not be too much older than me. Why do you say 'girl' as if I was small?"

I shrugged, taking a bite of warm, sweet goo from the broken bowl. "I wouldn't be any more scared of a crying woman."

"Even one with my talents?" She held up one finger, letting it glow blue. It never seemed to take the moment of concentration for her that it did for Krift to make the magic.

"I am not afraid of you." I told her, though that was not entirely true. "But, what you have done to our captain, and what the griffin might do to get you back, does worry me quite often."

"There must not be much you are afraid of." Karen returned, bowing her head over her breakfast with a bitter tone in her voice. I blinked, seeing images of flickering flames and imprisoning ice, but not understanding where she wanted this conversation to go. Was I supposed to tell her my worst fears, so that she could use them against me?

Well, I would not be led to that so easily. Going back to our original subject, I asked with a touch of mockery, "were you crying because your bed was too wet last night to sleep in? I could lay it out on the deck to dry this morning."

"No, it's fine." Turning away from me even further, she applied herself slowly to her food. With another shrug, I did the same, scraping out the last bits of oatmeal with the tip of my spoon when it got near the bottom. Then I ran a finger around the bowl, sucked the last trace of oatmeal off, and stood up.

"Well, I'll be leaving you then. Just set the bowl aside when you're done and it can be brought back to the cook later."

My hand reached out and touched the latch, just before I heard her say something quietly, almost as if to herself. Unsure if she was talking to me, I turned back. "What was that?"

"My tears were not for the wetness of the bed!" She replied fiercely, in a louder tone, trailing away once again into a quiet one as she added, "they were because I remembered."

Repenting of having made fun of her, I came back and sat near her on the floor. Whatever had come to her mind might be important to my quest, "what do you remember?"

She put a hand across her eyes, covering them as tears leaked silently down her face again. "How they killed my family...the men sent by the master. How they fund me. I was—but you don't want to hear. You have important things to do. And why should I want to tell you, my enemy?"

"I'm not your enemy." I assured her, feeling even worse for having spoken roughly earlier on. I could not help hoping that this small clearing of the clouds in her past would lead to a larger revealing before long, "and if you want to tell me, I will listen."

"I don't know." Karen shook her head, still hiding her face in her hands, "it just keeps coming to my mind, a few clear images from my past. I see myself, standing at a window, making patterns on it with ice to amuse the children inside. They are laughing, saying that I am Jack Frost...I think they are my siblings. Then the scene changes, it is later in the day and I see the men coming, breaking in the door, killing everyone inside. I attack them from behind with a hoe, which

I have been using in the garden. There is dirt on it, then there is blood. But there is more men than I can stop and they drag me away..."

I frowned in anger at her sorrow. It was almost the same story as the one Krift had told me. People killing their family and taking them away by force. Like the boy, she had a griffin and claw branded on her forehead, though it had faded to a dull scar with time. I wondered what would drive the griffin to do these things to people and how he could make his men do them as well. Not that I thought no one in the world would do those things without some unnatural force backing them, but because I knew there must be some incentive.

"I'm sorry," I told her, though part of me was glad that she had begun to remember the terrible things which the griffin had done. She could not possibly think of him as a perfect master now. "That is what Nightwing orders done to all the talented people he captures. He has their families killed and then their memory blurred so that they can not look back at it."

she nodded miserably, before straightening up and brushing a hand across her face. "But you have made me remember."

"It's the least I can do," with a self-depreciating shake of my head, I went back to the door to leave. She would not want to talk any longer and my other duties were calling to me.

Back on the deck, I helped put up a new wheel and then work on a shack for Chirn to cook in, so that if it happened to rain we would not have soup every night for dinner. All the time the conversation with Karen ran through the back of my mind, as I wondered how much she would tell me now, about where the griffin was hiding and what he was doing with his captives. The men around me worked mostly in silence as well, still depressed with the burned ship and frozen captain. They did not mutter against me too much, since I worked with them and never gave any order I would not have followed myself. Their quietness was a small comfort, knowing as I did how pirates can complain when they feel like it. Little did I know then, that things would get worse before they got any better.

MANY DAYS LATER WE were still going south, with the wind shifting between the north and the west. It was often cloudy and storms would blow up without warning to lash down rain and wind. The galley and the cabin had been at least partially repaired, to hold these storms off. We had also managed to come a little further west, toward the coast of Selland, but we were always being blown back the other way by contrary winds. The Middle islands were all around us as we sailed down their outer fringes, so that a watch had to be kept carefully both day and night so that we did not run aground. Most of the islands were small and rocky, just the sort to run up under your bow and hole you before you knew what was happening.

One day Chirn brought me the news about the food supplies. Feeding so many men every day used up supplies at a ferocious rate, as they came in hungry from a hard day's work in the cool weather. Then the cook told me that some of the previsions which had gotten wet when the hold leaked had now gone bad. Faced with starvation and even worse, a starving crew, I told Chirn to cut back on the rations. Meanwhile we would keep an eye out for any island large enough to go hunting and scavenging on.

As if to mock me, no islands bigger than a cluster of rocks was seen for days after that. Once, we stopped and killed a fat, colorful type of seabird on one of these little islands and had a good meal all around with the meat and their eggs. But after that we had to go on thinner and thinner rations again. Many of the men tried catching fish or sharks as we sailed, but only a few small ones ever came to the surface to be caught. Hunger bit into us all, accentuated by the fact that the days were cool and stormy. I had to be careful every day to encourage the men and promise that we would find something better soon. Mutiny could be around any corner. If it came to open rebellion, the hopes for the captain would become even thinner than they already were.

One of the things that galled the men the most was the fact that I still brought a meager ration to the prisoner, though she neither worked in the sails nor below. I ignored them when they hinted that we should throw her off into the sea to save her food for ourselves. I was adamant about keeping her, both for all of the practical reasons which I constantly reminded them of, and also because she was beginning to free herself from the griffin's mental grip. I could no longer think of her as a person to fear, or an enemy. Every day we spoke together more and she hesitantly told me about what she could remember of her past. In return, I told her a little of my own younger days, thinking of things which I had not cared to remember for many years. Such as how I used to play fight with my brother in the loft of our house at home, wrestling from the bed to the floor in a furious tangle. Or how my sister once found a little abandoned bird and tried to raise it, only to have it die on the morning of her birthday. I also told her a little of my adventures at sea and the things leading up to my fight with Skon Yew. This gave her an idea of Nightwing's history, without it seeming like I was trying to force the idea of his evil onto her. Also, it let both of us forget the ever-present drag of hunger for a little while, as we remembered and talked instead of having to worry about what was going on aboard the ship.

Finally one morning she told me what she knew about the griffin's hiding place and where it was located, "when they first brought me to his place, I was asleep. I awoke in the dark, in a strange room with stone walls and a stone floor. Old, rusty pipes ran along the wall. Later, I learned that it was underground, beneath a town called Littleton. The main entrance is hidden near the town. There is another, secret one in a shed beside a lighthouse nearby. But the master's place is very strange, full of twisting rooms like a maze and machines that I could not understand. If you go there to get the fiery one back, you will have to be very careful. I lived there for many days and still could never really understand how to navigate most of the rooms."

"A sort of maze, hmm?" I tried the imagine a maze underground, but I just kept thinking of a ridiculous hedge-maze with the griffin sitting in the middle. "But what is he capturing people for, Karen? Did he ever tell you why he wanted you there, or why he wants Krift?"

She looked a little perplexed at this question and at first I thought she would not answer at all. But then she explained hesitantly, "he rarely spoke to us directly and I did not often meet the other people whom he had captured. But I was given the feeling that he wanted our help in some great project, some plan of power or revenge that I did not know the particulars of, just an idea that haunted me with it's grandeur. The fiery one the master wanted because he was central to the plan in some way: he is to be a key piece in the whole thing."

I frowned, still not knowing as much as I wanted to, "so you don't really know what Nightwing is doing, just that he has some grand idea?"

"Yes, I'm sorry, I never really knew what his whole plan was." Karen shrugged, brushing back a strand of her pale hair with a gesture that I had become familiar with, when she was puzzled or trying to remember something, "only that he wished to capture people of talent, especially the fiery one, and keep them near him. Some he sent out on little missions now and then: to look for a person, or watch a place. It was always as if he was waiting for something in particular to happen before launching his grand scheme."

"Interesting." I sat back against the door, trying to put together all of the clues I had leaned by now to figure out what the griffin's plan could be. Sometimes, thinking of it, it almost seemed like there could be no grand scheme at all. What if he just wanted the powerful people working for him, collecting them as a sort of hobby?

I shook my head at the thought. That did not make any sense and would have held little point for the other people working for him. What made the most sense was if his idea was to eventually take over Selland and perhaps the other countries nearby. Now that they were at war with each other, it would be a good time to put such an action into effect. There was even the rumor that the king of Durny had been kidnapped, which could be connected to Nightwing. "Karen, was there anyone in the griffin's place that they called 'king?'"

"Not that I know of." She shook her head, "though he might have dropped the title in respect for the master."

"That's true." I tried to remember what the king of Durny's actual name was, but it kept escaping my grasp. Something like Rufgar, or Rifnik, was as close as I could get. As I sat puzzling over it, there came a knock at the door and someone began shoving on it trying to get in. Needless to say, that made it so that they were shoving the door against me.

"Hold on a minute!" I scooted toward the prisoner, out of the way, wondering what could be wrong now. I thought it would have to be something important, for one of the crew to come all the way down here and find me. To my surprise it was Wallace who came pushing in the door, followed by a few of the others whom he seemed to hang out with the oftenest. Before I could speak, the man from the *Highwind* pointed an accusing finger at me as if proving a point, "See, look at him! No more fear of that *thing* then as if it had been his sister, or his sweetheart!"

I glanced over at Karen, realizing that we were sitting rather close now that I had moved away from the door. To me it did not seem dangerous, or odd, as I knew that she meant me no harm now. But the men might see it in a different way.

"How much have you questioned her, chief?" Wallace looked down at me with a sneer. "What have you found out? Or have you been bewitched by this creature, who is nothing but a Jonah and an evil witch!"

At first I had felt uneasiness, but at his jabbing tone the feeling turned to firm resolve. Standing up slowly, I met his gaze, "For starters, I have found out where the griffin's lair is. It is below Littleton, and there is a secret entrance near the lighthouse of the same name."

My eyes swept across both of the men following him, before settling on his face again. His expression held a strange mixture of fear and hate, not so much for me, but for the thing that had once frozen his mind. Steadily, I went on, "and if you think that physical torture is the only way to get information, you forget what I am capable of doing with my mind. It is the very thing you owe your life to, mind magic. Because without it, you would be slowly dying in a prison of ice. Or already dead, rather, since starvation would have killed you long ago."

Wallace stepped back once, checked by my calm reply. The other two exchanged glances, before one said, "she might still be bad luck. What stops us from throwing her overboard now?"

"I do." with a gesture over my shoulder at Karen, I went on, "there is still things I have to learn from her: the griffin's weaknesses, the best ways to infiltrate his base, how many magicians he has working for him. Besides, you know that the famine aboard is not her fault. It is Dolgan's fault for making a fire boat of our enemies, which burnt down the galley and ruined more supplies in the hold. And Dolgan has already been banished."

This logic made them hesitate all the more, the two behind Wallace shruging, muttering agreements and backing away. They trusted me, basically, because they were my own men. But the crewman from the *Highwind* was still suspicious, which frustrated me after having saved his life and spent time throwing knives with him.

"That thing may still be useful to us." Wallace said, expression ugly with his fear and hatred. "But you are still far too friendly with her. If she gets free and freezes more of us, I'll hold you to blame, even if you are the first to go."

"That suits me." I stared at him hard until he left, before throwing a glance over my shoulder at the prisoner. She was still sitting by the center post on the floor, her head bowed and pale hair hiding her face. After a moment of silence she looked up at me to say quietly, "thank you."

"All in a day's work." I replied ironically, though the tone of real gratitude in her voice touched me, making me feel a little more light-heart as I left the room.

Topside I walked into the semi-repaired cabin and found Bowen sitting on the captain's bunk, unraveling a knotted length of thin line. His fingers stumbled over the knots, pulling them apart by feel alone. Seeing him sitting there, I was struck by how thin he looked and wondered if we had all become that gaunt from small meals. Then another thought came to me, and I asked sharply, "Bowen, have you been taking your rations?"

His fingers stilled for a minute, then went on with their work. "Why ask me such a question, chief?"

The truth coming together in my mind, I frowned at him, "you've been giving your share up for other people to eat, haven't you? What have you eaten today?"

"I don't think that is something you need to ask." He hedged, pulling too hard on one knot and tightening it instead of making it loosen, "you know exactly how much each of us are given."

"But I don't know how much of it you eat!" Going suddenly from a sense of cheerful recklessness to anger, I grasped the blind man by the shoulders and shook him, hard. "You don't need to play hero, Bowen! We'll make out without you starving yourself to death. Who would be here to tell me stories and give me advice then?"

frustrated at the wind that held us back, at the ship for sailing slowly with a hole in it's side, at myself for not being able to take better care of the crew, I stepped back to add forcefully, "you are going to eat the same ration as everyone else, do you understand?"

In his quiet, calm voice Bowen replied, "on Ullabar, a man is taught to go a long time with little provisions, if it is needed."

I still frowned, "I've also heard that on Ullabar if the tribe has to move far, quickly, or is running low on supplies, they will leave the old or crippled behind so that they can travel faster and have less mouths to feed. Is that what you were thinking, Bowen? Is it!"

He did not say anything, picking slowly away at the bit of string as if it was the most important job in the world. After waiting for a reply that never came, I turned about on my heel, "you stay right there. Don't try to go away, because I would only find you again."

I hurried out into the improvised galley, determined to see my old friend eat something before the day was any older. No one was in the kitchen right then, the temporary table having a knife laying out on it, as well as the bowls and spoons. I picked up one of each of these later two things and went over to where the cauldron stood over a heap of cooling coals. In the bottom of it was left a just little thin soup, enough for one person to make a meal of. I scooped it up with a ladle which hung nearby and put it into the bowl. Then I picked up a hard, slightly burnt biscuit from the counter and strode back to the cabin. Bowen still sat on the bunk, working quietly away at his string. I came up to him and yanked the line away from him, replacing it with the bowl and spoon. "Now I am going to watch you eat this. And you had better do as I say, because I'm the first mate now, you know."

When he hesitated, I went on, "think, Bowen, would you abandon the captain, because he is useless to us right now? Should we stop feeding him, because he can do nothing useful whatsoever? No, so don't be a fool when you know that you work as hard as any man aboard and help me with the hard decisions to boot. Eat it!"

Under such pressure he gave in and I could see by how he spooned the thin soup up that he had secretly avoided many meals lately. With a sigh, I went over to the chart table, muttering under my breath, "did the captain always have to watch over all of us in this way?"

I knew he had always been encouraging in the worst of times, or caustically abrasive when it was needed. But I had never realized how much work it took to keep a crew together, or how tired you could become simply from arguing with people all day.

Chapter 10: Edna's Ghost Returns

A few more days passed, everyone growing weaker and less alert from lack of nutrition. The last of the supplies were giving out altogether and no new provisions had been found. The wind was almost always from the west, with a rare burst from the north. We sailed partially against it, so that we could keep traveling south even if we were too far from the coast to make out the Littleton lighthouse. I sat consulting the charts once again, using the captain's instruments to find our position and mark it out with a red-headed pin. After many careful calculations, I found that we were almost directly across from Littleton, though still many miles to the east of the coast. With a sigh I sat back in my chair and closed my eyes, rubbing a hand across them tiredly. How were we going to get there in time?

Hungry and weary, I stood up slowly and looked down once more at the chart. There was one way which I knew of to go against the wind, other than rowing. And the crew were far too weak now to row us all the way. But my other method would require me to leave the ship, something I could not do with the crew of the *Seashooter* in such a state. I was pondering the quandary of captain or crew in a very dark mindset when suddenly I was electrified by a shout from the crow's nest up above, "Land ahoy! Straight ahead! Land!"

The watchman must mean a larger island to be shouting that way. Forgetting the problems weighing me down, I ran out into the prow of the ship, putting a flattened hand to my forehead to gaze under. At first there did not appear to be anything in front of us, but after a moment my eyes struck on something dead ahead. A low, pale line topped by dark smudges lay there on the level horizon. Above the smudges was an indistinct haze, hanging phantom-like in the air. Even at a distance the line was wider than any island we had seen recently and the darkness indicated trees. Remembering the spyglass, I hurried back and brought it out, training it on the land ahead with my hands shaking a little from anticipation. Brought into clear outline were the tops of trees, fronted by a wide beach of sand. Beyond the trees rose up a small mountain, a dead volcano heaved from the deep and surrounded by clouds. On the shore I thought I caught a speckling of square shapes like some tribe's huts, though it was hard to tell.

"Good job, watchman!" I called up to the crow's nest, feeling a surge of hope and new life flow into me, "it is land, looks like some sort of large island. There should be fruit in the trees and animals to hunt on the mountain. By tomorrow night we should all have a good meal before us!"

There was a cheer from the men who stood nearby, watching and hoping that it could not be a hungry man's mirage. Out of gloom, spirits rose all over the ship into a tangible feeling of excitement which filled the air. Everyone was talking about going ashore, eating roast wild pigs and drinking coconut milk until they could hold no more. With a will that had not been seen on board for days, they fell to their tasks. All day a holiday air prevailed and it did not dampen it for me when I went quietly to Caraway to tell him to make sure that everyone who went ashore the next day was well armed. I was not sure if it had been huts I had seen on the shore, but if it had been there was no way to tell how friendly the tribesmen would be.

The night passed restlessly, with everyone waiting impatiently to get to land. In the morning it was so close that we all could make out the tops of palm trees and the pyramidal mountain which rose above them. The clouds had blown away by now, leaving the slopes of the old volcano in plain sight. Part of the way up it was covered in a dense, lush vegetation of dark green, broken here and there by ridges and floes of dark stone. Above that point, the whole hillside turned into a cone of bare lava rock, coming to a peak which could be seen to be blown open on one side and shattered. But no steam or smoke rose from the mountain and it looked to have been many years since the hardened magma had flowed.

On the beach I could now see clearly the huts of the people native to the island, as well as the fishing boats pulled up on shore. But there was another thing which slowly came into view and surprised us all. Standing back from the clean beach, just inside the line of palm trees, was a fort built of adobe and native stones. It stood low and square in the shadow of the mountain, partially overgrown with vines and creepers. But it did not look broken down and among the boats of the natives I could now see a few which were of a different build, made of hewed wood instead of whole carved logs.

Slowly, we sailed up to this quiet beach, taking soundings until the water was not deep enough to support our ship any further. By then we were in close to the shore, as the island rose suddenly up out of the water without underwater ridges on this side.

People had come out of the huts to stand and stare at us on the beach. They were a little darker of skin then the northern tribesmen, but not nearly as browned as the cannibals who lived further south past the tip of Selland. These people were dressed in a mixture of skins, leaves and store-bought cloth in bright colors, showing that they had at least a trading knowledge of continental countries. The men lined up closest along the shore, watching us with spears and bows held in hand. Behind them, nearer their little houses, stood the women and children, looking on full of curiosity. I did not know any of the tribe's language, but hoped that they might know a little Sellish from trading with the continent. "Hello! We mean you no harm. But my men are very hungry, as we ran low on supplies, so we would like to come ashore."

There was a little pause in the group, before one of the men who was wearing a white cap on his head stepped forward out of the mass, "Sellander always welcome. You no harm, we no harm. Bring much fruit for hungry men!"

With a bright grin, he turned to wave to the women waiting further up on the sand. They broke ranks suddenly and went scurrying off, children screeching and howling after them, or running down the beach toward us. Within a few minutes dozens of little boats were putting out into the water and the tribe swarming around our ship like flies on a carcass. They called up for spirit water, coins and ribbons, vying to take us to shore for the lowest price. Barely containable, my men pressed to the railings, calling down to them in often ridiculously simplified pigeon Sellish. Some of the natives spoke back in our tongue, while others talked only in their own language. It was only by shouting that Caraway and I could get our men to listen to us and remind them to bring weapons, be on their alert, and not antagonize the natives. Hungry for food, and land, and fresh company, they agreed readily, only asking in return for freedom to go ashore. I gave it to all but a few, whom I set to watch the ship. These were promised ample food brought back to them as quickly as possible, then left to watch from the ship as the population of the island doubled with pirates being ferried to land. In a confusion of laughter and mixed languages, they met the women coming back with bowls of fruit and roast meat from their little palm-frond huts.

I was in one of the last boats coming to the beach, rowed by the native with the white cap. Curious at seeing no one come down from the fort to find out what the commotion was about, I asked my ferryman, "is there anyone living in that big house?"

"Ah, fort all empty for wet season." He shrugged with an islander's sense of carelessness about time and reason, "the Selland big-wigs only stay for trade when sunny. All gone when water come from skies too much. Not like you, ay?"

I knew that there was a question in those words: he wanted to know what we were doing here at this time and why the ship was in such a condition. I answered simply, but without any deviation from the truth, "yes, we were blown off course and attacked by a pirate ship, or else we would not be here at all. Are you the head man of this island?"

He shook his head, indicating someone whom I could not pick out of the mass on shore, "no, Massim Joe head man. Me Billy-Bahna, his son."

We came to the sand a moment later and both jumped out into the water to shove the boat up on it. "Well, thank you for taking me ashore, Billy."

I flicked him a small silver coin, turning to make my way up on the beach. The men were eating fruit, haggling for meat, giving away all of the little trinkets they could spare for the food that the tribe's women brought to them. A long shortage of food had made the bits of silver and gold we were loaded with seem small, compared to the fruit that was freely given.

Then, when the bowls were empty, they spread out on the island to hunt and forage for themselves, in able to resupply the ship. I told them to stay in large groups and be careful, warning them also to watch out for poisonous snakes. Euphoric with fresh food and a chance to roam freely on the land, they nodded and laughed carelessly before spreading out across the land. But I stayed behind on the beach near the hut, wishing to find the headman and ask him some questions.

With a few pointers I was able to locate him, sitting in front of his hut's doorway. He was a short, stocky man with a square head of curly hair and the expression of a contented dog guarding his porch and greeting any strangers with a friendly wag. I came up to him and he offered me a seat on the ground, waving for his woman to bring me coconuts and fruit. Settling on the sand, I waited until she had brought a tray with these things and left again, before asking, "do you speak my language, Massim Joe?"

"Yes, yes. Sellander I speak." The tribesman replies in a slow, slightly cracked voice, "what you want to ask of Massim, ay?"

"First of all, are all the other Sellanders gone from the fort and do they intend on returning anytime soon?" I put the question lightly, pretending that it would be a good thing for me if they were going to return. But the headman confirmed what his son had told me, "no come back until sky is sunny most the days and waves do not want to eat the sand any more. Sellander all gone from fort 'til then."

"Alright then." I nodded, secretly glad but trying not to show it. I did not want him to guess that we were pirates, though it might be obvious. "My men will have to fix our ship themselves. Would you let us pull our ship up onto the beach along here and stay on the island while it is being repaired? I will give you and your people many gifts if you will help us and let us stay here."

Massim Joe smiled, bobbing his head repeatedly in assent, "you stay, give my tribe many gifts and we will help with ship. You stay all'a longa you want."

His curly hair bounced with his moving head. Then he stopped nodding to hold out a hand toughened from fishing and hunting for me to shake. Afterwards, I stood up, bringing a bit of fruit to nibble on as I added, "I will bring you the gifts soon and also bring my right hand man, Caraway. He will be the one in charge of my men, because I have to go away soon."

The headman just waved and nodded again, picking up a broken coconut from the tray to drink it's milk. He was one of the cheerfullest and easiest to work with leaders I had ever met, giving me hopes that my people and his would get along well while I was gone. Because now that the crew had plenty of food and a safe place to stay, I had to turn my efforts back to saving the captain. There was one good way I knew of to go against the prevailing wind, or at least what was the prevailing wind at the height of the ocean. *Edna's Ghost*, the balloon which we had used to escape from the shadow city after being imprisoned there by the Dark Prince, and which we had afterwards deconstructed and stowed in the *Seashooter*'s hold. It was still there as far as I knew, taken to pieces and packed away beneath the other supplies. We had not used it since leaving Fraistia aboard our ship, so there must still be fuel in the canister which made it's heater run.

In a balloon, you could fly upwards until you hit a wind going in the direction which you wanted to travel. You dd not have to wait for it to come to you like we did on the sea. The only fears I had were that the balloon silk had rotted away by now, or that I could not find many of the crew to go with me. They would have to be willing to leave this tropical island, as well as to travel with Karen. Because she, too would have to be on the balloon with us, to help me navigate the griffin's lair.

I strolled along the sunny, open beach, feeling the sand dent beneath my feet as I made my way back to where the boats were drawn up on the shore. It was nice just to walk the land for a few minutes, feel the sun warm on my shoulders and smell the earth. The rich green and gray of the island inland was delicious to the eye after having spent so many days out in the monotonous waves of the sea. I knew the men were enjoying themselves hunting on the mountain after such a difficult sailing. As long as they did not offend the natives of the island in any way, they should be safe staying here for a time, repairing the ship and eating well after being on low rations for days. I would have to remind Caraway to give them a day off from repairing the ship now and then, so that they could go hunting again or just laze around on the beach. It was a good time to recharge and prepare for the inevitable launching out to sea once again.

Coming abreast of the ship, I found a tribesman who would go across in his boat and gave him a small coin to take me. He paddled us swiftly over in his sleek little canoe and I dismissed him with a wave once he had set me there. Stepping on deck, I located one of the men left on watch and called him over to help me pack the things I wanted from below up into one of our own, larger boats. First of all we put in a pile of old knives and daggers, as gifts for the tribe. Then I laid in a cutlass for Massim Joe, as well as a few bottles of wine from Fraistia. With these we put in a sack of shiny red beads which we had once found on a merchant ship and had kept for just such an occasion. With something for both the men and the women, as well as a special piece for the headman, our gift was ready to be given. I only wished we had some candy to give to the children, as there is no better way to win a people's friendship then to give things to their kids. But the younger ones could share in the beads, I supposed, as there was plenty to go around.

Once all this was neatly stowed, I had a few of the crew help me dig up and bring out the pieces of *Edna's Ghost*. To put it in storage, the basket had been cut along each corner, and then the walls detached from the base. It had not been meant to come apart in this way, but with some careful rope work it should not be too hard to put it back together again. Then there was the spidery metal frame, which held the burner and controls. The oiled sack which contained the balloon itself I unpacked on the deck of the ship to check for any rotten spots or holes and was gratified to find that there was none. Packing it back up, we put everything in the boat as best as we could, floating the basket pieces behind it on the water because they were so large. Luckily, they were meant to be water proof, having been varnished originally. All of this was rowed to shore and the balloon pieces left stacked near the boats. Then I went searching for Caraway, who had gone with a small group to look at the adobe fort.

Walking up through the palm trees, along a graveled path bordered by flowering bushes, my thoughts kept returning to which of the crew might agree to come with me. Ramses would come, if he was asked, of that I was sure. But I also knew that the men who had come with Wallace to accuse me of being too friendly with Karen would have to be left behind, as she was coming with me. I wanted about six men, I thought, all well armed and prepared to do whatever it took to save the captain. For no one knew how the griffin could be defeated, or what it would take to find him.

Coming around a curve in the path, I stopped to survey the fort which was clearly before me. It had been built on a rise in the land, a little plateau which was clear of trees and bushes. Behind it the mountain rose up suddenly, a thick wall of lush plants and lava rock. Directly around the fort the grass was green and smooth, almost like a lawn in it's height and formation. The structure itself was only one story tall, a wide, low building with a walled courtyard in front of it, boasting loop holes to shoot muskets out of and a few loops for cannons as well. The gate was made of wood re-enforced with iron, shaped in a tall arch which stuck up above the height of the dusty tan walls. This gate was open a little right now and I could hear voices inside of it. Recognizing that of the second mate, I strolled over to the open gate to peer inside.

Caraway stood gesturing at the main building of the fort, speaking to another one of the men about the how and why of it's construction. I listened for a minute, before coming quietly up behind him and remarking, "I didn't know that you knew so much about architecture, Caraway."

He turned with a small start, surprised to see me there. A touch of red came to his face as he replied, "oh, yes sir. I was studying to be an architect, before I ran away to sea and joined Captain Leighton. I suppose I never mentioned it, but then, it never really mattered."

"I guess you're right." I returned, amused to have brought such an admission from our usually taciturn second mate. It is easy to be surprised at what a person had done before becoming a pirate: many of us had started with a basic trade and then left it for the sea. It was not all of the crew who had always been pirates or seafarers of some sort, as the captain had been.

"Well, I need your help down at the beach, second." I told him, waving a hand around me. "As long as you are not too busy with all this?"

"No, sir." He followed me as I turned to go, leaving the other crewmen to explore the fort on their own. As we left through the gate I added, "by the way, how did you get in? I'd think that they would keep this gate locked."

Caraway shook his head, "just barred from the inside, with a door on the main building locked. We wanted to see what was inside, so Humper climbed over the wall and took down the bar."

"I see." distracted by a bright bunch of flowers with a sweet smell, I stopped for a moment and almost picked one. But then I thought better of it with the second mate following me and went on as if nothing had made me hesitate. Quickly we made our way along the path, down to the huts on the shore. Some of the tribesmen had already gathered near our boat, peering curiously in and speculating in their own tongue about what it contained. Massim Joe was among them, standing silently and watching as if to keep them from taking any of the things before they were given.

"Massim." I nodded to him before gesturing at my companion, "this is Caraway, the second mate of our ship. He will be supervising the men while I am away."

They shook hands solemnly, after which Caraway looked at me, "but I don't understand. Where are you going to, sir?"

"I have to try to get Krift back, both to save the captain and to rescue Krift himself." I lay a hand on Caraway's shoulder and met his gaze seriously. "He is my captain and my grandfather. I can not let him die. But the only way to go against the wind without constant rowing is to go above it. So I am going to take the balloon, along with some of the crew, to get the cabin boy back. You have to stay here and see that the ship gets repaired, as well as watching after the men. They might get rowdy and restless on land for so long. They need to be kept firmly in hand. Can you do that for me, Caraway?"

He nodded, straightening himself up tall with the importance of what I was asking him. He may have been older than me, but I had been in command up until that time. When I was gone, our whole piracy outfit would rest on his shoulders, "I will make sure everything goes smoothly, chief. Are you taking the captain with you, too?"

I shook my head as an answer. "We will bring Krift back if we can get him. It would be too dangerous for the captain where we are going. And if we die trying...well, you will have the ship and crew to yourself, to do with as you wish."

He bowed his head in acknowledgment. I turned to distributing the gifts to the tribesmen, who were all waiting nearby. The headman was given the sword with a little ceremony, as well as the bottles of wine to give away or keep as he chose. Every one of the tribe who came was given a knife or a bead and what was left over in our boat the chief would hold for others of his people who were not there at the time. Eventually everything was passed around and some of our men were starting to trickle back from their various expeditions on the mountain.

I waylaid a handful of them to help me put the balloon and basket back together, fixing everything in place with rope and lines, even the crude figurehead I had once carved meaning for it to go on the *Blue Bucket*. By the time *Edna's Ghost* was ready it was evening and the glow of camp fires lit up the sand all along the beach. The crew was roasting wild pigs and the tiny deer that the natives called Popara, laughing and talking into the night as if there had never been a famine on the ship and never would be again.

I went to join them, putting aside my worries about the next day, trying to enjoy myself as much as possible for one night. Earlier I had brought Karen fruit and meat from the shore, telling her briefly about the natives and the island. But I had not yet revealed my plan of taking her on the balloon. Not even to anyone on board, leaving that bridge for when I had to cross it. By flickering orange flames and glowing red coals we feasted, as the seafaring tales grew taller into the night. Some of the natives sat and watched, those who could understand our speech translating the stories for those who could not. Their eyes grew wide as they heard artistically embellished versions of the fight with the octopus, the run from the warships by Clydesfort, or other stories from further back in our history.

Eventually, tired out with fun and feasting, everyone dropped to sleep where they lay, or returned to the ship to take the next watch. I went back to the ship myself, standing a watch under the sharp stars of a clear sky before turning in to my own bunk in the cabin. Tomorrow would bring it's problems, but for tonight I could almost feel satisfied.

THE MORNING DAWNED cool and moist, with a thin, warm mist falling from pale clouds which had blown up late in the night. The men sleeping by the campfires had mostly ignored it, snoring in the damp as if it were nothing. Only a few of them had rowed themselves back to the boat, where they could find shelter and blankets on their beds. I had gone quietly in the early morning and assembled some of the crew whom I knew to be the most steady and faithful. Once they were around me, I told them of my plans and asked who would volunteer to go with me. Of the ones who offered to go, I picked out six of the best, including my old friend Ramses. After that my orders for the chosen crewmen were to get a good breakfast and pack whatever of theirs they would want to take with them, especially their best weapons.

While they got ready I went to check on Leighton one more time before we left.

He lay on a bed in the sawbones' personal quarters, blankets stacked on him in an attempt to keep him at a decent temperature. His face was barely recognizable, wasted and wrinkled with a bluish color like a man on a very cold night. His breathing was just perceptible, when I took his hand in mine it was as thin and cold as an icicle. My hand could only stand to touch his for a moment, before it became so cold that I let it drop. I paced up and down, torn about leaving him in that terrible condition. Then I said, just in case he could hear me through the prison of frozen lines, "I'm going to find a way to save you captain. Just hang on a little longer, you no-good old seadog."

Hoping that, if he heard my words, they would both give him hope and needle him into sticking around. After pausing in the thin hope of an answer, I looked over at the doctor, who stood stiff and frowning nearby. "You've done well to keep him alive this long. Just take care of him a little longer."

"Of course." Vulture replied with a tilt of his long nose and a shrug of his thin shoulders. There was little difference, to him, between mere duty and the best which could be done.

After that I went up to say farewell to Chirn and Bowen in the kitchen. My old friend was no longer in danger of starving himself, so I felt no qualms about leaving him. There was nothing else to do but go down to the carpentry shop. Feeling a little uneasy at letting Karen out, both for the crew's sake and hers, I unlocked the door and opened it slowly. She sat on the floor inside as always, one knee drawn up and her hands fastened around it as she gazed at the wall as if she could see right through. Coming in, I asked with care, "would you like to see the island, Karen?"

Her face whipped around to look at me intently. "Yes, very much."

"Then come with me." I held out a hand and forced myself to take hers without a flinch, wondering that someone who could freeze a man's mind so quickly had a warm palm like anyone else. Like hers, delicate and living. We walked over to the ladder and I climbed up first, helping her out as she came onto deck. there I took her hand again, just to show everyone that there was nothing to fear from her.

Karen's gaze went out to the island, then up to the sky as if she would breath it all in. She had not seen anything outside of her wooden cell for many days and could barely move with trying to see and feel everything around her to its fullest extant. The men on deck either stared at her in astonishment, or turned their backs pointedly and would not look. Wallace was standing near the makeshift galley door when we went by and spit on the planks in front of him as if to get a bad taste out of his mouth. I did not care: she was going with me and no one could stop me from bringing her.

We walked over to the side of the ship to climb down into the waiting boat, where the six companions I had picked sat with their bundles at their feet. They all edged uneasily away from Karen as she stepped down into the boat. suspicious glances were cast at her as she went to sit in the prow. Nothing was said except for the usual directions to shove off and start rowing, until we got to the shore and climbed out. Once the boat was beached Ramses sidled over to me to whisper quietly, "do you think this will be safe, my friend? She is a dangerous person."

I had already explained to my chosen companions that we would be bringing her with us for guidance once we reached Littleton, but the closer the time came to leave, the less they could believe it. It was odd enough to be leaving in a hot air balloon, which would fly us through the skies like a bird. But to be taking the one person who had caused the problem which we were trying to fix seemed extremely strange to them, especially since she was not tied or bound, but walking free.

"Does she look too dangerous for seven strong men to handle?" I gestured at the girl, who had gone a few steps away to stare up at the cloud-swathed mountain with wide, curious eyes. Beads of the warm mist caught in her hair and her hands were clasped in front of her as if she were silently begging for permission to stay gazing there for a long time.

"Ah, but you can never tell." Ramses shrugged, beginning to move away toward where *Edna's Ghost* sat ready to be filled with hot air. "She could be tricking us."

My face turned to a thoughtful frown, watching her. Could she really be tricking me, biding her time to freeze us all? But what would be the point for her to kill us now, when we were taking her right back to the griffin of our own will? If she wanted us dead, all she would have to do is wait for her master to find us in his home. I would have to stay alert and see that she did not betray us once we reached Nightwing's lair.

Catching sight of the men moving away toward the large basket set on its side in the sand, Karen pointed at it and asked, "what is that? Where are they going?"

"It is a hot air balloon. Have you ever heard of them before?"

She shook her head, so I explained, "see that big envelope of silk laying on the ground? We will fill it up with hot air from a burner in the basket and the hot air will make it rise. The basket gets flipped upright and we will get into it. With the balloon full, it will pick the basket up and carry us to where ever we want to go."

"It will fly?" Her expression held wonder and amazement, "and we are going in it? But where, and why? What about your ship?"

"I have to rescue Krift, remember?" I looked at her steadily, "You must come with us, both to help find the way to the griffin and because it would not be safe to leave you aboard the ship alone. We are going to fly to Littleton, using the higher winds that go in a different direction than the wind down here is blowing. I hope you are not too afraid of heights?"

She shook her head, reminding me, "I used to fly on the master's back where ever he wanted me to go. It was wonderful."

"Good." I waved for her to go ahead of me, still secretly too cautious to have her behind my back. We went over to where the men waited by the balloon, looking back at us. They had all been told what the balloon was and how it worked when it was stowed in our hold long ago. All of the crew knew that we were going to be flying in it today, as they had seen it being assembled on the beach the day before. But my companions were still a little nervous, as none had flown in it before or even seen it flying. One of them tugged at a lashing on the corner of the basket, muttering, "well, it looks stout, but I would hate to see it break while we were over the ocean."

"It will hold out." I assured him, moving past to inspect the burner on it's metal frame, "I checked the knots myself."

Carefully remembering what Myrmidon had taught us so long ago, Ramses and I got the heater forcing flames into the opened envelope, while the others held lines connected to the balloon and basket. Slowly it filled, rising with gentle majesty up into the air until the basket righted itself with a jerk. The balloon bobbed up above it, until *Edna's Ghost* was pulling at the lines like a boat in the ebb tide. We all climbed in, cutting the ropes holding it down to stakes all at once so that it was released smoothly. The whole thing lifted gently up into the air, jerking only slightly from one side to the other as the lower breezes played with it. As we rose, it steadied out, water dripping from the edges of the balloon where the mist caught and turned to solid trickles. I stood by the burner, pulling down on the lever which made the flames leap into the envelope above. It burned with a thin whooshing sound, heating the air and making it rise. The others stood around the edges, peering downwards as the ground slipped away beneath us. Some of them looked a little sick, while others just appeared interested or excited. Karen stood at a little distance from them, holding on to one of the lines which connected the envelope to the basket. Her head was turned downwards as well, watching the land sink away beneath us. After a moment she came to join me by the control lever as we rose above the clouds. The sun was suddenly shining down on us, reflecting white across the billowing top of the cloud cover. It blinded our eyes with it's brilliance, setting off the drops in everyone's hair so that they shone like veils of diamonds. The balloon rose above the billowing clouds, until all below us was a solid landscape of fluffy white. Eventually we struck a fresh wind and I let off on the fuel valve. The wind was blowing towards the west, and that was the direction which we wanted to take.

Chapter 11: Lighthouse Keeper

Karen stood next to me, looking uncertainly at the men I had brought with us. They had spread out now and were stowing their gear away or simply getting used to the big basket which was carrying us.

"I don't even know their names." The young woman remarked shyly, with a small flick of her hand at the others, "and I know they can't trust me."

I glanced around, startled to realize that she could, of course, have no way of knowing these men, though I had grown so accustomed to them through the years that just the sight of their faces brought their names and character to mind.

"Well, I can easily remedy the first problem." I told her, pointing out two of the crew who were still looking over the edge in interest, "Those two, of about my own age, are Felix and Humper. The first is a Friastian, as you can see by his classic orange hair, and the other a Sellander. But they came on our ship together and you rarely find them apart. Felix is cheerful, quick with a joke and also a deadly shot with a rifle. Humper is the quiet one, though he is one of the most agile men aboard the *Seashooter*."

I turned to some of the others, who were looking through their bundles on the wooden benches which lined the inside of the basket, "that is Henry, with the scars on his arm and the red sash. A real buccaneer, always ready to fight or feast. Next to him is the graybeard Don, a steady man who will recite poetry if you ask him a question he doesn't want to answer. Then there is Bready, as we call him because he once took a dare and ate ten loaves of bread in a sitting. Nicknames stick quickly on a ship full of pirates, who are always looking for a bit of fun."

The last person I pointed out was Ramses, who stood nearby with a look between amusement and wariness on his face as he watched. "This is my friend Ramses. We broke out of the Dark Prince's jail together, knocking out the guards and stealing the keys. He is always polite, quick to help and a pain to escape from if you don't want him around."

In acknowledgment he bowed to us, though he kept his place. He seemed to be the only one to have heard or understood at least a part of my introduction, which was of course spoken in Gracklandic so that Karen could understand. She gave a little, surprised nod of her head in to return his bow, before asking me, "you can trust all of these men, I suppose?"

"Without a question." I nodded, giving a small tug on the balloon control lever so that we would not fall too fast, "the first mate does not stay in the same quarters as the crew, but I've never liked to separate myself from them like some officers would. We work together, fight together and talk when there is time. In return they may grumbled about me sometimes, but their hearts are never really in it."

The girl was silent for a long space of time, before saying quietly, "Sarkin, I am scared."

"Of them? But I just told you, I trust them. They will not hurt you." My words held a touch of surprise, as she had never admitted to any form of fear before. But her head was shaking as she returned, "No, not of them. I—I am afraid of the master. What will he do when I come back with you? I am a traitor."

I had never thought of it from that point of view before. Nightwing would most likely be angry to find that I had partially won her over to our side and would aim a fraction of that anger at her. Which raised the question, why had he not tried to rescue her before? Surely she was worth something to him. I supposed the answer was in how much she was worth.

But it was important that she came with us and I did not want her to feel anxious the whole trip over.

"Don't worry too much." Was my advice, "we'll all look out for each other, keep our eyes open. He would be angry at us even if you weren't here. If the griffin attacks us, we'll just have to fight back. That's why I brought the best of my men."

She did not reply, just continued to look troubled and stood near me as if my presence alone could protect her from the griffin.

A little later in the day I called the others over to show them how to run the lever on the balloon. It was fairly simple to operate, so once I had explained the basics we could all take watches throughout the night without much trouble.

The clouds below us spit and cracked as the day went on, drawing apart into long streamers of curling white with patches of sea seen below. At the rate we were going, I guessed that we could be to the edge of Selland after about two days of flying. Littleton was a coastal town, so it would be right there. So it would not be long before we were landing at it and would have to figure out the next steps in our mission. To begin to get an idea of what we would have to work with, I asked Karen to take a bit of chalk which Don had gave me and draw a map of what she could remember of Nightwing's underground lair. We sat on the floor of the basket near the cupboard which held the food supplies and the tank which held the water. She took the white chalk and drew a handful of lines on the floor, erasing some and redrawing them when they did not suit her. Then she explained what rooms were along all of the lines and what she thought might be beyond them. She did not know where the secret entrance to the fortress came in compared to those rooms, but the main entrance and hall she marked out for me. In the end, the map of what Karen knew was very sketchy, the halls coming to abrupt ends and many of the rooms unlabeled. She said that even what she had drawn she was not sure of, and seemed confused whenever I pressed her for more details. Finally, I gave up trying to figure out what the warren looked like on the inside and asked her what other people she knew that the griffin had captured.

"There were two I met often and one whom I only met once." She gave a little shiver, "He was a strange one and not a person I would want to meet more. I never learned what his specialty was, or why he was there. He had a large, bald head and a small, narrow-featured face. And he seemed to be quite important to the master." She shook her head, seeming to flick the memory of him away with a gesture, "One of the other two was a man who was extremely quick and good at fighting. You could throw an apple at him suddenly and he would catch it before it hit. I know: I tried to hit him with one once. He took it and threw it against the wall so hard it splattered like a rotten egg, even though it was fresh. The other talented one I knew was an old woman who wove things out of string. What she wove them for I never learned, but they were strange shapes and symbols which seemed to have some deeper meaning."

Karen shrugged sadly, finishing, "I know there were more than that, because I would see them sometimes, going around corners or disappearing through doors. But I simply was not curious at that time...as you have said, my mind was twisted to follow only the master."

At least she admitted it now. I squinted thoughtfully up at the sky over the edge of the basket, considering the characters she had described. The quick one, the fighter, sounded like the most dangerous to me. We would have to be careful if we met him, he might be agile enough to avoid a gunshot or a sword slash, if he was skilled enough to have attracted the griffin's notice. The other two sounded strange, but without knowing exactly what they could do, my fear of them could not be fully formed.

"Let me ask just one more question for today." I pressed the girl, switching my gaze down to her face, "what about the griffin's soldiers, the ones whom he sends to kidnap people. How many of them is there and why do they follow him?"

"He pays them highly." Karen returned after a minute of thought, "and promises them a position in his vague dream of power. As to numbers...they were never around enough for me to see. At most, I would meet ten of them together at one time."

"Thank you." I nodded, accepting the bit of information. It was likely all I was going to get before having to search Nightwing out of his lair myself. What I would do when I found him was still a question that I could not answer. But wherever he was, Krift was sure to be nearby.

IN THE AFTERNOON OF the third day out from the island, we spotted the rocky point of land which was the nearest edge of Selland. It was a wide, rounded arm of land curling gently around both to the north and the west: for this was almost at the very southern end of the land, where it touched a new sea and ran away to the west out of sight. Selland was not nearly as wide as it was tall, but I had never before been around to the western edge or seen the ocean there. Somewhere beyond it, far to the west, lay the land of Ullabar, where Bowen had been raised by the natives after having been kidnapped from the Sellish colony. I had not yet seen that land, either, though I intended to one day.

Below us the rocks and shore became clearer, gray and wet beneath a clear, cool sky. We floated down out of this sky, landing with a gentle thump on the grassy headland. Here the grass was much thicker and more luxuriant than it had been up north on Petal point. The trees which stood nearby were a mixture of palm near the beaches, and thick, dark oaks up on the headland. To our right, set on the very edge of the slope which led to the sea, was the lighthouse. It was a tall, slightly tapering building of stone which had been whitewashed on the outside to make it more visible to the passing ships in the daytime. On the top of the stone pillar was set a cage of glass and steel, topped with a little roof of rusted metal. This was where the huge oil lantern burned throughout the night, reflected out to sea with curved pieces of metal to make it more intense. Its job was to warn sailors away from the long arm of rocks which reached out into the water at the bottom of the point. I had heard tell that the shore was haunted at specific times of the year, haunted by ghosts of drowned seamen who had died trying to round the point of Selland before the lighthouse was built.

With the basket sitting lightly on the thick, green grass we let the balloon deflate all of the way and packed it carefully into it's bag. Then we had too let it sit, as there was no way to disguise the basket from sight out in the open. Henry suggested that we cut palm fronds and oak branches to hide it, but that was not really practical with how little trees there was, and a heap of brush would have stuck out almost as badly as the basket did.

I moved around inside the basket for a minute, making sure that we had left nothing behind. Once satisfied, I hopped out and joined the others, who were waiting in a group.

"Well, let's go," I told them, striding past to lead the way toward the lighthouse. The grass swished as I went through it, leaving trails of moisture on my pant's legs. Far off I could see the roofs of the town glittering in the light and the rise of smoke from their chimneys. But the lighthouse stood out by itself, with a barely perceptible path running from it toward the houses far away. It did not look like the lighthouse tender kept up communication with the town very frequently.

Standing at the base of the tall, white tower which held up the light was a small cabin of slabbed logs, the bark facing outwards in rounded humps. Beside the lighthouse, almost behind it compared to the keeper's house, was a medium-sized shed with wooden walls and a shingle roof. It was too large to be an outhouse, but not quite big enough to work as a stable even for a single horse. What the lighthouse keeper thought it was for, I was not sure. But this was where we made for, Karen walking beside me and pointing it out as we went. "That is the place where the secret entrance starts."

"What's she saying?" Felix asked, skipping a few steps to catch up, "is that the place we're looking for?"

I nodded, not answering. Things seemed quiet enough on the headland, no shape moving except for some half-wild horses grazing off toward the town. And yet someone must have seen us land in our balloon and I persistently had the feeling that we were being scrutinized from a distance. Finally my feet came to a stop, bunching the others up behind me, and I swept my gaze across the scene. White tower, graying shed, green grass, brown cabin... then I noticed it. Standing in the shadow in front of the cabin's door was a half-hidden figure, turned toward us as if watching. He was wearing a long sea coat of dark gray, both hands tucked into the wide pockets, out of sight. From a distance his face was shadowed, but there was something strangely familiar about the way in which he stood. I stopped for a long minute, holding the others back with an upraised hand. If he wished to speak or attack, now was the time. But he still made no move. My hand dropped and we walked across the grass to confront him. He would want to know why we were here and, worse, we would have to make up a good reason to convince him that we needed to look in his shed.

We came to a stop again when we were directly in front of him. I was struck once again with the feeling that I should know this man. He had straight, dark hair which lay in a wave on his forehead and fell just below the ears on each side. His chin had a rough stubble on it and there was an expression in his cool gray eyes which I could not quite name.

"Sarkin." He said, before I had time to speak, "did you come all this way in that strange contraption only to force me back to your ship?"

Suddenly, recognition hit me. "Storm. So this is where you went after jumping ship?"

"It was better than what awaited me if I stayed on as your chief gunner." He shrugged, shifting to lean against the doorpost of the cabin. He had been the second gunner we had hired on the *Seashooter*, the one who had left with no word of warning when we were anchored along the coast near this spot. I had always preferred him to Dolgan, often wishing he would have stayed on longer as a pirate instead of leaving so quickly. Though he had always been rather quiet and hard to talk to, I had gained a great respect for him as our gunner. I had even liked him personally, despite his shadowy ways. But it had never occurred to me that we would see him again after he had left that once.

As he shifted on the post, I noticed a strange bulge in his left coat pocket and my eyes dropped to it, wondering if he could have a gun hidden in there to prevent us from forcing him to go back with us. Not that we actually had that in mind, but he might be worried about it.

He saw my glance and pulled his arm out of the pocket slowly.

"Pirates aren't the only ones that can have one of these," he held out an arm with a sharp metal hook attached on the end, held in place by a leather cup instead of a hand, "nor are clever thieves. I was sleeping in a cow barn one night, after I jumped ship. The cow stomped on my hand and the break never healed right. Had to cut it off because of the infection. But tell me, what are you doing here?"

My surprise at the sudden meeting was beginning to fade away, I told him the half-truth which I had prepared just a moment before, "we came looking for the entrance to a secret tunnel, which is said to be inside your shed over there. Didn't know it was you running this place, of course, but we still wanted to have a look. Heard there might be some treasure down there we would want."

"Still looking for treasures, hmm?" Storm regarded me for a long moment, then swept his eyes over the others. His gaze rested for a long moment on Karen, surprised, I suppose, to see a girl with us. "Well, let's go over to the shed and see. But I warn you, you might not like what you find in there."

"What do you mean? What does the shed hold?" I asked as he went passed me and began leading the way over to the shed. His shoulders under the thick coat shrugged as he explained, "the shed holds barrels of oil, for the lighthouse when it runs out. But that's not all I meant."

Puzzled, I watched as he unlocked the door with a little key and swung it open. When he stepped in and beckoned, we followed. There was a dusty square of glass in the wall, which let in a dim sort of light from the westering sun. The floor was made of cement, rough and chipped from use. A few barrels of oil stood to one side and a rusty metal ladder leaned against the opposite wall. Between them was an open slab of cement, with faint lines all around it in a square.

"That's what you're looking for, I take it?" Storm waved a hand at the cement, which was so obviously a removable piece that I wondered that no one had found the secret entrance before. Without waiting for an answer, the lighthouse keeper picked up a crowbar which lay nearby and prized up the thin slab on one side. With a grunt, he shoved it over to the side with his one good hand, exposing a dark hole underneath. A set of stone steps led steeply downwards, ending at a solid metal door. The door had no handle or latch visible, only a small slot in the center as if something was meant to fit in it.

"There is your secret entrance." Storm told us, his expression hard to read, "I've been through it before, but never found a way through the door on my own. A piece of wood or a wire stuck in the slot does nothing. Do you have any ideas?"

His tone was almost mocking, as if he thought we would never get through. I looked from the door to him, narrowing my eyes, "is that what you meant when you said we might find something down here we did not like?"

"Partially." His eyes cut toward mine, full of something unspoken. I tried to fathom what it might be, but was distracted by a tug on my sleeve. It was Karen, looking excitedly down at the door, "I remember now! There is a sort of key which opens that door, but it is not like other keys. It is flat and has glowing lines on it in an image. It uses some sort of magic."

"Does it look like this?" becoming excited as well, I whipped out the object which Krift had stolen and given to Bowen, before the blind man had given it to me. It was the thin, rectangular piece of metal with the glowing lighthouse on it, which had first given me the clue that the griffin lived in this direction.

"Yes, that looks right!" Karen clapped her hands together, before remembering herself and adding, "I only hope that no one knows we are here."

Jumping down the steps, I thrust the flat metal key into the slot. There was a sharp *click* from inside and the card was sucked out of my hand for a moment. It just disappeared into the wall like a tongue being withdrawn. Then it came bouncing back as if it had hit a spring and I was able to grasp it just in time. For the door began to slid sideways of it's own accord, slipping back into the wall until it had disappeared altogether. It was the strangest thing to see that thick stone slab moving out of our way by itself. Beyond it there lay a long passage with dark walls of some smooth stone, dimly lit by a glowing line on the roof, much like the ones on the flat key but pale blue instead of green. I had never seen anything like it before and it made me wonder who could have built this underground fortress originally, what sort of knowledge they had possessed.

"I wouldn't go any further." Storm warned from up above, as a few of my companions pressed around to get a better look, "there is nothing but pain down that way for you!"

His tone was so urgent that I backed up a step, to give him a hard look, "what do you mean? What is the meaning of all these vague warnings that you are giving us?"

"They are the truth." He leaned on the crowbar and waved a his metal hand at me, exclaiming in a low, painful tone, "my power tells me so! The master will capture you if you go any further!"

There was dead stillness for a moment after he had spoken these words. Breaking it, Henry smoothly drew a pistol and pointed it at Storm, while Bready pulled a long, leaf-bladed knife from it's sheath. The others stood by the entrance to the tunnels, looking on alertly. They all knew by now that 'the master' was what the griffin's servants called him. I walked a few steps back up the stone stairs, drawing one of my own hand guns to point at the lighthouse keeper, "tell me what you know about the master."

He stood leaning on his crowbar, looking back at me with a sullen sorrow in his eyes, like a wound that still ached even though it had long since healed. With a move of his right hand he brushed the wave of hair away from his forehead. Below it, burned deep in the skin, was the mark of the griffin.

"I know more than most." He told us, letting the hair fall back, "and more than I would ever ask to. But I don't work for him any longer, if that is what you are wondering. He had no use for me after all my news was bad news."

"Tell us what you know," I pressed him, taking another step forward with the pistol, "and how you know it."

"You might want to take a seat." Storm replied sardonically, letting down the crowbar and finding himself an old crate to sit on, heedless of the guns pointed at him. He did not seem entirely adverse to telling what he knew, though he really had little choice. We all stayed standing, even Karen, and did not put our weapons away. After letting his gaze run over all of us once, Storm shrugged, "I used to live near here, on the outskirts of Littleton. When I was young my parents died, leaving me with a baby sister to fend for. I took care of her myself, until—"

He was interrupted by Henry, who growled, "enough with the sob story. Get to the point or I'll blow your other hand off to match the first!"

Storm gave him a cold look, continuing without an answer, "until she was old enough to look after herself. Then I did various little jobs looking for work, until I hit on being a gunner's mate in the navy. That ended badly for me, you don't need the details, so I eventually joined up with you pirates as the gunner."

His hook hand clinked solidly on the wooden crate as he dug it into the wood, "up until then, I had never even heard of the griffin. But I began to hear rumors about you fighting him, Sarkin, all that sort of thing. Then, one day when we were anchored near here, my second sight told me that my sister was in danger of immanent death. So I—"

"Wait." It was me who interrupted him this time, holding up a hand to pause the story, "you still have not told us what this 'second sight' is. I suppose it's the talent which the griffin wanted you for?"

"That's right." Storm nodded, right hand clenching, "I can feel things...see just a little of how something is going to turn out, or get a glimpse of things happening far away. I've always had it and kept it secret, but it was in part of that 'gunner's mate' affair that I let the truth slip. A plague on me, all this wouldn't have happened if I had just kept quiet."

He fell silent, upon which one of the men made a motion as if to stir him up. But I stopped him with a wave of my hand, telling the informant quietly, "Go on. So you knew that your sister was in danger."

"Yes." Storm agreed, taking a deep breath to continue, "I knew that someone was going to kill her if I did not stop them soon. So I jumped ship, taking my things with me, and hurried home. There I found them waiting, the master's soldiers. They had my sister tied to a chair and one of them held a sword to her throat. somehow, they had heard of my talent, and knew I would come if she was threatened. Then...as I watched, and she looked back at me pleadingly, they killed her. Before I could do a thing, they killed her!"

He jumped up to his feet, leaving the hook behind him buried in the wood of the crate. The memory was hot and alive on his face, burning in his eyes. But after a moment he blinked, looked at Henry's pistol, and sat down again with a sigh, going on more calmly than he had before, explaining how the soldiers had captured him and dragged him off just as they had Karen and Krift. But they didn't have far to go, as they were in Littleton just above the griffin's lair at the time. They took him down into the caverns and brought him before the master. He had fought and struggled against them to exhaustion and was in a daze as someone stepped out beside the griffin to speak to him.

"I don't remember anything for a long time after that." Storm admitted, running his hand through his hair, "some sort of spell was put on me and I lived only to do as the master said. All that time is blurred, except for a few things which stick sharply out of it in my memory. The master had a room, mostly dark, lit by a single bright light. It shone down on a coffin holding a young man's body, laid out dead and white. He, the griffin I mean, wanted to find someone who could bring this corpse back to life. He collected the talented people partially for that, hoping one of them would have power enough to do it."

"Skon Yew. Kipper." I murmured under my breath, knowing who the dead person must be. It made sense. Nightwing had carried him off years before, after I had defeated Skon Yew in a battle. Now the griffin was looking for someone to bring him back to life, though it seemed odd to me that he had not tried to steal the queen of Grackland's wishing bone to do it with. I knew from experience that it had the power to bring ghosts back into our realm, so why not a corpse?

Storm did not hear the names I said, and went on with his explanation. It seems that the griffin had tried to make him prophesy who would be the one to bring the Dark Prince back to life, but Storm did not know the answer. The griffin asked him to tell if the Dark Prince would come back to life at all and the answer had been; "He will never truly live again."

Angered at these poor answers, the griffin had let him alone for a time and Storm had wandered in the strange rooms of the underground maze for what seemed like a long time, seeing strange things, many of which he did not understand. Finally, he had been brought before the griffin again and asked the same questions a second time.

"This time I saw an image in my head, when he asked me the first question. It was the image of a boy who had fire dancing on his fingers. So I told him he had to find the fiery one to even attempt to bring the dead one alive again. When he asked me if the body would ever live, I did not see life in my head. I only saw the dead one with fire in his eyes, laughing as he threw a sword at someone or something I could not clearly see. So I told the master the same thing I had before. The corpse would never truly live again."

I opened my mouth to speak, but the story was not over yet. Storm finished with explaining that the griffin had asked him many questions after that and every answer seemed to make Nightwing angrier. Finally, the master had decided that Storm was not worth keeping. He was thrown out of the secret lair and the fog that had been on his mind lifted.

"But they did not let me truly go free." He finished with a shake of his head, "oh, no. He would not do that, or else I might tell the world what I had seen."

"How did he keep you from telling?" Humper asked quietly, stepping up beside me for a moment. I let him speak, my mind full of what Storm had said. Now I knew why the griffin wanted Krift so badly and was beginning to understand part of his plan. It was to bring Skon Yew back to life again and ruin all my work in getting rid of him.

"He took something from me, or one of his talents did." Storm shook his head again, leaning it in his hands, "it is something which I can not name and you can not see. It was a piece of my spirit, I guess, and I just don't care any more. I don't care about anything; if you kill me, or if I live. If the master destroys the world, or if the world destroys him. The townsfolk think I'm crazy, they would never believe me even if I told them the truth...perhaps they are right."

He stood up, crossing his arms and sweeping us with his gaze once again. The expression on his face which I had not been able to name before made sense to me now. He was angry, and tired, and even a little afraid, but he just did not care. Nothing mattered to him any more, the only reason he lived was because he did not care enough to die.

"So that is that." He spoke abruptly, shrugging and moving towards the door, "I don't know why I have told you all this, but there it is. If you wish to kill me now, I won't stop you. Just remember; bad things wait for you if you go down that tunnel, Sarkin."

"Wait." he stopped as I spoke, "wouldn't sorrow wait for me just as much if I did not?"

He considered this for a minute, paused in the doorway, before answering, "yes, that is true. But remember, if you are caught by the griffin, you will become another weapon yourself. Not that I care."

With none of us having the heart to stop him, he walked out of the door.

Chapter 12: Into the Griffin's Lair

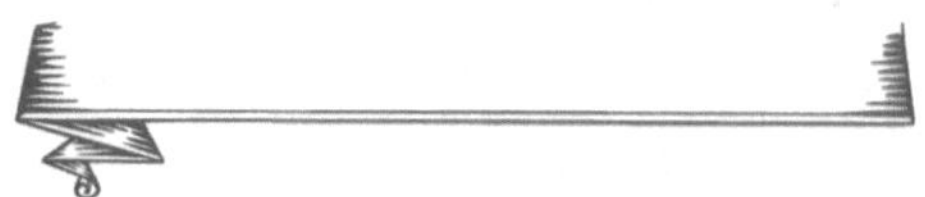

Everyone stood still for a space of time after the lighthouse keeper left. Eventually Karen took a step closer to me and asked, "What did he say?"

Reminding me that she could not understand very much of our language, though I had begun to teach her. In as few words as possible, I explained to her what Storm had said. Afterwards, she glanced at the tunnel, with it's pale lights and smooth floor, then back at me, "he must have tried to get his spirit back before, but could not open the door. I think he still cares a little more than he would like to believe."

It was a good observation, as he had obviously had a hard time controlling his emotions while telling the story. But whatever the griffin had taken from him was keeping him dangerously near the secret entrance, though he did not seem inclined to follow it now that it was open. I guessed that fear and the wish for revenge were always warring in him, driving him back and forth in his mind. It was a shame that he was too unstable now to be any help to us; I had always thought of him as someone steady of heart when he was our gunner. The trail of the griffin's dark deeds ran through everyone who met him.

Turning to the rest of my men, I said, "so, pain awaits me down that tunnel. And perhaps awaits you also, if you follow. But I am going forward, as there is unavoidable pain down every choice in life. Who will follow me?"

One by one, they all silently raised their hands. With a nod, I turned about, taking Karen's hand to comfort her as we entered the dimly lit tunnel.

Our footsteps clicked softly on the smooth floor. The light above shown around us with a strange, bluish glow. The air smelled of moist, secret places that few men ever traveled. It also smelled of seven pirates and a former prisoner in an enclosed space, but I did not really notice that after having been on the ship so long.

There was a faint humming from far back in the darkness, a sort of bee's nest sound that you did not notice at first. It sunk in slowly as you went along.

Feeling tense down every bone, I tried to make myself keep a cool head and stay calmly alert. At my side Karen walked stiffly and I could feel the fear in her hand at what might be ahead. Thinking of how comforting to me a good weapon always was, I offered her a dagger to hold in her other hand. But she just shook her head, preferring her icy natural weapon to a man-made one. Time went out of proportion as we walked deeper. None of us could tell how the sun was turning up above, while down in the tunnel. And the light above was unchanging, not even flickering as the moments slipped passed. We went down three sets of steps at three separate places, each one leading us further below and nearer to the underside of Littleton.

Eventually, after walking for what seemed like a ridiculous amount of time, we came to a longer, steeper set of steps which ended in a three-way split. A wide tunnel led off straight in front of us and two smaller ones went to each side. The one ahead was lit with the same bluish light; the one on the right was lit with red, and the left was green lighting. All of the lights were the same narrow stripe of glowing phosphorescence along the roof, with no obvious source and no flicker as an honest flame should have. If the lights were made by far off fires coming through glass panes or by some sort of strange magic, I could not tell. The latter seemed more likely, as it was like the lines on the metal key.

"Which way should we go?" I asked Karen, twisting my head to look down one path and then another. She pointed straight ahead, "I think that way will lead us towards the center. That is probably where he is now, if he is not out flying somewhere; in the center."

With a nod, I led the way down the blue lit passage, the men following behind me in a double file. Many more silent, dim tunnel slid past us as we went forward. Finally we came to another split, this one having only two directions to it. One curving gently off to the left, while the another bent in the opposite way, as if there was a mirror between them. Both ways were lit with red now, the blue ending abruptly at the division. The wall between the two paths pointed toward us in a wedge shape, blank, dark stone with no visible markings. This time the girl at my side had no suggestion as to which way we should go, so we put it to a vote and chose to take the right-hand passage.

In a strangely natural manner, unlike any man-made tunnel I had seen before, this passage curved gently around, so that you felt you were going to run into the other end any moment. But it was not a passage we came into at the end of the bending path, it was a wide, open area. Like the tunnels, this room was walled and floored in a smooth, black material unlike anything I had seen, except for in the walls of the Shadow City. Unlike the tunnels, this room was lit by many strange white globes suspended from the roof at different heights. Each of the spheres was about as big as my head and looked to be perfectly round. Inside them was a soft, white light which did not seem to have any particular source; it glowed without a flicker, like the lines on the wall. We walked into this room craning our heads around to look at the globes on every side, puzzled as to why they should be there at all. The rest of the room was blank, the floor a flat of unmarked stone with not even a chair set on it to view the spheres from in comfort. Most of the orbs were high up above us, out of reach. A few hung down near eye level, round and tempting. I walked toward one of them and reached out a finger to brush it, but Karen caught my hand and warned, "I would not do that. These orbs may like them, but I do not think they are the same as the lines on the key card. Listen."

Pulling my hand back, I leaned a little toward the globe and concentrated on listening. Faintly a noise reverberated out of the orb, a sort of far away tinkling or chiming that was just on the edge of my hearing. It was an oddly frightening noise once you heard it, like the bells of death ringing far away.

"You're right." I agreed with Karen, turning back to call to the others, "don't touch the globes! There is something I don't like about them. They may be dangerous."

Don nodded agreement, pulling his head up from listening to another one of them, "That's it, chief. They sound like fairy spells twinklin' in the dusky night."

Or something much worse, I thought, leading the way through the maze of orbs with more care than before. Soon we came to the far side of the room, where another tunnel led further off into the labyrinth.

"Is any of this familiar?" I asked Karen, but she just shook her head in a negative, running one hand nervously down the side of her shirt into the pocket of her pants, while the other hand pushed back a strand of hair. She was at least as puzzled as the rest of us.

We traveled on, every now and then coming to a split or turning, until we were all so confused that finding our way back out would have been just the same as finding our way to the griffin. Neither of the choices were easy.

After a bit we stopped and ate some of the provisions which we had brought with us, before pressing on. It was not long after this that Humper found a door in a recess on the side of the pathway and drew our attention to it.

"Look at this," he said, running a hand lightly over the metal door, "no lock or knob visible and not even one of those key-hole slots like before."

"Maybe you should just push on it." His pal Felix commented with a grin, obviously joking. But when Humper took the advice and pushed, the door swung open inwards. He held it open as we all gathered around to peer in, trying to understand what we were seeing in the room. There was a narrow bed up on metal trestles in the center of the room, with a thin white cushion and sheet, uncomfortably starched. On it lay a man dressed in a rich, scarlet hunting jacket, shiny black breeches and a long cloak of deep purple. But the sleeves were rolled up on the cloak, and a confusing array of metal bands, clear tubes and shiny copper wires were coming from across the room to attached to his arms. The same types of wires and tubes connected to a band of copper on his forehead, which seemed to fit painfully tight. The man's eyes were closed and his body completely limp. On the wall beyond him there hung a sheet of glass like a mirror, but without the silvering. Instead, a constantly changing image showed under the glass, like a picture which simply could not stand still. Many of the wires on the man connected to this living image, though the tubes and some of the other wires went over to a large tank of some sort against a different wall, or ran through a hole in that wall which went beyond where we could see.

The images under the glass seemed to be of places in different countries nearby. I saw a distinct picture of the palace in Fraistia, as clear and vivid as if I had been standing before it myself. Then it shifted away, and showed a group of buildings on a hill in a place that I did not recognize.

"What is all this?" I said in amazement, trying to understand what I was seeing.

"Mostly, I don't know either." Henry put in with a wave of his pistol, "but that fellow I recognize. Can't you see his royal duds? He's the King of Durny, who was kidnapped not so long ago!"

I had never seen the King of Durny before, though I had heard that he was kidnapped. Finding a man laying there all covered in wires and tubes was horrible, but at least it explained why none of the other countries had yet come forward with a ransom demand. None of the warring countries had the missing king.

"I've seen this room before." Karen gripped my hand tighter in her own narrow, strong fingers, "he's one of the talented ones, I think, though I had forgotten about him. He just lays here and dreams about the places he's seen. I don't know why the master wants him for that, but that is what he does."

I backed out of the entrance-way, shaking my head at the thing laying inside, "do you know the way from here to the center of the fort, then?"

She looked down the hallway, pushing her hair back once again and wrinkling her forehead in thought. "Maybe...I think you go ahead and then turn right at the next split in the path. After that, it's all fuzzy."

"It might clear as we go." The others fell in behind us again as we turned to follow the path, hoping to find a way to Krift and the griffin.

A LONG TIME LATER WE were still hoping. The paths became ever thicker and full of more turnings, as well as more rooms off to the sides. All of them contained things which to us were inexplicable; wires and lights, metal shapes and glass orbs suspended on chains or rods. They seemed to often be the apparatus for arcane experiments, or at least scientific ones. Once we came across a room holding a small, deep pool of cold water. In the pool floated a creature that was long and thin, like the large-headed eels seen in some parts of the sea. But it's fins glowed a dripping green and the color of it's skin was an unnatural yellowish-white. Slime covered it's smooth skin, dribbling off of it's upper jaw as it gaped open.

Not long after that, we came walking into a room that was occupied. There was a thick carpet on the floor, a fluffy, comfy chair in the center of the floor and beyond it a large, warm fire. After wandering in the dark, hard tunnels for so long, the warmth of the room was pleasant.

I saw no one inside at first, so most of us stepped in to rest in the natural light and homeliness of the room. As soon as we had come in, something shifted in the armchair before the fire and a figure arose from it. A tall, athletic man stood in front of us. His expression was one of mild surprise, until he saw Karen standing just behind me. Then his eyes got wide and his mouth opened into a little circle of shock. He blinked, his mouth coming shut. A blank expression crossed his face for a moment and I got the distinct impression that mind magic had been used nearby, perhaps to contact him.

The next moment he took a flying leap at me, one hand outstretched before him. With no time to react properly, I pulled the trigger on my pistol and it went off into the air beside him, just missing his left side. He hurtled forward and struck my chest with all him momentum, sending me stumbling backwards with a gasp. Then his other hand struck me on the side of the head, not particularly hard, but enough to put me completely off balance after already having been hit once. In a state of absolute surprise I was thrown off my feet to land on my side by a low table on the carpet. My shoulder hit hard, gaining a respectable bruise as I landed. Behind me I heard the sound of someone struck in the stomach and doubling over with a grunt. Close on its heels there was a shot and a cry of pain.

Quickly, I rolled over and jumped to my feet, seeing Felix staring in shock at his friend Humper, while holding his rifle loosely in his hands. Blood was running down the front of Humper's shirt from a small hole in it, as he blinked blankly back at the shooter. Meanwhile Don grappled with our strange assailant, holding him desperately by one arm as he jerked, spun and lashed out at everyone around him. As I watched, he pulled free of Don, hitting him on the back of the neck so that he fell to the ground momentarily stunned. Then the crazy, whirling fighter turned on Karen, who was approaching him quietly from behind. There was not much room to maneuver in the small room, but he managed to dodge out of her way as she lunged toward him with one hand glowing icy blue. This made her trip over Don and stumble against the armchair. With the jump he also hit Henry square in the face, as my man tried to draw a long cutlass he carried at his side. The pirate was on his guard by now, able to keep his ground and hit back. With a jerk, the fighter made the blow simply glance off the side of his face, and turned around as if to attack the just rising Karen once again.

Finally fumbling my sword into my hand, I shouted, "Karen!" in warning and moved across the floor to take the swift fighter on once again. He saw me coming and jumped forward, preparing to fight me with only his closed hands. But at that moment Don rolled over, grabbing on to the fighter's ankle. With a strong jerk he pulled the man off balance and flung him to the floor beside him. Then another shot went off and at the same time a dagger flashed in Don's hand.

With a gurgle and a gasp, the fighter fell silent, laying stiff on the floor. The graybeard's knife stuck out of his throat at an odd angle, while a bullet hole leaked redness at his side. Felix stood with his gun in his hands, tightly this time and with an expression of hate on his face, "I've never missed before. But he hit the barrel and made me."

His voice was bleak as he turned back to where Humper lay on the carpet, kneeling beside him and pressing a hand tightly against the wound which he had been made to shoot in his friend's chest.

"You'll make it yet, brother. Just hang on a little longer." He murmured, as Humper breathed heavily in pain.

Don stood up and yanked his dagger out of the fighter, kicking the dead body with the toe of his boot. "What a fighter. Too bad he is dead instead of working for us. Eight people against one and it took that long to fell him!"

It was then that I became aware of someone banging on the closed door of the room and shouting something about letting them in. The entrance had not been closed by us, but now it was both shut and latched on the inside. Either the fighter had done it with incredible swiftness, or the door had shut and locked itself, but both Ramses and Bready were caught on the outside of it, kept away from the fight.

"Only six against one," I corrected Don, letting those two in to the room.

"What happened?" Ramses asked, glancing around at us, and down at Humper.

"That happened." I pointed at the dead man, stepping over him to join Felix. The wounded man was still breathing and the gunshot looked like it had hit higher up, near his shoulder, missing the lung. But it was bleeding heavily and the crewman was only half-conscious. I was at a loss what to do, other than giving Felix a piece of cloth from a blanket which lay nearby to press down with. There were no herbs growing down here and no doctors which we would want to consult. The only thing I could think of was cauterizing the wound with a blade heated on the fire, though it would be painful for the patient.

At that moment Karen moved over beside me, leaning down to ask, "did the bullet go through both sides?"

I relayed the question, to which Felix nodded tightly, "I think so, but I can't tell without letting up on the wound."

"If the bullet is out, I know how I can stop the bleeding." Karen told me once I had explained what he said, "but they would have to trust me to use my talent on him."

I nodded, leaning over to pat a hand on the wounded man's cheek and get his attention, "Humper, listen to me."

His eyes focused on me, dim and blurry as he made a sound to show that he was awake. My voice was steady, though I was afraid he would refuse, "Karen wants to help you. She needs to stop the bleeding. Will you let her?"

His eyes flicked to the girl, then back to me.

"Okay, chief," he spoke in a strained voice, "if you trust her, it suits me."

Reluctantly, Felix gave up his place and Karen moved to take it. With a knife borrowed from me, she cut away the fabric of his shirt around the bullet hole. Then she took a deep breath as if to prepare herself, and held out a hand on which the pointer finger glowed with a frosty blue light. Everyone in the room seemed to be watching that finger, afraid that she would use it to freeze his mind instead of save him. Humper watched it too, then squeezed his eyes shut as it descended to touch him. Karen drew the finger in a circle around the wound, then pressed her hand tightly against it. The injured man let out a small gasp, making some of the crew move their hands toward their weapons. But he said as if in surprise, "it's cold!"

"Yes." I agreed, holding his other shoulder down so that he would not try to move away. After a moment the girl moved her hand away and I could see that the edges of the bullet hole had drawn a little closer together, tinted a bluish shade under the drying blood.

"It doesn't feel so bad now." Humper told us with widened eyes, moving his other hand to feel gingerly over the injury. "It's a little numb. She...she made it cold and numb!"

"And stopped the bleeding, too." I remarked, before telling Karen, "Good job. He says it does not hurt as much anymore."

"Yes, I made it very cold all the way through." She explained, "but it will wear off after about a day. It is not permanent like what...what I did to the captain."

Seeing that his friend was not in as much danger any more, Felix looked up from him to Karen with grateful eyes. He did a surprising thing and reached out to take her hand in both of his, shaking it once, "Thank you."

I translated this to Gracklandic and the girl looked embarrassed, pulling her hand away to stand up, "it is only a small thing. I have done so much harm, it is just a little bit to pay the debt back."

Humper was still too hurt to go further into the tunnels, though, and I came to the difficult decision of breaking my forces up. Felix, Henry and Bready were left to make a stretcher out of anything they could find in the room and try to transport the injured man up out of the tunnels as best as they could. Meanwhile I took Don, Ramses and Karen to look further into the confusing maze of the warren. It was not a sure thing that either party would find their way out, making Humper protested many times that I should not take only half of my force because of him. But it was my decision to make, besides the fact that it was really no more dangerous for us than it was for them. If either party found the griffin, they would have to find a way to defeat him. And if neither party did, we might wander down here until our supplies ran out and we all starved to death.

Taking my crew, I left Henry in command of the other group and we set off down the passages once again. Twists, turns and the ever glowing halls met us, sometimes lined with doors and sometimes empty. Strangely, we ran into at least one room we had seen before, but they did not ever seem to be in the same sort of hallways as we remembered them, or near any room which they had been next to before. It was almost as if the rooms were shifting around while we were not watching, moving from place to place in the endless maze. I looked into one knob-less door and saw again the figure of the king of Durny, laying on his white bed and dreaming of things which appeared as images on the wall. Curious if there was anything in this room that we had missed before, I stepped into the room and walked around all of the wires and tubes running across it, moving toward the glass pane on the wall. Karen still followed at my side, though since she had helped Humper there had been little or no hard feelings against her from the other two crew members. They both stood just inside the door, looking warily at the sleeping king and speaking quietly together.

As we stepped up in front of the screen there was an ominous creaking sound under our feet. We both looked down, puzzled, at the solid stone floor as we tried to figure out where it was coming from. Then I grabbed Karen's arm and jerked both her and me off of the stone slab of that part of the floor. Our feet left it just as it began to collapse. With a crumbling noise and a crash, a piece of the floor big enough for us both to have fallen through went smashing down out of sight, into a pit of darkness.

"Are you alright, my friends?" Ramses stepped carefully closer, as stone dust puffed up into the room and then settled back downwards.

"Yes." I told him tightly, looking back at the hole, "it was a trap of some sort. Be careful, there may be more."

Walking with light footsteps, Karen and I made our way over to where the others stood, before gazing back at the pit again. We could not tell how deep it was, nor what was down below. The girl let out a shaky breath, while I let go of her arm, "that was a close one. We will have to be more careful from now on."

"Maybe we shouldn't go into the rooms through the doors." Don suggested, running a hand through his thin gray hair, "they all seem dangerous."

I agreed, expecting to stick to that sound advice. But soon we came to a room which we had to go through, a wide one that the path ran into on one side and out of on the other. The only thing in the room was a mosaic on the floor, made out of large slabs of what looked like white and black marble. There was no furniture or ornaments to be seen. It looked like just the sort of place for another trap, so I made the others go behind as I led the way. I prodded every slab with my sword before I stepped on it, testing for weakness. The pattern had white lines on a black background, seeming to form a large, curving symbol which we could not make out from so close to it. Everything was quiet in the room except for the clinking of my blade against the stone. Every step, I worried would be my last. Something told me that there was at least one trap here, hiding in the stones. Then I stepped forward once and the world dropped out from under me. The edge of the stone whooshed by before I could grab it, just as I felt someone snatch for the back of my shirt. They got it, but instead of hauling me back up, my weight jerked them over the brink. We were falling through darkness so rapidly that we had no time to think, or even for me to put my sword out of the way. It whistled through the air in my hand, cutting darkness. Though I had pressed on the stone with my blade and it had felt firm, it had not held a human's weight.

With a solid thump we landed on a hard floor, falling in a tangled heap and rolling wildly around before we could be untangled. I had landed on the bottom, of course, and had gotten flattened against the hard stone like a salted fish in the lower end of a barrel. Finally, we got disentangled and I saw that it was Karen who had tried to stop me, unsuccessfully. Luckily, my sword had not cut either of us and though I was bruised none of my bones felt broken.

Karen held her head for a minute, looking around in confusion, while I stood stiffly to look back up toward where we had come from. Above us a square hole of light shone in the roof, with a notch in it where someone was looking down, "Sarkin! Karen! Are you alright?"

"As much as we could be, Ramses!" I shouted back up, taking a deep breath and looking around at my surroundings before answering, "but I don't think there is a way to get back up there."

The walls down here were much different than they had been up above, being made of pale gray stone and a rough layer of cement which was not smoothed or finished at all. Rusty pipes and bits of metal stuck out of it here and there, while the wall dented in and out like a model of the waves at sea. The only light we had, came from the square hole up above, shining down around us in a limited area. By it, I could tell those rough walls were too high to scale in an attempt to get back to the opening and that the place we were in was more of a tunnel than a square pit.

"Should we find something to lower down, for you to climb up?" Ramses inquired, leaning over the edge.

"Like what?" I thought of the bare room up above, shaking my head, "no, just continue on and we will try to rejoin you soon. It looks like this passage down here goes in the same direction as we were traveling up there. Maybe they meet up. Just don't join us the hard way: you might land on our heads."

"Alright, my friend." Ramses pulled back from the opening, "good luck!"

Helping Karen to her feet, I pulled a candle from my pocket and lit it with a flint and steel. The candle I had brought in case the griffin's lair was unlit, thugh up until now it had been unnecessary. But now we were in darkness and had to move forward under the flickering light of the single flame. Bruised and covered in dust, we must have looked like a pair of children exploring the family attic for the first time.

This pathway was cooler than the ones up above had been, and there seemed to be the echoing plunk of falling water just on the edge of your hearing. Strange old rusty things still poked out of the cement; large pipes with metal gratings, small pipes oozing dried algae and bits of iron rod. Also large gears and bolts, caught in the cement like frogs trying to crawl out of the mud. Wires like the ones which had been hooked to the metal bands on the king of Durny also bristled here, but so worn that they did not gleam in the candle's light.

"Who would have built all this?" I wondered, seeing what looked like a metal door tilted at a crazy angle in the wall. Trying to open it, I found that it was sealed shut with mortar, "bits of metal and cement, under a rambling maze of smooth stone and glowing lights. Why would the griffin want all this?"

"I don't think it was built by him," my companion returned quietly, "these things are far older. And as for the upper parts...I don't know. Sometimes I wonder if he is crazy."

"Oh, he must be." I affirmed, brushing through a hanging wall of cobwebs. To have all these things and do as little with them as he had, he must be been mad. And the further we walked, the more a strange dreamlike feeling pressed upon me, as if nothing we said or did was real. The candle light, the cement walls and even my own footsteps seemed fuzzy with unreality.

After a little while we came to a split in the pathway, the first we had found. One of the directions led off into what appeared to be a large cave, filled with a dim, spooky red light. The other was closed by a wooden door about fifteen feet down, with a handle shaped like a griffin's head.

"I think we'll go this way." I gestured at the door blindly, while gazing into the cavern. It was so dim inside that I could not make out anything except for the dark lumps of rock sticking off of the wall, but there was a deep feeling of menace wafting out toward us from it. After a moment, I decided not to look into it any further. Karen peered in with me, still looking that way as I went to open the wooden door. Though it was neither sealed with cement nor locked, it seemed to be jammed on the inside. Yanking and shoving, pushing the griffin handle roughly, I was able to get it open, though it grated raggedly as I pushed it.

"Come on." I called back over my shoulder, stepping through, "That place feels—"

I let go of the door handle and it slammed shut behind me. Frustrated, I stepped back to start yanking and jerking on it, trying to get it back open. At first, nothing happened. Then there was a groaning noise above my head and I looked up to see a wooden trap door coming open, with dust and gravel starting to fall out. In instant reaction, I threw myself backwards, tripping over a bit of protruding rock and falling onto what felt like the bottom of a staircase. In front of me the trap door let loose, dumping a heap of fist-sized stones and gravel where I had been standing just a moment before. The air filled with dust, making me cough and choke. When it finally cleared, I heard Karen calling from the other side and beating on the door, "Sarkin! Are you there? Sarkin!"

Hoarsely, I called back, "I'm here! One of the griffin's traps almost got me, that's all. But I was too quick for him."

"What happened?"

"There's a spill of stones across the door," I moved over to throw a few out of the way, before letting out a growl of frustration, "Agh, there's a ton of this stuff here! It will take a long time to shift it all."

"Maybe I can go—" Karen's words were cut off by a scream. A woman's scream; hers. And she was not the type to be shrieking at pointless things like a spider running across her toes, either. Instantly, I scrambled further up the pile towards the top, where it lay above the top of the door and closest to the wall, "Karen! What is it? Karen!"

There was no reply, or any sound at all from the other side of the stone wall. Pounding on it with the hilt of my sword, I called for her again. But there was no sound from the other side. Desperate, I threw my mind that way in an attempt to find her or whatever had attacked her. But my thoughts hit a fuzzy barrier at the wall, one which it could not penetrate. Even going through the door in my mind I could not cross this barrier. It appeared as a fine network of black threads, gleaming with tiny yellow lights. If I rammed against it, the threads bent slightly, but would not give or allow me through. Whoever was creating it was very powerful with their mind magic, because I could not force a way or find a route around it. In fact, my thoughts were confined to a small space in the tunnel I occupied physically, so there was no way to find either Karen or the griffin.

Angrily, I tried to dig the stones away, but gravel kept slipping down into place so that I made no real headway. Finally, with fingers torn from the rocks and dust working down through all of my clothes, I had to give up. There was no way to get back the way I had come from easily. Whatever had happened to Karen, I could only go on and demand answers from the griffin himself.

Chapter 13: Fire and Ice

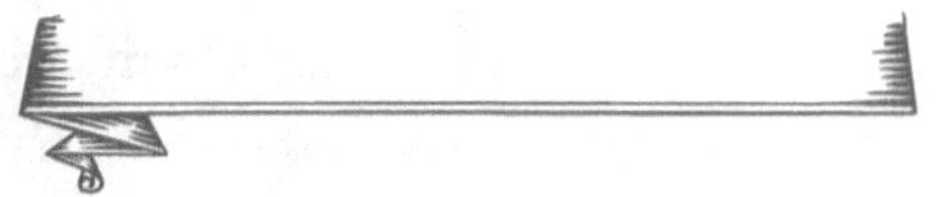

The staircase I had fallen on earlier led up at a steep angle away from the gravel trap and covered door. It was built much like the last, wooden with a brass handle depicting a griffin's head. I hesitated for a moment, feeling the bite of fear as I realized that there was no one else left. I was alone.

But whatever had happened to Karen and the rest of my crew by now, I could not help them by standing there on the stairs with my hand on the door-pull. The only thing to do was go on. So I opened the door, stepping quickly through into a room lit by beams falling down from a hole far up in the roof above.

For a long moment I stood blinking, blinded by the yellow beams. When my vision cleared I saw what was around me. I stood in a large, oval room which was lit in the center by a wide hole high up in the roof. This looked like it could be open and shut with some sort of metal shutters which were hanging downwards from the sides, latches dangling. The floor was tiled in white and black marble, just as the room I had fallen through earlier was, but with a simple checkered pattern instead of a mosaic. In the middle of the floor, where the light fell strongest, was a pyramid of glistening pale sandstone, so brilliant in the light that it looked almost like pure gold. The top of the triangle did not come to a sharp peak, being cut off flat so that there was a wide, open space on top. On the open space lay an open coffin, or low-walled bier, with a figure dressed in dark clothes laying on it in full view.

There was a rank of steps up each side of the pyramid, meeting at the top. Quietly, I ascended them to come face to face with my old friend and more recent enemy, Skon Yew. His features were white and calm in death, unmarked by any sign of rot or decay. His hands lay at his sides, one of them resting on the hilt of the cutlass I had run him through with on our last meeting. On the front of his black uniform was a long, rusty stain where the blade had gone in, but that was the only clear mark that he was dead instead of simply in a deep sleep. Besides the fact that he was not breathing, snoring or otherwise unconsciously proclaiming himself among the living, that is.

For a long moment I stood there in the shine of the sunlight from above, looking down at him. He had my sword and I had his. I was living and he was dead. Could that trifling circumstance be reversed?

A soft footstep broke into my musings, and someone stepped up on the other side of the pyramid. My gaze came up to him and my daydreams were broken by a sudden shock. It was Krift.

"Sarkin." He said in an odd, far-away tone, "you have come. The master said that you were coming and that we should wait for the final ceremony until you were here. Good."

His thick, dark hair and strong young frame were the same as ever, but there was a horrible blankness in his eyes, and his plain, dark clothes had been changed for a suit of flaming orange and red. The expression on his face gave me a shock, especially as I realized just what ceremony he was speaking of. An attempt to bring the Dark Prince back to life.

I stepped around the coffin toward where he stood, keeping my voice calm and my hand on my sword as I said, "Krift. It has been some time since I saw you. Has the griffin been treating you well?"

He ignored me, closing his eyes and crossing his arms as he always did to prepare for working his magic. I slid slowly toward him, drawing my blade not with the intention of really harming him, but hopefully to help me capture him. He opened his eyes and held out a hand with the ember of magic glowing brightly on it's tip. At that moment I stepped forward quickly, reaching towards that hand to stop him from using the magic on any nearby bodies, including mine. But right before my fingers touched him, a hunting bird's shriek rang through the air and a gust of wind almost blew me off of the pyramid.

Distracted from my attack, I looked up to see the griffin circling down from the opening in the roof up above. His metallic wings were spread, catching the light and reflecting it back with a silver sheen. His beak was open in a wild cry, while one eye gleamed fiery orange.

Nightwing swept passed us, flying around to land at the bottom of the pyramid. I caught myself from falling and wondered what I was going to do now, as the griffin crouched, watching me from the base of the stairs. Caught between Krift and Nightwing, I was starting to slip through the door in my mind to fight them both on another level when the griffin spoke, calling me back.

"Sarkin." His voice was low and harsh, a hate-filled whisper through the metal beak, "you have come to see the ceremony. How...good of you."

"I've come to *stop* the ceremony, you metallic crow," I returned, remembering what was going on behind me. Swiftly, I spun around and curled my fingers into the back of Krift's shirt, bringing my sword up under his chin to make him a hostage. The griffin would not want his only hope of bringing Skon Yew back destroyed, and could not have known that I had just as much hope in the boy's abilities myself. But in the moment I grasped Krift's shirt his hand finished a sweeping gesture of power over Skon Yew's whole body, leaving a trail of flames in the sky. The boy seemed to be in a trance, barely even noticing what was going on around him. I drew him back with the sword to his throat, but it was too late.

The body of Skon Yew stirred, a strange symbol glowing on his brow where the boy had touched it in the ceremony. His face was just as deathly white as a moment before, but his eyes snapped open and stared at the roof above. They were not human eyes now, more like white glass filled with embers of fire. As of yet he seemed to see nothing, and he barely breathed. But the flames in his eyes were slowly glowing brighter.

As I dragged Krift away from the waking monster, he suddenly twisted in my arms, touching my sword hand with the tip of his finger. It felt like a red hot iron, so that I let out a cry, dropping the blade to the ground. The boy yanked out of my grasp, grabbing tightly onto my hand with his own. He faced me now, his expression twisted with another person's fury. Fire seemed to leap along my arm, burning in to the bone. It ran along my shoulder and touched the edge of my mind, orange agony like nothing I had ever known before. With another inarticulate cry I fell to my knees, seeing only a raging fire burning through my mind. The thing I feared most in all the world, alive inside me.

I tried to retreat through the mystical door, beyond myself, but fire hemmed me in on all sides. I was trapped, burning like a ship at sea. I had failed: the captain would die in his prison of ice while I perished in a cage of fire.

I was falling into darkness through endless flames when something miraculous happened. In among the fire, my mind felt the touch of something cold. The coolness spread, wonderful as a sunrise and as life-giving as water in a desert. The pain was washed away by patterns of flowing water and frost, reminding me once again that I loved the color blue.

My vision cleared and I saw blue. It was Karen, standing nearby with her hand resting on my arm. Her eyes were closed and there was an expression of concentration on her face as she washed away the fire with her magic.

Krift had backed away now, looking confused and disarmed. His right hand was held out in front of him, open, on it a glittering symbol of ice. It was melting, slowly, but until it was gone he could not use his fire. I stood up while Karen opened her eyes. I was so grateful to her and so glad to see her safe and alive, for a moment I barely noticed what was around us, "You saved me...I thought you were gone."

She nodded, "I thought so too. But I froze the one that grabbed me. From there I wandered until I found my way to you."

Before I could tell her how glad it made me that she was with me, the griffin screamed. To my dismay the sound still did not hold fear or anger, but a ringing triumph.

Something moved behind Karen. I looked past her to see Skon Yew, holding the silver sword which I had dropped. In a moment slowed to unreality by horror I saw him raise it above his head, glinting in the sunlight. His eyes were solid orange with flame, fearful to see. With a crackling laugh he threw the sword directly toward me like a spear. But there was something between us. Karen.

There was a sickening thump and the girl's mouth opened in shock. The sword stuck through her entirely, just as it had through Skon Yew. Slowly, she took a step forward to collapse into my arms.

"No!" I held her, kept her from falling to the cold ground, and felt her gasping raggedly for her last breaths. Skon Yew stood looking on with his fiery eyes, which seemed to gloat at my pain. Behind me, I heard a harsh voice whisper through it's metal beak, "now you know what it feels like to see a sword in the one you love."

I looked down at Karen and she looked up at me, eyes dimming as her life faded. The sword slid from the wound in her back, clattering to the floor. Until that moment I had not known the depths of what she meant to me, but when it was too late I realized that the griffin was right. She was someone I loved.

A deep, hot fury rose all through me, as hot as Krift's flames. "No! She will not die!"

Still holding her from falling on the sword, I went through the door in my mind. There I saw the dimness of her light as it began to fade away into eternity. I also saw the unnatural brilliance which surrounded Skon Yew's head: not a true mind, but the power of life invested in something that would not live again. It was a frightening spectacle, bu I could not do anything about it at the moment. Desperately, I flung my power around what was left of Karen's frosty blue light, to hold it back from the brink. Our minds faded into one another, mixing and melding. With all of my energy I held her into place, feeding my own life force into the pit to keep her from dying. But the hole the sword made was sucking us away like water draining from an open spigot in a barrel. I felt the edges of darkness and cold, a grayness like the time just before dawn. Somewhere on the other side of the grayness was an immortal light.

Just in time I pulled back from it, using my last resources to fling an arm of magic out to the light around Skon Yew's head. There was true life in that fire, though not for him. It was for anyone that was not yet dead. Like a greedy animal gulping up their dinner, I sucked the power away from him, using it to block the gap in the life that was both mine and Karen's. Energy rushed through us in a torrent, bright and powerful.

Pulling away from Karen's light, I made our minds separate, feeding the power only into her. The blue aura around her mind glowed brighter, like a fire catching on wood or frost freezing across water. Her life came back in a spurt and I wielded it to force her body to heal, to live and contain her spirit instead of letting it go. Skon Yew, I drained dry of life, so that he fell back to the bier like a pale ghost. Meanwhile Karen glowed with energy like a lantern lit at night to keep away the cold.

At that moment something struck me a tremendous blow in the world back through the door and I was shocked back through it. I found myself knocked away from Karen, tumbling wildly down the stairs of the pyramid. The griffin had jumped up to slap us apart with his giant claws, knocking me off the pyramid. As I rolled down it, he followed in short bounds.

It seemed that I hit every stair on the way down, jolting from one to the next like a cannon ball. Pain shot through my ankle as it twisted wrong and I felt a stinging lash across my face where the griffin had hit me. In fact, the stairs battered me so much that I hurt everywhere, indiscriminately. Finally coming to a stop, I lay on the floor gasping for breath, exhausted by my use of magic and beaten to what felt very close to a pulp by the fall down the steps. With a last effort, I rolled over onto my back to see the griffin rising over me.

"Twice!" He shrieked so loudly that the room echoed and my head hurt even more, "twice you have destroyed my master, my Prince. Now I will destroy you!"

One great metal talon went up, sharp tip gleaming in the light from above. I could not have moved in time to avoid it and none of my weapons would have done anything against his metallic hide. But his wish for a dramatic ending gave me one last chance to save myself.

"Wait." I said, both with my ragged voice and with the last strength of my mind, impressing it deeply into his. His claw hesitated and I slid through the door into his mind.

Inside his mind was strange and dark, lit with twinkling lights that shifted and whirred just beyond reach. I got the strong impression that his mind was not like ours, it was not a living mind at all. It was made of wires, magic, gears and electricity like what flowed in a lightening strike. But there was understanding there and emotion. Right now it was filled with an overwhelming loneliness like that of a lost dog. His collecting of people, his attempts to awaken the Dark Prince, his wish to have powerful, talented people around him, these things were all connected to that loneliness. It was a deep sorrow in him, the wish for a strong master to lead him to glory.

In that longing I saw a glimpse of what he had originally been made for. To be the Whispering Brethren's weapon, a tool to raise them from their broken status to glory. He had been built to be a weapon wielded by a powerful leader. When that leader died all he wanted was to have him back, or find a new one.

For a moment it crossed my mind that I could be his master, a replacement for Skon Yew. But in the next one I realized that no crew would ever have this thing on a ship: it wouldn't even fit on the *Seashooter* without knocking the masts over whenever it tried to fly. And I would never give up the life of a pirate, wild and free on the waves, just to own a metallic griffin.

So instead I found the part of it's mind that had rested in long sleep, like a statue, before he had been brought awake. It was still there, a part of his mechanical brain that could force all of him into hibernation.

Softly, gently, I lulled him back into this state, drawing his mind into blankness and nothing with the promise that when he awoke again, he would have a new master more powerful than any before. Like the shard of pottery, there had to be something to activate his awaking when the time came. So I told him to sleep until someone came and called his original name to him with these words, *"Awake, Hope, and fly free!"*

Returning dazedly to the world, I let my eyes slide open wearily. Above me reared a black, metal statue of a griffin, one claw upraised and wings half spread like the image seen on some old shields or banners. Too tired to move at first, I just lay there looking up at him, before pulling myself slowly up into a sitting position. Nightwing was waiting now for the next master who came along with the right words to awake him, while Skon Yew was safely dead and out of the way. Amazingly, I was still alive.

But the show was not over yet. There was a deep clang somewhere in the depths of the warren below us, like a bell announcing an important person's entrance. A door opened on the far side of the room and someone came walking in. It was a man dressed in black clothes, with a large, bald head shaped like an egg set up on point. He came and stood in front of me, looking down at the floor with his hands clasped in front of him, the fingers and thumbs touching in a triangle.

"Remarkable." He said in a grave voice which gave me the chills, "you have defeated the griffin, saved a young woman from the brink of death and made sure that someone dead did not act as if he was alive. I say again, remarkable."

No kidding. And I had thought we were all just playing party games. Grim with tiredness, I just looked up at him, wondering what he wanted, but saying nothing. He raised one hairless eyebrow at me, going on without a prompt, "you know, I am the one who built this place. All the experimental equipment, it is mine. To me, the griffin was just a useful tool. I need all these talented people for my grand experiment and I convinced him that he needed them too. I am the Mentalist. But it seems you have great powers of your own. Will you join me?"

He extended a hand as if expecting me to take it, to jump up and shout for joy because he had asked me to join him. Instead I just looked at him through narrowed eyes.

"Come now, I know all about you." He said, starting to get impatient, "I have watched you through the link which I still have in Karen's mind. You have great skills and a determination that I can respect. Won't you join me, help me with my great plan?"

"How can I answer that." I managed finally, flatly, "if I don't know what your plan is?"

"Quite right." He crossed his arms, leaving me to sit on the floor if I chose, "it is a great plan, a grand one. The griffin could only understand the edges of it and I made sure that all the people put under his command saw no more. Of course, I made sure that Nightwing thought Skon Yew would be at the head of it, while I would be the real master. Here is the plan itself;"

He began pacing back and forth on the checkered floor, laying out to me his grand vision. In his twisted mind he saw all of the talented people of the world becoming his tools, his slaves to use as he pleased. He would learn more about their powers, perhaps even discovering how they worked so that he could teach the talents to others. Then he would have an army of people unlike any others in the world, more powerful than the normal humans around them. The Mentalist wanted to infiltrate high positions in the governments of nearby countries, slowly replacing their leaders with his Talented Ones. Eventually only his minions would have any say in the ruling of the countries around the Middle sea, effectually making him the king of it all.

Normal people would cease to be of much value in this kingdom. They would become the slaves and serfs, while Talented Ones ruled from on high.

"Can you just imagine it?" He said, stopping for a moment to gesture wildly in the air, caught up in his mad fantasy, "people like me, like Karen and Krift, like you, Sarkin, would be the rulers. We would expand our powers until we could use them to shape anything we desired, to do anything we could wish! And the rest of the people would be in awe of us, helpless, happy slaves. They would think we were gods!"

He stopped for a minute, as if savoring this image. Then he repeated softly, "yes, powerful beyond any human measure!"

By now he was a dozen paces from me as he turned and held out his hands, "you can see how powerful I am already. What I can do to hold a person's mind to my will. You see what I am. I can make you the same. Will you join me and become this powerful, too?"

I pulled myself to my feet, looking at him with eyes wide with wonder at what he had described. There was never really any choice about what I would say to him. "Yes, I see what you are. You are a complete madman."

At my words his face twisted in anger, "I'm not mad, you fool! I'm brilliant, a genius! But if you will not serve me willingly, I will make you against your will. No one can stand against me!"

His eyes turned to dark slits in his egg-shaped head. I felt a terrible pressure come against me, a wall of willpower slam against my mind. Tired as I was, I had no hope of defeating him or fighting back. I struggled to hold him off, frozen in place on the checkered floor. My vision blurred, the world becoming nothing but a fuzzy battle between his mind and mine. I fought to hold him off long enough to slip through the door in my mind, but I was exhausted already and could feel myself failing. After all that had happened, all I had won, we were about to lose to this madman.

Something happened and the pressure wavered. Surprised, I rallied myself to push back. The waved of his domination abruptly came to a halt, frozen through with icy lines which held them in place. My mind was freed and my vision cleared. I saw Karen standing beside the Mentalist, her fingers glowing with a frosty light. He was staring in horror at a glowing symbol sketched on his hand. In the next moment he collapsed, falling limply to the floor like a doll. His head hit the stones with a painful thump. All of the pressure sent against me was gone.

"You stopped him," I let out a long sigh of relief, before giving Karen a weary smile, "You saved me again."

Moving forward, I drew a knife and plunged it into the collapsed form of the Mentalist, ending his life for good. Nothing could unfreeze him or save him now. Now all the people whom he held in bondage, all the Talented Ones whom he wanted to rule the world with, they would all be freed from his bonds.

In that moment that he died something strange happened around us. The whole room, the pattern on the floor and the smooth walls, shifted. Like ice left near a fire, it melted away, leaving only a bare cave of gray stone, a griffin like a statue, and a pyramid of sandstone with a dead man on top. Krift had moved down to the floor and now stood there like frightened child looking around in amazement.

"Illusion." I shook my head, "He was powerful...but crazy. This whole place is made out of illusion built into a natural cavern system. Now I don't know what is real or fake."

After a moment of thought, I added, "but I'm so tired it doesn't matter. Come on, you two, we have to find our way out of here and get back to the captain as soon as possible."

Krift came over to stand by me, still bewildered, with tears in his eyes as he remembered what he had done when he was under the Mentalist's spell, "Sarkin, I—"

"Don't mention it." I knew he was going to apologize for things that weren't his fault, "you couldn't help it, Krift. Just come back with me to free the captain, will you?"

He nodded, adding quietly, "I would still like to be part of your crew, if you'll take me."

"Of course." I told him. Then I looked over at Karen, standing as if she did not know what to do or say now. In her left hand she held the sword which had tried to kill her earlier, Skon Yew's silver one. She had not used it against the Mentalist, trusting her innate talent more. Mutely, she offered it to me hilt-first. I went over and took it from her, before flinging it off into the shadows at the edges of the room, where it disappeared with a disapproving clank.

"I never want to see that blade again." I told her simply, taking her arm in mine, "Now let's get going before I fall to the floor asleep."

WE WALKED OUT OF THE oval cavern up a rough, stony tunnel. Gone was the strange, glowing lights and smooth, featureless floors. I marveled at the scale of the illusions that the Mentalist had sustained. We had seen them, felt them and walked in them as if they were real. But what had they really been? There was no way for me to know. Just more air-castles from his insane mind, I supposed.

Thinking of it reminded me of what had happened when Karen and I had been split up. Still holding her arm in mine tightly, I said, "Tell me what happened when you were left behind the door. I heard you scream, and you say that something captured you. What was it?"

Karen shuddered, "Perhaps just one of the Mentalist's illusions, I don't know. It was a tall man, bigger than any I have seen before. He was wearing ragged skins and carried a curved sword in his belt. He grabbed me and I screamed, before he covered my mouth and dragged me into the cavern. But my hand was free and I was able to freeze him. After that, I wandered through that cave, up a curving pathway, and found myself to you."

"To save my life twice," I added, giving her another weary smile.

She returned it this time, "You've done much more for me."

"Never as much," I returned, remembering with a sense of horror the fire licking at my mind. Just then we heard the sound of footsteps hurrying towards us, and I braced myself for an attack. But the figure that came into view did not look like he was in any state to harm us. Tubes and wires dangled wildly from a band around his forehead, while drops of blood trickled from a few small punctures in his arm.

It was the king of Durny. He stopped his wild career down the hall just in front of us, staring from one to the other in horrified dismay. His mouth opened in a circle of fear, before he started babbling out words in Durnaic that I could not understand.

"Calm down," I told him, holding up a hand to show that it was empty of weapons, "Sellish. Do you know Sellish, your majesty?"

He gaped, gasped and choked a little before saying in a slippery accent, "Ah, Sellish. Yes, yes. A little. You, er, work for metal bird?"

He flapped his hands to show what he meant. I shook my head, "The metal bird is asleep now, your majesty. You have nothing to fear. Do you want to come out with us?"

The idea of a royal ransom was starting to grow in the back of my mind, though it would be dangerous with so many countries already looking for him. But the king shook his head and pushed passed us, hurrying on down the tunnel, "Ruffians! I find my own way...somewhere. Tlaffa! Floundink tlaffa."

He was out of sight in in instant, running around a bend in the path. I shook my head, "He'll get quite a shock when he come out in the room with the griffin in it."

"Poor fellow," Krift said, "Is he really the king of Durny?"

Nodding, I continued to lead the way up the path. We came to a few smaller caves, one of which held the bed and screen which the king had been connected to not long before. Another held a comfortable stool, set up in front of a painting easel with colors splattered on it. Looking at it, I recalled the strange girl named 'Mistress Painter' who had tried to take me captive in the house of Krift's aunt. This must have been her studio, stripped of its illusion comforts. I was glad that she was not there, though she might have been kinder to me now that she was free of the Mentalist.

Further on, we found Ramses and Don, who were still trying to find a way to the griffin and utterly bewildered at the change in scenery. After everything had been explained to them, they joined us to carry on. The tunnels were less confusing now, since they did not seem to switch around and rearrange as they had before. But they were still a vast network, some of it with ancient pieces of ironwork sticking out of the walls or dangling from the roof. Someone had been here before the Mentalist, but they were long gone now.

Up one tunnel, we came to an old, wooden door hanging by rusty hinges. Using the tip of a dagger, I pried it open and we went through. Beyond it was a small, cramped cavern with a bunk against one wall made of splintery wood and a chair of the same material set on the floor beside it. A man was sitting on the chair, bent over a large book that he was writing in. As he wrote, he sputtered out the words that he was setting down, "Day *four* since the master last spoke to me. *Three hours* since I was given anything to eat or drink. The door is *Shut,* meaning that I am not to move around the halls. And my room has *suddenly* gone *entirely devoid* of any comforts. Namely, *blankets, pillows, carpets* and *proper lighting!* I don't know how I can stand any more of this. End of entry."

He did not seem to notice us in the least, but upon seeing him Karen put a hand to her mouth in surprise, before whispering to me, "I know this man. He...he was the captain of a ship we raided. Oh, the things I did then! I remember it all clearly, now. Freezing a poor man, killing a child..."

She was close to tears, so I pulled her away, out of the door. If the fool inside was not clever enough to get out of his self-manufactured prison, he could starve in it. But I hated to see the look on Karen's face.

"It wasn't your fault," I reminded her, "Not at all. It was the Mentalist doing it. But he was the captain of the *Highwind,* I suppose? Bogan?"

She nodded, before mastering her emotions with a gulp and adding, "I forgot about him. But the griffin said that he had a talent that might be useful to us...something about being able to call up winds and change weather."

"That would make sense, because any captain would covet those abilities," I replied dryly, remembering the times I had shifted small weather patterns for Leighton, "Now come on, this must be a dead end. We'll have to try a different way."

IT DID NOT TAKE US nearly as long to get out as it had for us to get in to the center of the griffin's lair. Or perhaps I should say the Mentalist's lair, as he had been the one pulling the strings.

When we emerged in the shed by the lighthouse it was late evening. The sun had just sunk below the horizon, sending streamers of ember and gold back through the top of the lighthouse and across the trees. The sky above was deep purple, fading to cobalt blue. In the dimness of the grassy plains a camp fire burned, a flickering light in the shadows. We made our way there, finding the rest of the crew laying around the fire, toasting fish and bread together over the coals. Humper was pillowed comfortably on coats near the fire, looking a little feverish but not near as bad as he might have been. The others of the crew were also playing a game of Leaflow's Paradise while they ate, a dice game which had been nicknamed that because of a famous game between the king of Selland and a mysterious cloaked man by the name of Leaflow, years before. It was also called liar's dice.

When the crew saw us step up into the fire's light they all stared for a moment in silence, before jumping up with shouts of glee at seeing us alive and Krift with us. Worn to what felt like little more than a wraith, I was nonetheless pleased, grinning at them as they slapped us on the back and explained how they had made their way out. It seems that after leaving me, they had found their way eventually to the top and decided to wait anxiously there for us. if I had not returned after that one night, Felix and Henry would have come back in to find me.

After eating the food they had cooked, I fell immediately into a deep sleep near the fire, feeling mostly content at having brought both myself and everyone else out of that nightmare alive. The only worry that prickled me now was the question of if Captain Leighton was still alive, back at our ship. I knew that he would be well cared for, with Vulture, Bowen and Caraway all watching him, but what he really needed was to be thawed.

In the clear light of early morning we packed our things and filled the balloon with hot air for flight. While I worked, I often cast glances over at the Littleton lighthouse, wondering if Storm had received his spirit back when the Mentalist died and if he would rejoin us now because of it. But he had not appeared by the time we were ready to take off, so I gave up that idea. He was happiest on his own, now, with no one near to remind him of his past.

Soon everything was ready to go and we lifted up into the air in the basket of *Edna's Ghost*. The lighthouse dwindled away on the grassy point of land beneath us. As if in a signal, it's light flashed once, pale with the morning sun on it. Storm knew we were leaving and was giving a silent farewell. What had happened to the rest of the talented people, including the king of Durny, I did not know. They were still down in the caverns of the griffin. But I hoped that they would all escape safely in the end. Even Mistress Painter.

Krift was delighted by this way of travel, watching the flames shoot into the envelope and gazing down into the sea below. It seems that in all the time he was captive, the griffin never once took him flying. It was a new sensation to him, and one that he enjoyed hugely. Karen and I spoke quietly together in Gracklandic as we flew, making our plans in a language that the rest could not understand. I Thought that the most difficult part was going to be getting the captain to forgive her, judging by how Wallace had reacted to being frozen. And I was determined not to live without either one or the other of them if it could be helped.

A few days later we landed on the island and immediately entrusted Humper to the doctor. I learned from him that the captain was still alive, though barely. Without losing a moment, I took Krift and we hurried to the captain's cabin. Leighton looked even worse than before and I wondered anxiously if he would hold on once we thawed him with our magic. The only thing to do was try.

IT TOOK THREE LONG months for captain Leighton to recover. the first weeks had been full of anxiety for me, as he was almost out of his mind altogether by the time we saved him. For days he shivered as if in cold and had to be spoken to often so that he knew he was not alone. With the help of Vulture and Bowen I watched after him, as well as organizing the crew to finish the repairs on the ship. By the time three months was up it was in good condition and so was the crew. But we lingered just a little longer on the island, enjoying the sun while it was out and letting the captain ease into life once again.

One evening I sat with him on the beach, high enough to be out of reach of the waves, and watched the wielders of fire and ice playing in the sand together as if they were both younger and less experience in life. Karen had helped me in watching over Leighton and when he was well enough to understand it, I had laid out the whole story to him, explaining how she had been used and manipulated beyond her will. I also told him how she had saved me twice from the Mentalist's magic. Afterwards she begged his forgiveness and he had not had the heart to refuse. Free of the Mentalist's repression she was a quiet, though at times fierce, young lady with a gentle disposition and a lot of courage. Not only that, but she was to be my wife by the time we sailed.

"You know, Sarkin." The captain said, after we had been watching the other two play in the sun for a long space of comfortable silence, "Lately, I have been thinking deeply about giving up my seafaring ways."

I laughed, then looked at him and realized that he was not joking, "oh, come now captain, you still have a lot of good days in you. Surely you can't be serious."

"Ah, but I am my boy, I am." He lay a hand on my shoulder, still thin and weakened from his fight against the ice. It had taken a lot out of him, though I had not thought it had taken enough to make him give up his position as our captain.

"I have enjoyed my years sailing the oceans and living freely off of anything that came my way. But at some point a man just begins to feel tired, as if he would like a place to rest without the heaving of the ship always under him. And I know that there is a good man to take my place, so I am not worried about the crew."

I bowed my head and stared at the sand, flicking a grain of it with my finger. Trying to see the days at sea with no Captain Leighton, with me as the captain of the ship, almost escaped me. It had been responsibility enough being the first mate and sole commander for a time. Could I really take on the command by myself, permanently?

"Yes." Leighton went on as if reading my thoughts, "it is lonely and there is hard decisions to be made. But you won't be alone, will you? Lady Karen will be at your side and my loyal old friend Bowen still takes to the sea even though he is blind. You will be a good captain, Sarkin. I have faith in you."

"I just never had any ambition for such things," I explained, shaking my head, "but I suppose if you really intend to leave...where will you settle down?"

"Somewhere along the Sellish coast." Leighton shrugged, "where there is a port, so that you can still come see you're dilapidated old captain sometimes, eh? So, buck up and stop worrying about the responsibility. You've had your time for fun and games, m'lad, now it's time to get some real work done. And, since I am still your commanding officer as of yet, you have to take that as an order!"

With a sudden half-smile at his description of my adventures as all fun and games, I replied lazily, "okay, gramps. No need to get your head in a stew. I'll take the job."

"You young whippersnapper." He threw a handful of sand in my face, before I rolled out of the way laughing. Then I sat up and said seriously, "there is one problem that has been bothering me. Do you think I should take Karen home to meet my family, or just let be?"

My father had never liked the fact that my mother's family ran strong with piracy, and I doubt he would want to know that his son had become one as well. On the other hand, it seemed a little cruel to never tell them that they had a new daughter in the family, or even explain that I was still alive.

Leighton's face screwed up thoughtfully for a moment, after which he clicked his fingers together. "You should probably send my daughter, your mother, a letter. That way they will know, but we can avoid any unpleasant scenes."

"Good idea, if I knew how to write," I gave him a handful of sand back, then added, "I'll see if Krift will write one for me. Hey Krift! Get up here! I would ask Karen, but she can only write Gracklandic, even if she is learning to speak Sellish."

The boy looked up from their sandcastle before coming up to me at a run.

"Yes?" He panted breathlessly.

"Could you write a letter for me this evening?" I asked, "I'll dictate it then. Its to my parents."

"Okay, Sarkin." He nodded, and gestured down at Karen, who was watching the sea, "we were just thinking that you should tell us about how you first came to meet Skon Yew and the ways you defeated him. I could write them down, too, and it could be a book."

"Hmm...a book." I mused, trying to imagine what that would be like. It would take a lot of time and a lot of honesty on my part, too. But it might be an interesting thing to do, sometime in the future. Krift ran off to play again after making the suggestion, but the thought stayed in my mind and the words I would use to describe the first part began to form there, *"Under a flaming sunset the sailing ship Blue Bucket rode gently at anchor..."*

Don't miss out!

Visit the website below and you can sign up to receive emails whenever Rachael S Lucas publishes a new book. There's no charge and no obligation.

https://books2read.com/r/B-A-XHJJ-XZGKC

BOOKS2READ

Connecting independent readers to independent writers.

Did you love *The Griffin's Claw*? Then you should read *Dimensions*[1] by Rachael S Lucas!

[2]

Lenny Staff's life runs on simple wheels in the oppressive city of Belltoh. That is, until his best friend Sara disappears mysteriously, his employer and hero Dr. Devi shuts down shop and the police find out that Lenny is illegally cybernetic...

Enter Jax, a young man with a dimension travelling habit and a flare for riding hoverboard. He hates staying still, especially when someone else is making him do it. And when an evil form of corruption cramps him in a ring of nine worlds, he jumps through Lenny's window looking for help.

---

1. https://books2read.com/u/3R5Jon

2. https://books2read.com/u/3R5Jon

Together with seven other quirky adventurers, one from every dimension in the ring of nine, they travel dimensions to find out what is destroying their worlds, and why.

About the Author

Rachael Lucas is a quiet girl from the mountains of northern California. She loves reading, writing, gardening and Asian art among many other things. She also lives with a varying number of cats and dogs who are always on call for inspiration.

9 798223 876403